Warwick Woodlands

Henry William Herbert

(AKA Frank Forester)

Contents

WARWICK WOODLANDS

BY

Henry William Herbert
(AKA Frank Forester)

MY FIRST VISIT, DAY THE FIRST

It was a fine October evening when I was sitting on the back stoop of his cheerful little bachelor's establishment in Mercer street, with my old friend and comrade, Henry Archer. Many a frown of fortune had we two weathered out together; in many of her brightest smiles had we two reveled--never was there a stauncher friend, a merrier companion, a keener sportsman, or a better fellow, than this said Harry; and here had we two met, three thousand miles from home, after almost ten years of separation, just the same careless, happy, dare-all do-no-goods that we were when we parted in St. James's street,--he for the West, I for the Eastern World--he to fell trees, and build log huts in the backwoods of Canada,--I to shoot tigers and drink arrack punch in the Carnatic. The world had wagged with us as with most others: now up, now down, and laid us to, at last, far enough from the goal for which we started--so that, as I have said already, on landing in New York, having heard nothing of him for ten years, whom the deuce should I tumble on but that same worthy, snugly housed, with a neat bachelor's menage, and every thing ship-shape about him?--So, in the natural course of things, we were at once inseparables.

Well--as I said before, it was a bright October evening, with the clear sky, rich sunshine, and brisk breezy freshness, which indicate that loveliest of the American months,--dinner was over, and with a pitcher of the liquid ruby of Latour, a brace of half-pint beakers, and a score --my contribution--of those most exquisite of smokables, the true old Manila cheroots, we were consoling the inward man in a way that would have opened the eyes, with abhorrent admiration, of any advocate of that coldest of comforts--cold water--who should have got a chance peep at our snuggery.

Suddenly, after a long pause, during which he had been stimulating his ideas by assiduous fumigation, blowing off his steam in a long vapory cloud that curled a minute afterward about his temples,--"What say you, Frank, to a start tomorrow?" exclaimed Harry,--"and a week's right good shooting?"

"Why, as for that," said I, "I wish for nothing better--but where the deuce would you go to get shooting?"

"Never fash your beard, man," he replied, "I'll find the ground and the game too, so you'll find share of the shooting!--Holloa! there--Tim, Tim Matlock."

And in brief space that worthy minister of mine host's pleasures made his appearance, smoothing down his short black hair, clipped in the orthodox bowl fashion, over his bluff good-natured visage with one hand, while he employed its fellow in hitching up a pair of most voluminous unmentionables, of thick Yorkshire cord.

A character was Tim--and now I think of it, worthy of brief description. Born, I believe--bred, certainly, in a hunting stable, far more of his life passed in the saddle than elsewhere, it was not a little characteristic of my friend Harry to have selected this piece of Yorkshire oddity as his especial body servant; but if the choice were queer, it was at least successful, for an honester, more faithful, hard-working, and withal, better hearted, and more humorous varlet never drew curry-comb over horse-hide, or clothes-brush over broad-cloth.

His visage was, as I have said already, bluff and good-natured, with a pair of hazel eyes, of the smallest--but, at the same time, of the very merriest--twinkling from under the thick black eyebrows, which were the only hairs suffered to grace his clean-shaved countenance. An indescribable pug nose, and a good clean cut mouth, with a continual dimple at the left corner, made up his phiz. For the rest, four feet ten inches did Tim stand in his stockings, about two-ten of which were monopolized by his back, the shoulders of which would have done honor to a six foot pugilist,--his legs, though short and bowed a little outward, by continual horse exercise, were right tough serviceable members, and I have seen them bearing their owner on through mud and mire, when straighter, longer, and more fair proportioned limbs were at an awful discount.

Depositing his hat then on the floor, smoothing his hair, and hitching up his smalls, and striving most laboriously not to grin till he should have cause, stood Tim, like "Giafar awaiting his master's award!"

"Tim!" said Harry Archer.

"Sur!" said Tim.

"Tim! Mr. Forester and I are talking of going up to-morrow--what do you say to it?"

"Oop yonner?" queried Tim, in the most extraordinary West-Riding Yorkshire, indicating the direction, by pointing his right thumb over his left shoulder--"Weel, Ay'se nought to say aboot it--not Ay!"

"Soh! the cattle are all right, and the wagon in good trim, and the dogs in exercise, are they?"

"Ay'se warrant um!"

"Well, then, have all ready for a start at six to-morrow,--put Mr. Forester's Manton alongside my Joe Spurling in the top tray of the case, my single gun and my double rifle in the lower, and see the magazine well filled--the Diamond gunpowder, you know, from Mr. Brough's. You'll put up what Mr. Forester will want, for a week, you know--he does not know the country yet, Tim;--and, hark you, what wine have I at Tom Draw's?"

"No but a case of claret."

"I thought so, then away with you! down to the Baron's and get two baskets of the Star, and stop at Fulton Market, and get the best half hundred round of spiced beef you can find--and then go up to Starke's at the Octagon, and get a gallon of his old Ferintosh--that's all, Tim--off with you!--No! stop a minute!" and he filled up a beaker and handed it to the original, who, shutting both his eyes, suffered the fragrant claret to roll down his gullet in the most scientific fashion, and then, with what he called a bow, turned right about, and exit.

The sun rose bright on the next morning, and half an hour before the appointed time, Tim entered my bed-chamber, with a cup of mocha, and the intelligence that "Measter had been oop this hour and better, and did na like to be kept waiting!"--so up I jumped, and scarcely had got through the business of rigging myself, before the rattle of wheels announced the arrival of the wagon.

And a model was that shooting wagon--a long, light-bodied box, with a low rail--a high seat and dash in front, and a low servant's seat behind, with lots of room for four men and as many dogs, with guns and luggage, and all appliances to boot, enough to last a month, stowed away out of sight, and out of reach of weather. The nags, both nearly thorough-bred, fifteen two inches high, stout, clean-limbed, active animals--the off-side horse a gray, almost snow-white--the near, a dark chestnut, nearly black--with square docks setting admirably off their beautiful round quarters, high crests, small blood-like heads, and long thin manes--spoke volumes for Tim's stable science; for though their ribs were slightly visible, their muscles were well filled, and hard as granite. Their coats glanced in the sunshine--the white's like statuary marble; the chestnut's like high polished copper--in short the whole turn-out was perfect.

The neat black harness, relieved merely by a crest, with every strap that could be needed, in its place, and not one buckle or one thong superfluous; the bright steel curbs, with the chains jingling as the horses tossed and pawed impatient for a start; the tapering holly whip; the bear-skins covering the seats; the top-coats spread above them-- every thing, in a word, without bordering on the slang, was perfectly correct and gnostic.

Four dogs--a brace of setters of the light active breed, one of which will out-work a brace of the large, lumpy, heavy-headed dogs,--one red, the other white and liver, both with black noses, their legs and sterns beautifully feathered, and their hair, glossy and smooth as silk, showing their excellent condition--and a brace of short-legged, bony, liver-colored spaniels--with their heads thrust one above the other, over or through the railings, and their tails waving with impatient joy --occupied the after portion of the wagon.

Tim, rigged in plain gray frock, with leathers and white tops, stood, in true tiger fashion, at the horses' heads, with the forefinger of his right hand resting upon the curb of the gray horse, as with his left he rubbed the nose of the chestnut; while Harry, cigar in mouth, was standing at the wheel, reviewing with a steady and experienced eye the gear, which seemed to give him perfect satisfaction. The moment I appeared on the steps,

"In with you, Frank--in with you," he exclaimed, disengaging the hand-reins from the terrets into which they had been thrust, "I have been waiting here these five minutes. Jump up, Tim!"

And, gathering the reins up firmly, he mounted by the wheel, tucked the top-coat about his legs, shook out the long lash of his tandem whip, and lapped it up in good style.

"I always drive with one of these"--he said, half apologetically, as I thought--

"they are so handy on the road for the cur dogs, when you have setters with you--they plague your life out else. Have you the pistol-case in, Tim, for I don't see it?"

"All raight, sur," answered he, not over well pleased, as it seemed, that it should even be suspected that he could have forgotten any thing --"All raight!"

"Go along, then," cried Harry, and at the word the high bred nags went off; and though my friend was too good and too old a hand to worry his cattle at the beginning of a long day's journey--many minutes had not passed before we found ourselves on board the ferry-boat, steaming it merrily towards the Jersey shore.

"A quarter past six to the minute," said Harry, as we landed at Hoboken.

"Let Shot and Chase run, Tim, but keep the spaniels in till we pass Hackensack."

"Awa wi ye, ye rascals," exclaimed Tim, and out went the high blooded dogs upon the instant, yelling and jumping in delight about the horses-- and off we went, through the long sandy street of Hoboken, leaving the private race-course of that stanch sportsman, Mr. Stevens, on the left, with several powerful horses taking their walking exercise in their neat body clothes.

"That puts me in mind, Frank," said Harry, as he called my attention to the thorough-breds, "we must be back next Tuesday for the Beacon Races-- the new course up there on the hill; you can see the steps that lead to it--and now is not this lovely?" he continued, as we mounted the first ridge of Weehawken, and looked back over the beautiful broad Hudson, gemmed with a thousand snowy sails of craft or shipping--"Is not this lovely, Frank? and, by the by, you will say, when we get to our journey's end, you never drove through prettier scenery in your life. Get away, Bob, you villain--nibbling, nibbling at your curb! get away, lads!"

And away we went at a right rattling pace over the hills, and through the cedar swamp; and, passing through a toll-gate, stopped with a sudden jerk at a long low tavern on the left-hand side.

"We must stop here, Frank. My old friend, Ingliss, a brother trigger, too, would think the world was coming to an end if I drove by-- twenty-nine minutes these six miles," he added, looking at his watch, "that will do! Now, Tim, look sharp--just a sup of water! Good day--good day to you, Mr. Ingliss; now for a glass of your milk punch"--and mine host disappeared, and in a moment came forth with two rummers of the delicious compound, a big bright lump of ice bobbing about in each among the nutmeg.

"What, off again for Orange county, Mr. Archer? I was telling the old woman yesterday that we should have you by before long; well, you'll find cock pretty plenty, I expect; there was a chap by here from Ulster --let me see, what day was it--Friday, I guess--with produce, and he was telling, they have had no cold snap yet up there! Thank you, sir, good luck to you!"

And off we went again, along a level road, crossing the broad, slow river from whence it takes its name, into the town of Hackensack.

"We breakfast here, Frank"--as he pulled up beneath the low Dutch shed projecting over half the road in front of the neat tavern--"How are you, Mr. Vanderbeck--we want a beefsteak, and a cup of tea, as quick as you can give it us; we'll make the tea ourselves; bring in the black tea, Tim--the nags as usual."

"Aye! aye! sur"--"tak them out--leave t' harness on, all but their bridles"--to an old gray-headed hostler. "Whisp off their legs a bit; Ay will be oot enoo!"

After as good a breakfast as fresh eggs, good country bread--worth ten times the poor trash of city bakers--prime butter, cream, and a fat steak could furnish, at a cheap rate, and with a civil and obliging landlord, away we went again over the red-hills--an infernal ugly road, sandy, and rough, and stony--for ten miles farther to New Prospect.

"Now you shall see some scenery worth looking at," said Harry, as we started again, after watering the horses, and taking in a bag with a peck of oats--"to feed at three o'clock, Frank, when we stop to grub, which must do al fresco--" my friend explained--"for the landlord, who kept the only tavern on the road, went West this summer, bit by the land mania, and there is now no stopping place 'twixt this and Warwick," naming the village for which we were bound. "You got that beef boiled, Tim?"

"Ay'd been a fouil else, and aye so often oop t' road too," answered he with a grin, "and t' moostard is mixed, and t' pilot biscuit in, and a good bit o' Cheshire cheese! wee's doo, Ay reckon. Ha! ha! ha!"

And now my friend's boast was indeed fulfilled; for when we had driven a few miles farther, the country became undulating, with many and bright streams of water; the hill sides clothed with luxuriant woodlands, now in their many-colored garb of autumn beauty; the meadow-land rich in unchanged fresh greenery--for the summer had been mild and rainy--with here and there a buckwheat stubble showing its ruddy face, replete with promise of quail in the present, and of hot cakes in future; and the bold chain of mountains, which, under many names, but always beautiful and wild, sweeps from the Highlands of the Hudson, west and south-wardly, quite through New Jersey, forming a link between the White and Green Mountains of New Hampshire and Vermont, and the more famous Alleghenies of the South.

A few miles farther yet, the road wheeled round the base of the Tourne Mountain, a magnificent bold hill, with a bare craggy head, its sides and skirts thick set with cedars and hickory--entering a defile through which the Ramapo, one of the loveliest streams eye ever looked upon, comes rippling with its crystal waters over bright pebbles, on its way to join the two kindred rivulets which form the fair Passaic. Throughout the whole of that defile, nothing can possibly surpass the loveliness of nature; the road hard, and smooth, and level, winding and wheeling parallel to the gurgling river, crossing it two or three times in each mile, now on one side, and now on the other--the valley now barely broad enough to permit the highway and the stream to pass between the abrupt masses of rock and forest, and now expanding into rich basins of green meadow-land, the deepest and most fertile possible--the hills of every shape and size--here bold, and bare, and rocky--there swelling up in grand round masses, pile above pile of verdure, to the blue firmament of autumn. By and by we drove through a thriving little village, nestling in a hollow of the hills, beside a broad bright pond, whose waters keep a dozen manufactories of cotton and of iron--with which mineral these hills abound--in constant operation; and passing by the tavern, the departure of whose owner Harry had so pathetically mourned, we wheeled again round a projecting spur of hill into a narrower defile, and reached another hamlet, far different in its aspect from the busy bustling place we had left some five miles behind.

There were some twenty houses, with two large mills of solid masonry; but of these not one building was now tenanted; the roof-trees broken, the doors and shutters either torn from their hinges, or flapping wildly to and fro; the mill wheels cumbering the stream with masses of decaying timber, and the whole presenting a most desolate and mournful aspect.

"Its story is soon told," Harry said, catching my inquiring glance--"a speculating, clever New York merchant--a waterpower--a failure--and a consequent desertion of the project; but we must find a birth among the ruins!"

And as he spoke, turning a little off the road, he pulled up on the green sward; "there's an old stable here that has a manger in it yet! Now, Tim, look sharp!" And in a twinkling the horses were loosed from the wagon, the harness taken off and hanging on the corners of the ruined hovels, and Tim hissing and rubbing away at the gray horse, while Harry did like duty on the chestnut, in a style that would have done no shame to Melton Mowbray!

"Come, Frank, make yourself useful! Get out the round of beef, and all the rest of the provant--it's on the rack behind; you'll find all right there. Spread our table-cloth on that flat stone by the waterfall, under the willow; clap a couple of bottles of the Baron's champagne into the pool there underneath the fall; let's see whether your Indian campaigning has taught you anything worth knowing!"

To work I went at once, and by the time I had got through--"Come, Tim," I heard him say, "I've got the rough dirt off this fellow, you must polish him, while I take a wash, and get a bit of dinner. Holloa! Frank, are you ready!"

And he came bounding down to the water's edge, with his Newmarket coat in hand, and sleeves rolled up to the elbows, plunged his face into the cool stream, and took a good wash of his soiled hands in the same natural basin. Five minutes afterward we were employed most pleasantly with the spiced beef, white biscuit, and good wine, which came out of the waterfall as cool as Gunter could have made it with all his icing. When we had pretty well got through, and were engaged with our cheroots, up came Tim Matlock.

"T' horses have got through wi' t' corn--they have fed rarely so I harnessed them, sur, all to the bridles--we can start when you will."

"Sit down, and get your dinner then, sir--there's a heel tap in that bottle we have left for you--and when you have done, put up the things, and we'll be off. I say, Frank, let us try a shot with the pistols--I'll get the case--stick up that fellow-commoner upon the fence there, and mark off a twenty paces."

The marking irons were produced, and loaded--"Fire--one--two--three"-- bang! and the shivering of the glass announced that never more would that chap hold the generous liquor; the ball had struck it plump in the centre, and broken off the whole above the shoulder, for it was fixed neck downward on the stake.

"It is my turn now," said I; and more by luck, I fancy, than by skill, I took the neck off, leaving nothing but the thick ring of the mouth still sticking on the summit of the fence.

"I'll hold you a dozen of my best Regalias against as many of Manillas, that I break the ring."

"Done, Harry!"

"Done!"

Again the pistol cracked, and the unerring ball drove the small fragment into a thousand splinters.

"That fotched 'um!" exclaimed Tim, who had come up to announce all ready. "Ecod, measter Frank, you munna wager i' that gate[1] wi' master, or my name beant Tim, but thou'lt be clean bamboozled."

Well, not to make a short story long, we got under way again, and, with speed unabated, spanked along at full twelve miles an hour for five miles farther. There, down a wild looking glen, on the left hand, comes brawling, over stump and stone, a tributary streamlet, by the side of which a rough track, made by the charcoal burners and the iron miners, intersects the main road; and up this miserable looking path, for it was little more, Harry wheeled at full trot. "Now for twelve miles of mountain, the roughest road and wildest country you ever saw crossed in a phaeton, good master Frank."

And wild it was, indeed, and rough enough in all conscience; narrow, unfenced in many places, winding along the brow of precipices without rail or breast-work, encumbered with huge blocks of stone, and broken by the summer rains! An English stage coachman would have stared aghast at the steep zigzags up the hills, the awkward turns on the descents, the sudden pitches, with now an unsafe bridge, and now a stony ford at the bottom; but through all this, the delicate quick finger, keen eye, and cool head of Harry, assisted by the rare mouths of his exquisitely bitted cattle, piloted us at the rate of full ten miles the hour; the scenery, through which the wild track ran, being entirely of the most wild and savage character of woodland; the bottom filled with gigantic timber trees, cedar, and pine, and hemlock, with a dense undergrowth of rhododendron, calmia, and azalia, which, as my friend informed me, made the whole mountains in the summer season one rich bed of bloom. About six miles from the point where we had entered them we scaled

---

1   Gate-- Yorkshire; Anglice, way.

the highest ridge of the hills, by three almost precipitous zigzags, the topmost ledge paved by a stratum of broken shaley limestone; and, passing at once from the forest into well cultivated fields, came on a new and lovelier prospect--a narrow deep vale scarce a mile in breadth--scooped, as it were, out of the mighty mountains which embosomed it on every side--in the highest state of culture, with rich orchards, and deep meadows, and brown stubbles, whereon the shocks of maize stood fair and frequent; and westward of the road, which, diving down obliquely to the bottom, loses itself in the woods of the opposite hill-side, and only becomes visible again when it emerges to cross over the next summit--the loveliest sheet of water my eyes has ever seen, varying from half a mile to a mile in breadth, and about five miles long, with shores indented deeply with the capes and promontories of the wood-clothed hills, which sink abruptly to its very margin.

"That is the Greenwood Lake, Frank, called by the monsters here Long Pond!--'the fiends receive their souls therefor,' as Walter Scott says-- in my mind prettier than Lake George by far, though known to few except chance sportsmen like myself! Full of fish, perch of a pound in weight, and yellow bass in the deep waters, and a good sprinkling of trout, towards this end! Ellis Ketchum killed a five-pounder there this spring! and heaps of summer-duck, the loveliest in plumage of the genus, and the best too, me judice, excepting only the inimitable canvass-back. There are a few deer, too, in the hills, though they are getting scarce of late years. There, from that headland, I killed one, three summers since; I was placed at a stand by the lake's edge, and the dogs drove him right down to me; but I got too eager, and he heard or saw me, and so fetched a turn; but they were close upon him, and the day was hot, and he was forced to soil. I never saw him till he was in the act of leaping from a bluff of ten or twelve feet into the deep lake, but I pitched up my rifle at him, a snap shot! as I would my gun at a cock in a summer brake, and by good luck sent my ball through his heart. There is a finer view yet when we cross this hill, the Bellevale mountain; look out, for we are just upon it; there! Now admire!"

And on the summit he pulled up, and never did I see a landscape more extensively magnificent. Ridge after ridge the mountain sloped down from our feet into a vast rich basin ten miles at least in breadth, by thirty, if not more, in length, girdled on every side by mountains--the whole diversified with wood and water, meadow, and pasture-land, and corn-field--studded with small white villages--with more than one bright lakelet glittering like beaten gold in the declining sun, and several isolated hills standing up boldly from the vale!

"Glorious indeed! Most glorious!" I exclaimed.

"Right, Frank," he said; "a man may travel many a day, and not see any thing to beat the vale of Sugar-loaf--so named from that cone-like hill, over the pond there--that peak is eight hundred feet above tide water. Those blue hills, to the far right, are the Hudson Highlands; that bold bluff is the far-famed Anthony's Nose; that ridge across the vale, the second ridge I mean, is the Shawangunks; and those three rounded summits, farther yet--those are the Kaatskills! But now a truce with the romantic, for there lies Warwick, and this keen mountain air has found me a fresh appetite!"

Away we went again, rattling down the hills, nothing daunted at their steep pitches, with the nags just as fresh as when they started, champing and snapping at their curbs, till on a table-land above the brook, with the tin steeple of its church peering from out the massy foliage of sycamore and locust, the haven of our journey lay before us.

"Hilloa, hill-oa ho! whoop! who-whoop!" and with a cheery shout, as we clattered across the wooden bridge, he roused out half the population of the village.

"Ya ha ha!--ya yah!" yelled a great woolly-headed coal-black negro. "Here 'm massa Archer back again--massa ben well, I spect--"

"Well--to be sure I have, Sam," cried Harry. "How's old Poll? Bid her come up to Draw's to-morrow night--I've got a red and yellow frock for her--a deuce of a concern!"

"Ya ha! yah ha ha yaah!" and amid a most discordant chorus of African merriment, we passed by a neat farm-house shaded by two glorious locusts on the right, and a new red brick mansion, the pride of the village, with a flourishing store on the left--and wheeled up to the famous Tom Draw's tavern--a long white house with a piazza six feet wide, at the top of eight steep steps, and a one-story kitchen at the end of it; a pump with a gilt pineapple at the top of it, and horse-trough, a wagon shed and stable sixty feet long; a sign-post with an indescribable female figure swinging upon it, and an ice house over the way!

Such was the house, before which we pulled up just as the sun was setting, amid a gabbling of ducks, a barking of terriers, mixed with the deep bay of two or three large heavy fox-hounds which had been lounging about in the shade, and a peal of joyous welcome from all beings, quadruped or biped, within hearing.

"Hulloa! boys!" cried a deep hearty voice from within the barroom. "Hulloa! boys! Walk in! walk in! What the eternal h-ll are you about there?"

Well, we did walk into a large neat bar-room, with a bright hickory log crackling upon the hearth-stone, a large round table in one corner, covered with draught-boards, and old newspapers, among which showed preeminent the "Spirit of the Times;" a range of pegs well stored with great-coats, fishing-rods, whips, game-bags, spurs, and every other stray appurtenance of sporting, gracing one end; while the other was more gaily decorated by the well furnished bar, in the right-hand angle of which my eye detected in an instant a handsome nine pound double barrel, an old six foot Queen Ann's tower-musket, and a long smooth-bored rifle; and last, not least, outstretched at easy length upon the counter of his bar, to the left-hand of the gang-way--the right side being more suitably decorated with tumblers, and decanters of strange compounds--supine, with fair round belly towering upward, and head voluptuously pillowed on a heap of wagon cushions--lay in his glory--but no! hold!--the end of a chapter is no place to introduce--Tom Draw![2]

---

2   It is almost a painful task to read over and revise this chapter. The "twenty years ago" is too keenly visible to the mind's eye in every line. Of the persons mentioned in its pages, more than one have passed away from our world forever; and even the natural features of rock, wood, and river, in other countries so vastly more enduring than their perishable owners, have been so much altered by the march of improvement, Heaven save the mark! that the traveler up the Erie railroad, will certainly not recognize in the description of the vale of Ramapo, the hill-sides all denuded of their leafy honors, the bright streams dammed by unsightly mounds and changed into foul stagnant pools, the snug country tavern deserted for a huge hideous barn-like depot, and all the lovely sights and sweet harmonies of nature defaced and drowned by the deformities consequent on a railroad, by the disgusting roar and screech of the steam-engine. One word to the wise! Let no man be deluded by the following pages, into the setting forth for Warwick now in search of sporting. These things are strictly as they were twenty years ago! Mr. Seward, in his zeal for the improvement of Chatauque and Cattaraugus, has certainly destroyed the cock-shooting of Orange county. A sportsman's benison to him therefor.

DAY THE THE SECOND

Much as I had heard of Tom Draw, I was I must confess, taken altogether aback when I, for the first time, set eyes upon him. I had heard Harry Archer talk of him fifty times as a crack shot; as a top sawyer at a long day's fag; as the man of all others he would choose as his mate, if he were to shoot a match, two against two--what then was my astonishment at beholding this worthy, as he reared himself slowly from his recumbent position? It is true, I had heard his sobriquet, "Fat Tom," but, Heaven and Earth! such a mass of beef and brandy as stood before me, I had never even dreamt of. About five feet six inches at the very utmost in the perpendicular, by six or--"by'r lady"--nearer seven in circumference, weighing, at the least computation, two hundred and fifty pounds, with a broad jolly face, its every feature--well-formed and handsome, rather than otherwise--mantling with an expression of the most perfect excellence of heart and temper, and overshadowed by a vast mass of brown hair, sprinkled pretty well with gray!--Down he plumped from the counter with a thud that made the whole floor shake, and with a hand outstretched, that might have done for a Goliah, out he strode to meet us.

"Why, hulloa! hulloa! Mr. Archer," shaking his hand till I thought he would have dragged the arm clean out of the socket--"How be you, boy? How be you?" "Right well, Tom, can't you see? Why confound you, you've grown twenty pound heavier since July!--but here, I'm losing all my manners!--this is Frank Forester, whom you have heard me talk about so often! He dropped down here out of the moon, Tom, I believe! at least I thought about as much of seeing the man in the moon, as of meeting him in this wooden country--but here he is, as you see, come all the way to take a look at the natives. And so, you see, as you're about the greatest curiosity I know of in these parts, I brought him straight up here to take a peep!

Look at him, Frank--look at him well! Now, did you ever see, in all your life, so extraordinary an old devil?--and yet, Frank, which no man could possibly believe, the old fat animal has some good points about him--he can walk some! shoot, as he says, first best! and drink--good Lord, how he can drink!"

"And that reminds me," exclaimed Tom, who with a ludicrous mixture of pleasure, bashfulness, and mock anger, had been listening to what he evidently deemed a high encomium; "that we hav'nt drinked yet; have you quit drink, Archer, since I was to York? What'll you take, Mr. Forester? Gin? yes, I have got some prime gin! You never sent me up them groceries though, Archer; well, then, here's luck! What, Yorkshire, is that you? I should ha' thought now, Archer, you'd have cleared that lazy Injun out afore this time!"

"Whoy, measter Draa--what 'na loike's that kind o' talk? coom coom now, where'll Ay tak t' things tull?"

"Put Mr. Forester's box in the bed-room off the parlor--mine up stairs, as usual," cried Archer. "Look sharp and get the traps out. Now, Tom, I suppose you have got no supper for us?"

"Cooper, Cooper! you snooping little devil," yelled Tom, addressing his second hope, a fine dark-eyed, bright-looking lad of ten or twelve years; "Don't you see Mr. Archer's come?--away with you and light the parlor fire, look smart now, or I'll cure you! Supper--you're always eat! eat! eat! or, drink! drink!--drunk! Yes! supper; we've got pork! and chickens..."

"Oh! d--n your pork," said I, "salt as the ocean I suppose!"

"And double d--n your chickens," chimed in Harry, "old superannuated cocks which must be caught now, and then beheaded, and then soused into hot water to fetch off the feathers; and save you lazy devils the trouble of picking them. No, no, Tom! get us some fresh meat for to-morrow; and for to-night let us have some hot potatoes, and some bread and butter, and we'll find beef; eh, Frank? and now look sharp, for we must be up in good time tomorrow, and, to be so, we must to bed betimes. And now, Tom, are there any cock?"

"Cock! yes, I guess there be, and quail, too, pretty plenty! quite a smart chance of them, and not a shot fired among them this fall, any how!"

"Well, which way must we beat to-morrow? I calculate to shoot three days with you here; and, on Wednesday night, when we get in, to hitch up and drive into Sullivan, and see if we can't get a deer or two! You'll go, Tom?"

"Well, well, we'll see any how; but for to-morrow, why, I guess we must beat the 'Squire's swamp-hole first; there's ten or twelve cock there, I know; I see them there myself last Sunday; and then acrost them buck-wheat stubbles, and the big bog meadow, there's a drove of quail there; two or three bevys got in one, I reckon; leastwise I counted thirty-three last Friday was a week; and through Seer's big swamp, over to the great spring!"

"How is Seer's swamp? too wet, I fancy," Archer interposed, "at least I noticed, from the mountain, that all the leaves were changed in it, and that the maples were quite bare."

"Pretty fair, pretty fair, I guess," replied stout Tom, "I harnt been there myself though, but Jem was down with the hounds arter an old fox t'other day, and sure enough he said the cock kept flopping up quite thick afore him; but then the critter will lie, Harry; he will lie like thunder, you know; but somehow I concaits there be cock there too; and then, as I was saying, we'll stop at the great spring and get a bite of summat, and then beat Hellhole; you'll have sport there for sartin! What dogs have you got with you, Harry?"

"Your old friends, Shot and Chase, and a couple of spaniels for thick covert!"

"Now, gentlemen, your suppers are all ready."

"Come, Tom," cried Archer; "you must take a bite with us--Tim, bring us in three bottles of champagne, and lots of ice, do you hear?"

And the next moment we found ourselves installed in a snug parlor, decorated with a dozen sporting prints, a blazing hickory fire snapping and spluttering and roaring in a huge Franklin stove; our luggage safely stowed in various corners, and Archer's double gun-case propped on two chairs below the window.

An old-fashioned round table, covered with clean white linen of domestic manufacture, displayed the noble round of beef which we had brought up with us, flanked by a platter of magnificent potatoes, pouring forth volumes of dense steam through the cracks in their dusky skins; a lordly dish of butter, that might have pleased the appetite of Sisera; while eggs and ham, and pies of apple, mince-meat, cranberry, and custard, occupied every vacant space, save where two ponderous pitchers, mantling with ale and cider, and two respectable square bottles, labelled "Old Rum" and "Brandy-1817," relieved the prospect. Before we had sat down,

Timothy entered, bearing a horse bucket filled to the brim with ice, from whence protruded the long necks and split corks of three champagne bottles.

"Now, Tim," said Archer, "get your own supper, when you've finished with the cattle; feed the dogs well to-night; and then to bed. And hark you, call me at five in the morning; we shall want you to carry the game-bag and the drinkables; take care of yourself, Tim, and good night!"

"No need to tell him that," cried Tom, "he's something like yourself; I tell you, Archer, if Tim ever dies of thirst, it must be where there is nothing wet, but water!"

"Now hark to the old scoundrel, Frank," said Archer, "hark to him pray, and if he doesn't out-eat both of us, and out-drink anything you ever saw, may I miss my first bird to-morrow--that's all! Give me a slice of beef, Frank; that old Goth would cut it an inch thick, if I let him touch it; out with a cork, Tom! Here's to our sport to-morrow!"

"Uh; that goes good!" replied Tom, with an oath, which, by the apparent gusto of the speaker, seemed to betoken that the wine had tickled his palate--"that goes good! that's different from the darned red trash you left up here last time."

"And of which you have left none, I'll be bound," answered Archer, laughing; "my best Latour, Frank, which the old infidel calls trash."

"It's all below, every bottle of it," answered Tom: "I wouldn't use such rot-gut stuff, no, not for vinegar. 'Taint half so good as that red sherry you had up here on-cet; that was poor weak stuff, too, but it did well to make milk punch of; it did well instead of milk."

"Now, Frank," said Archer, "you won't believe me, that I know; but it's true, all the same. A year ago, this autumn, I brought up five gallons of exceedingly stout, rather fiery, young brown sherry--draught wine, you know!--and what did Tom do here, but mix it, half and half, with brandy, nutmeg, and sugar, and drink it for milk punch!"

"I did so, by the eternal," replied Tom, bolting a huge lump of beef, in order to enable himself to answer--"I did so, and good milk punch it made, too, but it was too weak! Come, Mr. Forester, we harn't drinked yet, and I'm kind o' gittin dry!"

And now the mirth waxed fast and furious--the champagne speedily was fin-ished, the supper things cleared off, hot water and Starke's Ferintosh succeeded, cheroots were lighted, we drew closer in about the fire, and, during the circulation of two tumblers--for to this did Harry limit us, having the prospect of unsteady hands and aching heads before him for the morrow--never did I hear more genuine and real humor, than went round our merry trio.

Tom Draw, especially, though all his jokes were not such altogether as I can venture to insert in my chaste paragraphs, and though at times his oaths were too extravagantly rich to brook repetition, shone forth resplendent. No longer did I wonder at what I had before deemed Harry Archer's strange hallucination; Tom Draw is a decided genius--rough as a pine knot in his native woods--but full of mirth, of shrewdness, of keen mother wit, of hard horse sense, and last, not least, of the most genuine milk of human kindness. He is a rough block; but, as Harry says, there is solid timber under the uncouth bark enough to make five hundred men, as men go now-a-days in cities!

At ten o'clock, thanks to the excellent precautions of my friend Harry, we were all snugly berthed, before the whiskey, which had well justified the high praise I had heard lavished on it, had made any serious inroads on our understanding, but not before we had laid in a quantum to ensure a good night's rest.

Bright and early was I on foot the next day, but before I had half dressed myself I was assured, by the clatter of the breakfast things, that Archer had again stolen a march upon me; and the next moment my bed-room door, driven open by the thick boot of that worthy, gave me a full view of his person--arrayed in a stout fustian jacket--with half a dozen pockets in full view, and Heaven only knows how many more lying perdu in the broad skirts. Knee-breeches of the same material, with laced half-boots and leather leggins, set off his stout calf and well turned ankle.

"Up! up! Frank," he exclaimed, "it is a morning of ten thousand; there has been quite a heavy dew, and by the time we are afoot it will be well evaporated; and then the scent will lie, I promise you! make haste, I tell you, breakfast is ready!"

Stimulated by his hurrying voice, I soon completed my toilet, and entering the parlor found Harry busily employed in stirring to and fro a pound of powder on one heated dinner plate, while a second was undergoing the process of preparation on the hearthstone under a glowing pile of hickory ashes.

At the side-table, covered with guns, dog-whips, nipple-wrenches, and the like, Tim, rigged like his master, in half boots and leggins, but with a short roundabout of velveteen, in place of the full-skirted jacket, was filling our shot-pouches by aid of a capacious funnel, more used, as its odor betokened, to facilitate the passage of gin or Jamaica spirits than of so sober a material as cold lead.

At the same moment entered mine host, togged for the field in a huge pair of cow-hide boots, reaching almost to the knee, into the tops of which were tucked the lower ends of a pair of trowsers, containing yards enough of buffalo-cloth to have eked out the main-sail of a North River sloop; a waistcoat and single-breasted jacket of the same material, with a fur cap, completed his attire; but in his hand he bore a large decanter filled with a pale yellowish liquor, embalming a dense mass of fine and worm-like threads, not very different in appearance from the best vermicelli.

"Come, boys, come--here's your bitters," he exclaimed; and, as if to set the example, filled a big tumbler to the brim, gulped it down as if it had been water, smacked his lips, and incontinently tendered it to Archer, who, to my great amazement, filled himself likewise a more moderate draught, and quaffed it without hesitation.

"That's good, Tom," he said, pausing after the first sip; "that's the best I ever tasted here; how old's that?"

"Five years!" Tom replied: "five years last fall! Daddy Tom made it out my own best apples--take a horn, Mr. Forester," he added, turning to me --"it's first best cider sperrits--better a darned sight than that Scotch stuff you make such an eternal fuss about, toting it up here every time, as if we'd nothing fit to drink in the country!"

And to my sorrow I did taste it--old apple whiskey, with Lord knows how much snake-root soaked in it for five years! They may talk about gall being bitter; but, by all that's wonderful, there was enough of the amari aliquid in this fonte, to me by no means of leporum, to have given an extra touch of bitterness to all the gall beneath the canopy; and with my mouth puckered up, till it was like anything on earth but a mouth, I set the glass down on the table; and for the next five minutes could do nothing but shake my head to and fro like a Chinese mandarin, amidst the loud and prolonged roars of laughter that burst like thunder claps from the huge jaws of Thomas Draw, and the subdued and half respectful cachinnations of Tim Matlock.

By the time I had got a little better, the black tea was ready, and with thick cream, hot buckwheat cakes, beautiful honey, and--as a stand by-- the still vener-able round, we made out a very tolerable meal.

This done, with due deliberation Archer supplied his several pockets with their accustomed load--the clean-punched wads in this--in that the Westley Richards' caps--here a pound horn of powder--there a shot-pouch on Syke's lever principle, with double mouth-piece--in another, screw-driver, nipple-wrench, and the spare cones; and, to make up the tale, dog-whip, dram-bottle, and silk handkerchief in the sixth and last.

"Nothing like method in this world," said Harry, clapping his low-crowned broad-brimmed mohair cap upon his head; "take my word for it. Now, Tim, what have you got in the bag?"

"A bottle of champagne, sur," answered Tim, who was now employed slinging a huge fustian game-bag, with a net-work front, over his right shoulder, to counter-balance two full shot-belts which were already thrown across the other--"a bottle of champagne, sur--a cold roast chicken--t' Cheshire cheese--and t' pilot biscuits. Is your dram-bottle filled wi' t' whiskey, please sur?"

"Aye, aye, Tim. Now let loose the dogs--carry a pair of couples and a leash along with you; and mind you, gentlemen, Tim carries shot for all hands; and lun-cheon--but each one finds his own powder, caps, &c.; and any one who wants a dram, carries his own--the devil a-one of you gets a sup out of my bottle, or a charge out of my flask! That's right, old Trojan, isn't it?" with a good slap on Tom's broad shoulder.

"Shot! Shot--why Shot! don't you know me, old dog?" cried Tom, as the two setters bounded into the room, joyful at their release--"good dog! good Chase!" feeding them with great lumps of beef.

"Avast! there Tom--have done with that," cried Harry; "you'll have the dogs so full that they can't run."

"Why, how'd you like to hunt all day without your breakfast--hey?"

"Here, lads! here, lads! wh-e-ew!" and followed by his setters, with his gun under his arm, away went Harry; and catching up our pieces likewise, we followed, nothing loth, Tim bringing up the rear with the two spaniels fretting in their cou-ples, and a huge black thorn cudgel, which he had brought, as he informed me, "all t' way from bonny Cawoods."

It was as beautiful a morning as ever lighted sportsmen to their labors. The dew, exhaled already from the long grass, still glittered here and there upon the shrubs and trees, though a soft fresh south-western breeze was shaking it thence momently in bright and rustling showers; the sun, but newly risen, and as yet partially enveloped in the thin gauze-like mists so frequent at that season, was casting shadows, seemingly endless, from every object that intercepted his low rays, and chequering the whole landscape with that play of light and shade, which is the loveliest accessory to a lovely scene; and lovely was the scene, indeed, as e'er was looked upon by painter's or by poet's eye--how then should humble prose do justice to it?

Seated upon the first slope of a gentle hill, midway of the great valley heretofore described, the village looked due south, toward the chains of mountains, which we had crossed on the preceding evening, and which in that direction bounded the landscape. These ridges, cultivated half-way up their swelling sides, which lay mapped out before our eyes in all the various beauty of orchards, yellow stubbles, and rich pastures dotted with sleek and comely cattle, were rendered yet more lovely and romantic, by here and there a woody gorge, or rocky chasm, channeling their smooth flanks, and carrying down their tributary rills, to swell the main stream at their base. Toward these we took our way by the same road which we had followed in an opposite direction on the previous night--but for a short space only--for having crossed the stream, by the same bridge which we had passed on entering the village, Tom Draw pulled down a set of bars to the left, and strode out manfully into the stubble.

"Hold up, good lads!--whe-ew--whewt!" and away went the setters through the moist stubble, heads up and sterns down, like fox-hounds on a breast-high scent, yet under the most perfect discipline; for at the very first note of Harry's whistle, even when racing at the top of their pace, they would turn simultaneously, alter their course, cross each other at right angles, and quarter the whole field, leaving no foot of ground unbeaten.

No game, however, in this instance, rewarded their exertions; and on we went across a meadow, and two other stubbles, with the like result. But now we crossed a gentle hill, and, at its base, came on a level tract, containing at the most ten acres of marsh land, overgrown with high coarse grass and flags. Beyond this, on the right, was a steep rocky hillock, covered with tall and thrifty timber of some thirty years' growth, but wholly free from under-wood. Along the left-hand fence ran a thick belt of underwood, sumac and birch, with a few young oak trees interspersed; but in the middle of the swampy level, covering at most some five or six acres, was a dense circular thicket composed of every sort of thorny bush and shrub, matted with cat-briers and wild vines, and overshadowed by a clump of tall and leafy ashes, which had not as yet lost one atom of their foliage, although the underwood beneath them was quite sere and leafless.

"Now then," cried Harry, "this is the 'Squire's swamp-hole!' Now for a dozen cock! hey, Tom? Here, couple up the setters, Tim; and let the spaniels loose. Now Flash! now Dan! down charge, you little villains!" and the well broke brutes dropped on the instant. "How must we beat this cursed hole?"

"You must go through the very thick of it, consarn you!" exclaimed Tom; "at your old work already, hey? trying to shirk at first!"

"Don't swear so! you old reprobate! I know my place, depend on it," cried Archer; "but what to do with the rest of you!--there's the rub!"

"Not a bit of it," cried Tom--"here, Yorkshire--Ducklegs--here, what's your name--get away you with those big dogs--atwixt the swamp-hole, and the brush there by the fence, and look out that you mark every bird to an inch! You, Mr. Forester, go in there, under that butter-nut; you'll find a blind track there, right through the brush--keep that 'twixt Tim and Mr. Archer; and keep your eyes skinned, do! there'll be a cock up before you're ten yards in. Archer, you'll go right through, and I'll..."

"You'll keep well forward on the right--and mind that no bird crosses to the hill; we never get them, if they once get over. All right! In with you now! Steady, Flash! steady! hie up, Dan!" and in a moment Harry was out of sight among the brush-wood, though his progress might be traced by the continual crackling of the thick underwood.

Scarce had I passed the butter-nut, when, even as Torn had said, up flapped a woodcock scarcely ten yards before me, in the open path, and rising heavily to clear the branches of a tall thorn bush, showed me his full black eye, and tawny breast, as fair a shot as could be fancied.

"Mark!" holloaed Harry to my right, his quick ear having caught the flap of the bird's wing, as he rose. "Mark cock--Frank!"

Well--steadily enough, as I thought, I pitched my gun up! covered my bird fairly! pulled!--the trigger gave not to my finger. I tried the other. Devil's in it, I had forgot to cock my gun! and ere I could retrieve my error, the bird had topped the bush, and dodged out of sight, and off--"Mark! mark!--Tim!" I shouted.

"Ey! ey! sur--Ay see's urn!"

"Why, how's that, Frank?" cried Harry. "Couldn't you get a shot?"

"Forgot to cock my gun!" I cried; but at the self-same moment the quick sharp yelping of the spaniels came on my ear. "Steady, Flash! steady, sir! Mark!" But close upon the word came the full round report of Harry's gun. "Mark! again!" shouted Harry, and again his own piece sent its loud ringing voice abroad. "Mark! now a third! mark, Frank!"

And as he spoke I caught the quick rush of his wing, and saw him dart across a space, a few yards to my right. I felt my hand shake; I had not pulled a trigger in ten months, but in a second's space I rallied. There was an opening just before me between a stumpy thick thorn-bush which had saved the last bird, and a dwarf cedar; it was not two yards over; he glanced across it; he was gone, just as my barrel sent its charge into the splintered branches.

"Beautiful!" shouted Harry, who, looking through a cross glade, saw the bird fall, which I could not. "Beautiful shot, Frank! Do all your work like that, and we'll get twenty couple before night!"

"Have I killed him!" answered I, half doubting if he were not quizzing me.

"Killed him? of course you have; doubled him up completely! But look sharp! there are more birds before me! I can hardly keep the dogs down, now! There! there goes one--clean out of shot of me, though! Mark! mark, Tom! Gad, how the fat dog's running!" he continued. "He sees him! Ten to one he gets him! There he goes--bang! A long shot, and killed clean!"

"Ready!" cried I. "I'm ready, Archer!"

"Bag your bird, then. He lies under that dock leaf, at the foot of yon red maple! That's it; you've got him. Steady now, till Tom gets loaded!"

"What did you do?" asked I. "You fired twice, I think!"

"Killed two!" he answered. "Ready, now!" and on he went, smashing away the boughs before him, while ever and anon I heard his cheery voice, calling or whistling to his dogs, or rousing up the tenants of some thickets into which even he could not force his way; and I, creeping, as best I might, among the tangled brush, now plunging half thigh deep in holes full of tenacious mire, now blundering over the moss-covered stubs, pressed forward, fancying every instant that the rustling of the briers against my jacket was the flip-flap of a rising woodcock. Suddenly, after bursting through a mass of thorns and wild-vine, which was in truth almost impassable, I came upon a little grassy spot quite clear of trees, and covered with the tenderest verdure, through which a narrow rill stole silently; and as I set my first foot on it, up jumped, with his beautiful variegated back all reddened by the sunbeams, a fine and full-fed woodcock, with the peculiar twitter which he utters when surprised. He had not gone ten yards, however, before my gun was at my shoulder and the trigger drawn; before I heard the crack I saw him cringe; and, as the white smoke drifted off to leeward, he fell heavily, completely riddled by the shot, into the brake before me; while at the same moment, whir-r-r! up sprung a bevy of twenty quail, at least, startling me for the moment by the thick whirring of their wings, and skirring over the underwood right toward Archer. "Mark, quail!" I shouted, and, recovering instantly my nerves, fired my one remaining barrel after the last bird! It was a long shot, yet I struck him fairly, and he rose instantly right upward, towering high! high! into the clear blue sky, and soaring still, till his life left him in the air, and he fell like a stone, plump downward!

"Mark him! Tim!"

"Ey! ey! sur. He's a de-ad un, that's a sure thing!"

At my shot all the bevy rose a little, yet altered not their course the least, wheeling across the thicket directly round the front of Archer, whose whereabout I knew, though I could neither see nor hear him. So high did they fly that I could observe them clearly, every bird well defined against the sunny heavens. I watched them eagerly. Suddenly one turned over; a cloud of feathers streamed off down the wind; and then, before the sound of the first shot had reached my ears, a second pitched a few yards upward, and, after a heavy flutter, followed its hapless comrade.

Turned by the fall of the two leading birds, the bevy again wheeled, still rising higher, and now flying very fast; so that, as I saw by the direction which they took, they would probably give Draw a chance of getting in both barrels. And so indeed it was; for, as before, long ere I caught the booming echoes of his heavy gun, I saw two birds keeled over, and, almost at the same instant, the cheery shout of Tim announced to me that he had bagged my towered bird! After a little pause, again we started, and, hailing one another now and then, gradually forced our way through brake and brier toward the outward verge of the dense covert. Before we met again, however, I had the luck to pick up a third woodcock, and as I heard another double shot from Archer, and two single bangs from Draw, I judged that my companions had not been less successful than myself. At last, emerging from the thicket, we all converged, as to a common point, toward Tim; who, with his game-bag on the ground, with its capacious mouth wide open to receive our game, sat on a stump with the two setters at a charge beside him.

"What do we score?" cried I, as we drew near; "what do we score?"

"I have four woodcocks, and a brace of quail," said Harry.

"And I, two cock and a brace," cried Tom, "and missed another cock; but he's down in the meadow here, behind that 'ere stump alder!"

"And I, three woodcock and one quail!" I chimed in, naught abashed.

"And Ay'se marked doon three woodcock--two more beside yon big un, that measter Draa made siccan a bungle of--and all t' quail--every feather on um--doon t' bog meadow yonner--ooh! but we'se mak grand sport o't!" interposed Tim, now busily employed stringing bird after bird up by the head, with loops and buttons in the game-bag!

"Well done then, all!" said Harry. "Nine timber-doodles and five quail, and only one shot missed! That's not bad shooting, considering what a hole it is to shoot in. Gentlemen, here's your health," and filling himself out a fair sized wine-glassfull of Ferintosh, into the silver cup of his dram-bottle, he tossed it off; and then poured out a similar libation for Tim Matlock. Tom and myself, nothing loth, obeyed the hint, and sipped our modicums of distilled waters out of our private flasks.

"Now, then," cried Archer, "let us pick up these scattering birds. Tom Draw, you can get yours without a dog! And now, Tim, where are yours?"

"T' first lies oop yonner in yon boonch of brachens, ahint t' big scarlet maple; and t' other--"

"Well! I'll go to the first. You take Mr. Forester to the other, and when we have bagged all three, we'll meet at the bog meadow fence, and then hie at the bevy!"

This job was soon done, for Draw and Harry bagged their birds cleverly at the first rise; and although mine got off at first without a shot, by dodging round a birch tree straight in Tim's face, and flew back slap toward the thicket, yet he pitched in its outer skirt, and as he jumped up wild I cut him down with a broken pinion and a shot through his bill at fifty yards, and Chase retrieved him well.

"Cleverly stopped, indeed!" Frank halloaed; "and by no means an easy shot! and so our work's clean done for this place, at the least!"

"The boy can shoot some," observed Tom Draw, who loved to bother Timothy; "the boy can shoot some, though he does come from Yorkshire!"

"Gad! and Ay wush Ay'd no but gotten thee i' Yorkshire, measter Draa!" responded Tim.

"Why! what if you had got me there?"

"What? Whoy, Ay'd clap thee iv a cage, and hug thee round t' feasts and fairs loike; and shew thee to t' folks at so mooch a head. Ay'se sure Ay'd mak a fortune o' t!"

"He has you there, Tom! Ha! ha! ha!" laughed Archer. "Tim's down upon you there, by George! Now, Frank, do fancy Tom Draw in a cage at Borough-bridge or Catterick fair! Lord! how the folks would pay to look at him! Fancy the sign board too! The Great American Man-Mammoth! Ha! ha! ha! But come, we must not stay here talking nonsense, or we shall do no good. Show me, Tim, where are the quail!"

"Doon t' bog meadow yonner! joost t' slack,[3] see thee, there!" pointing with the stout black-thorn; "amang yon bits o' bushes!"

"Very well--that's it; now let go the setters; take Flash and Dan along with you, and cut across the country as straight as you can go to the spring head, where we lunched last year; that day, you know, Tom, when McTavish frightened the bull out of the meadow, under the pin-oak tree. Well! put the champagne into the spring to cool, and rest yourself there till we come; we shan't be long behind you."

Away went Tim, stopping from time to time to mark our progress, and over the fence into the bog meadow we proceeded; a rascally piece of broken tussockky ground, with black mud knee-deep between the hags, all covered with long grass. The third step I took, over I went upon my nose, but luckily avoided shoving my gun-barrels into the filthy mire.

"Steady, Frank, steady! I'm ashamed of you!" said Harry; "so hot and so impetu-

---

3   Slack--Yorkshire. Anglice, Moist hollow

ous; and your gun too at the full cock; that's the reason, man, why you missed firing at your first bird, this morning. I never cock either barrel till I see my bird; and, if a bevy rises, only one at a time. The birds will lie like stones here; and we cannot walk too slow. Steady, Shot, have a care, sir!"

Never, in all my life, did I see any thing more perfect than the style in which the setters drew those bogs. There was no more of racing, no more of impetuous dash; it seemed as if they knew the birds were close before them. At a slow trot, their sterns whipping their flanks at every step, they threaded the high tussockks. See! the red dog straightens his neck, and snuffs the air.

"Look to! look to, Frank! they are close before old Chase!"

Now he draws on again, crouching close to the earth. "Toho! Shot!" Now he stands! no! no! not yet--at least he is not certain! He turns his head to catch his master's eye! Now his stern moves a little; he draws on again.

There! he is sure now! what a picture--his black full eye intently glaring, though he cannot see any thing in that thick mass of herbage; his nostril wide expanded, his lips slavering from intense excitement; his whole form motionless, and sharply drawn, and rigid, even to the straight stern and lifted foot, as a block wrought to mimic life by some skilful sculptor's chisel; and, scarce ten yards behind, his liver-colored comrade backs him--as firm, as stationary, as immovable, but in his attitude, how different! Chase feels the hot scent steaming up under his very nostril; feels it in every nerve, and quivers with anxiety to dash on his prey, even while perfectly restrained and steady. Shot, on the contrary, though a few minutes since he too was drawing, knows nothing of himself, perceives no indication of the game's near presence, although improved by discipline, his instinct tells him that his mate has found them. Hence the same rigid form, stiff tail, and constrained attitude, but in his face--for dogs have faces--there is none of that tense energy, that evident anxiety; there is no frown upon his brow, no glare in his mild open eye, no slaver on his lip!

"Come up, Tom; come up, Frank, they are all here; we must get in six barrels; they will not move: come up, I say!"

And on we came, deliberately prompt, and ready. Now we were all in line: Harry the centre man, I on the right, and Tom on the left hand. The attitude of Archer was superb; his legs, set a little way apart, as firm as if they had been rooted in the soil; his form drawn back a little, and his head erect, with his eye fixed upon the dogs; his gun held in both hands, across his person, the muzzle slightly elevated, his left grasping the trigger guard; the thumb of the right resting upon the hammer, and the fore-finger on the trigger of the left hand barrel; but, as he had said, neither cocked. "Fall back, Tom, if you please, five yards or so," he said, as coolly as if he were unconcerned, "and you come forward, Frank, as many; I want to drive them to the left, into those low red bushes; that will do: now then, I'll flush them; never mind me, boys, I'll reserve my fire."

And, as he spoke, he moved a yard or two in front of us, and under his very feet, positively startling me by their noisy flutter, up sprang the gallant bevy: fifteen or sixteen well grown birds, crowding and jostling one against the other. Tom Draw's gun, as I well believe, was at his shoulder when they rose; at least his first shot was discharged before they had flown half a rood, and of course harmlessly: the charge must have been driven through them like a single ball; his second barrel instantly succeeded, and down came two birds, caught in the act of crossing. I am myself a quick shot, too quick if anything, yet my first barrel was exploded a moment after Tom Draw's second; the other followed, and I had the satisfaction of bringing both my birds down handsomely; then up went Harry's piece--the bevy being now twenty or twenty-five yards distant--cocking it as it rose, he pulled the trigger almost before it touched his shoulder, so rapid was the movement; and, though he lowered the stock a little to cock the second barrel, a moment scarcely passed between the two reports, and almost on the instant two quail were fluttering out their lives among the bog grass.

Dropping his butt, without a word, or even a glance to the dogs, he quietly went on to load; nor indeed was it needed: at the first shot they dropped into the grass, and there they lay as motionless as if they had been dead, with their heads crouched between their paws; nor did they stir thence till the tick of the gun-locks announced that we again were ready. Then lifting up their heads, and rising on their fore-feet, they sat half erect, eagerly waiting for the signal.

"Hold up, good lads!" and on they drew, and in an instant pointed on two several birds. "Fetch!" and each brought his burthen to our feet; six birds were bagged at that rise, and thus before eleven o'clock we had picked up a dozen cock, and within one of the same number of fine quail, with only two shots missed. The poor remainder of the bevy had dropped, singly, and scattered, in the red bushes, whither we instantly pursued them, and where we got six more, making a total of seventeen birds bagged out of a bevy, twenty strong at first.

One towered bird of Harry's, certainly killed dead, we could not with all our efforts bring to bag; one bird Tom Draw missed clean, and the remaining one we could not find again; another dram of whiskey, and into Seer's great swamp we started: a large piece of woodland, with every kind of lying. At one end it was open, with soft black loamy soil, covered with docks and colts-foot leaves under the shade of large but leafless willows, and here we picked up a good many scattered woodcock; afterward we got into the heavy thicket with much tangled grass, wherein we flushed a bevy, but they all took to tree, and we made very little of them; and here Tom Draw began to blow and labor; the covert was too thick, the bottom too deep and unsteady for him.

Archer perceiving this, sent him at once to the outside; and three times, as we went along, ourselves moving nothing, we heard the round reports of his large calibre. "A bird at every shot, I'd stake my life," said Harry, "he never misses cross shots in the open;" at the same instant, a tremendous rush of wings burst from the heaviest thicket: "Mark! partridge! partridge!" and as I caught a glimpse of a dozen large birds fluttering up, one close upon the other, and darting away as straight and nearly as fast as bullets, through the dense branches of a cedar brake, I saw the flashes of both Harry's barrels, almost simultaneously discharged, and at the same time over went the objects of his aim; but ere I could get up my gun the rest were out of sight. "You must shoot, Frank, like lightning, to kill these beggars; they are the ruffed grouse, though they call them partridge here: see! are they not fine fellows?"

Another hour's beating, in which we still kept picking up, from time to time, some scattering birds, brought us to the spring head, where we found Tim with luncheon ready, and our fat friend reposing at his side, with two more grouse, and a rabbit which he had bagged along the covert's edge. Cool was the Star champagne; and capital was the cold fowl and Cheshire cheese; and most delicious was the repose that followed, enlivened with gay wit and free good humor, soothed by the fragrance of the exquisite cheroots, moistened by the last drops of the Ferintosh qualified by the crystal waters of the spring. After an hour's rest, we counted up our spoil; four ruffed grouse, nineteen woodcocks, with ten brace and a half of quail beside the bunny, made up our score-- done comfortably in four hours.

"Now we have finished for to-day with quail," said Archer, "but we'll get full ten couple more of woodcock; come, let us be stirring; hang up your game-bag in the tree, and tie the setters to the fence; I want you in with me to beat, Tim; you two chaps must both keep the outside--you all the time, Tom; you, Frank, till you get to that tall thunder-shivered ash tree; turn in there, and follow up the margin of a wide slank you will see; but be careful, the mud is very deep, and dangerous in places; now then, here goes!"

And in he went, jumping a narrow streamlet into a point of thicket, through which he drove by main force. Scarce had he got six yards into the brake, before both spaniels quested; and, to my no small wonder, the jungle seemed alive with woodcock; eight or nine, at the least, flapped up at once, and skimmed along the tongue of coppice toward the high wood, which ran along the valley, as I learned afterward, for full three miles in length--while four or five more wheeled off to the sides, giving myself and Draw fair shots, by which we did not fail to profit; but I confess it was with absolute astonishment that I saw two of those turned over, which flew inward, killed by the marvelously quick and unerring aim of Archer, where a less thorough sportsman would have been quite unable to discharge a gun at all, so dense was the tangled jungle. Throughout the whole length of that skirt of coppice, a hundred and fifty yards, I should suppose at the utmost, the birds kept rising as it were incessantly--thirty-five, or, I think, nearly forty, being flushed in less than twenty minutes, although comparatively few were killed, partly from the difficulty of the ground, and partly from their getting up by fours and fives at once. Into the high wood, however, at the last we drove them; and there, till daylight failed us, we did our work like men. By the cold light of the full moon we wended homeward, rejoicing in the possession of twenty-six couple and a half of cock, twelve brace of quail--we found another bevy on our way home and bagged three birds almost by moonlight--five ruffed grouse, and a rabbit. Before our wet clothes were well changed, supper was ready, and a good blow-out was followed by sound slumbers and sweet dreams, fairly earned by nine hours of incessant walking.

DAY THE THIRD

So thoroughly was I tired out by the effects of the first day's fagging I had undergone in many months, and so sound was the slumber into which I sank the moment my head touched the pillow, that it scarcely seemed as if five minutes had elapsed between my falling into sweet forgetfulness, and my starting bolt upright in bed, aroused by the vociferous shout, and ponderous tramping, equal to nothing less than that of a full-grown rhinoceros, with which Tom Draw rushed, long before the sun was up, into my chamber.

"What's this, what's this now?" he exclaimed; "why the plague arn't you up and ready?--why here's the bitters mixed, and Archer in the stable this half hour past, and Jem's here with the hounds--and you, you lazy snorting Injun, wasting the morning here in bed!"

My only reply to this most characteristic salutation, was to hurl my pillow slap in his face, and--threatening to follow up the missile with the contents of the water pitcher, which stood temptingly within my reach, if he did not get out incontinently--to jump up and array myself with all due speed; for, when I had collected my bewildered thoughts, I well remembered that we had settled on a fox-hunt before breakfast, as a preliminary to a fresh skirmish with the quail.

In a few minutes I was on foot and in the parlor, where I found a bright crackling fire, a mighty pitcher of milk punch, and a plate of biscuit, an apt substitute for breakfast before starting; while, however, I was discussing these, Archer arrived, dressed just as I have described him on the preceding day, with the addition of a pair of heavy hunting spurs, buckled on over his half-boots, and a large iron-hammered whip in his right hand.

"That's right, Frank," he exclaimed, after the ordinary salutations of the morning.

"Why that old porpoise told me you would not be ready these two hours; he's grumbling out yonder by the stable door, like a hog stuck in a farm-yard gate. But come, we may as well be moving, for the hounds are all uncoupled, and the nags saddled--put on a pair of straps to your fustian trowsers and take these racing spurs, though Peacock does not want them--and now, hurrah!"

This was soon done, and going out upon the stoop, a scene--it is true, widely different from the kennel door at Melton, or the covert side at Billesdon Coplow, yet not by any means devoid of interest or animation-- presented itself to my eyes. About six couple of large heavy hounds, with deep and pendant ears, heavy well-feathered sterns, broad chests, and muscular strong limbs, were gathered round their feeder, the renowned Jem Lyn; on whom it may not be impertinent to waste a word or two, before proceeding to the mountain, which, as I learned, to my no little wonder, was destined to be our hunting ground.

Picture to yourself, then, gentle reader, a small but actively formed man, with a face of most unusual and portentous ugliness, an uncouth grin doing the part of a smile; a pair of eyes so small that they would have been invisible, but for the serpent-like vivacity and brightness with which they sparkled from their deep sockets, and a profusion of long hair, coal-black, but lank and uncurled as an Indian's, combed smoothly down with a degree of care entirely out of keeping with the other details, whether of dress or countenance, on either cheek. Above these sleek and cherished tresses he wore a thing which might have passed for either cap or castor, at the wearer's pleasure; for it was wholly destitute of brim except for a space some three or four inches wide over the eye-rows; and the crown had been so pertinaciously and completely eaten in, that the sides sloped inward at the top, as if to personate a bishop's mitre; a fishing line was wound about this graceful and, if its appearance belied it not most foully, odoriferous headdress; and into the fishing line was stuck the bowl and some two inches of the shank of a well-sooted pipe. An old red handkerchief was twisted rope-wise about his lean and scraggy neck, but it by no means sufficed to hide the scar of what had evidently been a most appalling gash, extending right across his throat, almost from ear to ear, the great cicatrix clearly visible like a white line through the thick stubble of some ten days' standing that graced his chin and neck.

An old green coat, the skirts of which had long since been docked by the encroachment of thorn-bushes and cat-briers, with the mouth-piece of a powder-horn peeping from its breast pocket, and a full shot-belt crossing his right shoulder; a pair of fustian trowsers, patched at the knees with corduroy, and heavy cowhide boots completed his attire. This, as it seemed, was to be our huntsman; and Booth to say, although he did not look the character, he played the part, when he got to work, right handsomely. At a more fitting season, Harry in a few words let me into this worthy's history and disposition. "He is," he said, "the most incorrigible rascal I ever met with--an unredeemed and utter vagabond; he started life as a stallion-leader, a business which he understands-- as in fact he does almost every thing else within his scope--thoroughly well. He got on prodigiously!--was employed by the first breeders in the country!--took to drinking, and then, in due rotation, to gambling, pilfering, lying, every vice, in short, which is compatible with utter want of any thing like moral sense, deep shrewdness, and uncommon cowardice.

"He cut his throat once--you may see the scar now--in a fit of delirium tremens, and Tom Draw, who, though he is perpetually cursing him for the most lying critter under heaven, has, I believe, a sort of fellow feeling for him--nursed him and got him well; and ever since he has hung about here, getting at times a country stallion to look after, at others hunting, or fishing, or doing little jobs about the stable, for which Tom gives him plenty of abuse, plenty to eat, and as little rum as possible, for if he gets a second glass it is all up with Jem Lyn for a week at least.

"He came to see me once in New York, when I was down upon my back with a broken leg--I was lying in the parlor, about three weeks after the accident had happened. Tim Matlock had gone out for something, and the cook let him in; and, after he had sat there about half an hour, telling me all the news of the races, and making me laugh more than was good for my broken leg, he gave me such a hint, that I was compelled to direct him to the cupboard, wherein I kept the liquor-stand; and unluckily enough, as I had not for some time been in drinking tune, all three of the bottles were brimful; and, as I am a Christian man, he drank in spite of all I could say--I could not leave the couch to get at him--two of them to the dregs; and, after frightening me almost to death, fell flat upon the floor, and lay there fast asleep when Tim came in again. He dragged him instantly, by my directions, under the pump in the garden, and soused him for about two hours, but without producing the least effect, except eliciting a grunt or two from this most seasoned cask.

"Such is Jem Lyn, and yet, absurd to say, I have tried the fellow, and believe him perfectly trustworthy--at least to me!

"He is a coward, yet I have seen him fight like a hero more than once, and against heavy odds, to save me from a threshing, which I got after all, though not without some damage to our foes, whose name might have been legion.

"He is the greatest liar I ever met with; and yet I never caught him in a false-hood, for he believes it is no use to tell me one.

"He is most utterly dishonest, yet I have trusted him with sums that would, in his opinion, have made him a rich man for life, and he accounted to the utmost shilling; but I advise you not try the same, for if you do he most assuredly will cheat you!"

Among the heavy looking hounds, which clustered round this hopeful gentle-man, I quickly singled out two couple of widely different breed and character from the rest; your thorough high-bred racing fox-hounds, with ears rounded, thin shin-ing coats, clean limbs, and all the marks of the best class of English hounds.

"Aye! Frank," said Archer, as he caught my eye fixed on them, "you have found out my favorites. Why, Bonny Belle, good lass, why Bonny Belle!-- here Blossom, Blossom, come up and show your pretty figures to your countryman! Poor Han-bury--do you remember, Frank, how many a merry day we've had with him by Thorley Church, and Takely forest?--poor Hanbury sent them to me with such a letter, only the year before he died; and those, Dauntless and Dangerous, I had from Will, Lord Harewood's huntsman, the same season!"

"There never was sich dogs--there never was afore in Orange," said Tom. "I will say that, though they be English; and though they be too fast for fox, entirely, there never was sich dogs for deer"

"But how the deuce," I interrupted, "can hounds be too fast, if they have bone and stanchness!"

"Stanchness be darned; they holes them!"

"No earthstoppers in these parts, Frank," cried Harry; "and as the object of these gentlemen is not to hunt solely for the fun of the thing, but to destroy a nox-ious varmint, they prefer a slow, sure, deep-mouthed dog, that does not press too closely on Pug, but lets him take his time about the coverts, till he comes into fair gunshot of these hunters, who are lying perdu as he runs to get a crack at him."

"And pray," said I, "is this your method of proceeding?"

"You shall see, you shall see; come get to horse, or it will be late before we get our breakfast, and I assure you I don't wish to lose either that, or my day's quail-shooting. This hunt is merely for a change, and to get something of an appetite for breakfast. Now, Tim, be sure that every thing is ready by eight o'clock at the latest--we shall be in by that time with a furious appetite."

Thus saying he mounted, without more delay, his favorite, the gray; while I backed, nothing loth, the chestnut horse; and at the same time to my vast astonishment, from under the long shed out rode the mighty Tom, bestriding a tall powerful brown mare, showing a monstrous deal of blood combined with no slight bone--equipped with a cavalry bridle, and strange to say, without the universal martingal; he was rigged just as usual, with the exception of a broad-brimmed hat in place of his fur cap, and grasped in his right hand a heavy smooth-bored rifle, while with the left he wheeled his mare, with a degree of active skill, which I should certainly have looked for any where rather than in so vast a mass of flesh as that which was exhibited by our worthy host.

Two other sportsmen, grave, sober-looking farmers, whom Harry greeted cheerily by name, and to whom in all due form I was next introduced, well-mounted, and armed with long single-barreled guns, completed our party; and away we went at a rattling trot, the hounds following at Archer's heels, as steadily as though he hunted them three times a week.

"Now arn't it a strange thing," said Tom, "arn't it a strange thing, Mr. Forester, that every critter under Heaven takes somehow nat'rally to that are Archer--the very hounds--old Whino there! that I have had these eight years, and fed with my own hands, and hunted steady every winter, quits me the very moment he claps sight on him; by the eternal, I believe he is half dog himself."

"You hunted them indeed," interrupted Harry, "you old rhinoceros, why hang your hide, you never so much as heard a good view-holloa till I came up here--you hunted them--a man talk of hunting, that carries a cannon about with him on horseback; but come, where are we to try first, on Rocky Hill, or in the Spring Swamps?"

"Why now I reckon, Archer, we'd best stop down to Sam Blain's--by the blacksmith's--he was telling t'other morning of an eternal sight of them he'd seen down hereaway--and we'll be there to rights!--Jem, cus you, out of my way, you dumb nigger--out of my way, or I'll ride over you"-- for, traveling along at a strange shambling run, that worthy had contrived to keep up with us, though we were going fully at the rate of eight or nine miles in the hour.

"Hurrah!" cried Tom, suddenly pulling up at the door of a neat farm-house on the brow of a hill, with a clear streamlet sweeping round its base, and a fine piece of woodland at the farther side. "Hurrah! Sam Blain, we've come to make them foxes, you were telling of a Sunday, smell h-ll right straight away. Here's Archer, and another Yorker with him--leastwise an Englisher I should say--and Squire Conklin, and Bill Speers, and that white nigger Jem! Look sharp, I say! Look sharp, cuss you, else we'll pull off the ruff of the old humstead."

In a few minutes Sam made his appearance, armed, like the rest, with a Queen Ann's tower-musket.

"Well! well!" he said, "I'm ready. Quit making such a clatter! Lend me a load of powder, one of you; my horn's leaked dry, I reckon!"

Tom forthwith handed him his own, and the next thing I heard was Blain exclaiming that it was "desperate pretty powder," and wondered if it shot strong.

"Shoot strong? I guess you'll find it strong enough to sew you up, if you go charging your old musket that ways!" answered Tom. "By the Lord, Archer, he's put in three full charges!"

"Well, it will kill him, that's all!" answered Harry, very coolly; "and there'll be one less of you. But come! come! let's be bustling; the sun's going to get up already. You'll leave your horses here, I suppose, gentlemen, and get to the old stands. Tom Draw, put Mr. Forester at my old post down by the big pin-oak at the creek side; and you stand there, Frank, still as a church-mouse. It's ten to one, if some of those fellows don't shoot him first, that he'll break covert close by you, and run the meadows for a mile or two, up to the turnpike road, and over it to Rocky hill--that black knob yonder, covered with pine and hemlock. There are some queer snake fences in the flat, and a big brook or two, but Peacock has been over every inch of it before, and you may trust in him implicitly. Good bye! I'm going up the road with Jem to drive it from the upper end."

And off he went at a merry trot, with the hounds gamboling about his stirrups, and Jem Lyn running at his best pace to keep up with him. In a few minutes they were lost behind a swell of woodland, round which the road wheeled suddenly. At the same moment Tom and his companions reappeared from the stables where they had been securing their four-footed friends; and, after a few seconds, spent in running ramrods down the barrels to see that all was right, inspecting primings, knapping flints, or putting on fresh copper caps, it was announced that all was ready; and passing through the farm-yard, we entered, through a set of bars, a broad bright buckwheat stubble. Scarcely an hundred yards had we proceeded, before we sprung the finest bevy of the largest quail I had yet seen, and flying high and wild crossed half-a-dozen fields in the direction of the village, whence we had started, and pitched at length into an alder brake beside the stream.

"Them chaps has gone the right way," Tom exclaimed, with a deep sigh, who had with wondrous difficulty refrained from firing into them, though he was loaded with buckshot; "right in the course we count to take this forenoon. Now, Squire, keep to the left here, take your station by the old earths there away, under the tall dead pine; and you, Bill, make tracks there, straight through the middle cart-way, down to the other meadow, and sit you down right where the two streams fork; there'll be an old red snooping down that side afore long, I reckon. We'll go on, Mr. Forester; here's a big rail fence now; I'll throw off the top rail, for be darned if I climb any day when I can creep--there, that'll do, I reckon; leastwise if you can ride like Archer--he d--ns me always if I so much as shakes a fence afore he jumps it-- you've got the best horse, too, for lepping. Now let's see! Well done! well done!" he continued, with a most boisterous burst of laughter--"well done, horse, any how!"-- as Peacock, who had been chafing ever since he parted from his comrade Bob, went at the fence as though he were about to take it in his stroke --stopped short when within a yard of it, and then bucked over it, without touching a splinter, although it was at least five feet, and shaking me so much, that, greatly to Tom's joy, I showed no little glimpse of day-light.

"I reckon if they run the meadows, you'll hardly ride them, Forester," he grinned; "but now away with you. You see the tall dark pin oak, it hasn't lost one leaf yet; right in the nook there of the bars you'll find a quiet shady spot, where you can see clear up the rail fence to this knob, where I'll be. Off with you, boy--and mind you now, you keep as dumb as the old woman when her husband cut her tongue out, 'cause she had too much jaw."

Finishing his discourse, he squatted himself down on the stool of a large hem-lock, which, being recently cut down, cumbered the woodside with its giant stem, and secured him, with its evergreen top now lowly laid and withering, from the most narrow scrutiny; while I, giving the gallant horse his head, went at a brisk hand-gallop across the firm short turf of the fair sloping hill-side, taking a moderate fence in my stroke, which Peacock cleared in a style that satisfied me Harry had by no means exaggerated his capacity to act as hunter, in lieu of the less glorious oc-cupation, to which in general he was doomed.

In half a minute more I reached my post, and though an hour passed before I heard the slightest sound betokening the chase, never did I more thoroughly enjoy an hour.

The loveliness of the whole scene before me--the broad rich sweep of mead-owland lying, all bathed in dew, under the pale gray light of an autumnal morning, with groups of cattle couched still between the trees where they had passed the night; the distant hills, veiled partially in mist, partially rearing their round leafy heads toward the brightening sky; and then the various changes of the landscape, as slowly the day broke behind the eastern hill; and all the various sounds of bird, and beast, and insect, which each succeeding variation of the morning served to call into life as if by magic. First a faint rosy flush stole up the eastern sky, and nearly at the self-same moment, two or three vagrant crows came flapping heavily along, at a height so immeasurable that their harsh voices were by distance modified into a pleasing murmur. And now a little fish jumped in the streamlet; and the splash, trifling as it was, with which he fell back on the quiet surface, half startled me.

A moment afterward an acorn plumped down on my head, and as I looked up, there sat, on a limb not ten feet above me, an impudent rogue of a gray squirrel, half as big as a rabbit, erect upon his haunches, working away at the twin brother of the acorn he had dropped upon my hat to break my reverie, rasping it audibly with his chisel-shaped teeth, and grinning at me just as coolly as though I were a harmless scare-crow.

When I grew tired of observing him, and looked toward the sky again, behold the western ridge, which is far higher than the eastern hills, had caught upon its summits the first bright rays of the yet unseen day-god; while the rosy flush of the east had brightened into a blaze of living gold, exceeded only by the glorious hues

with which a few bright specks of misty cloud glowed out against the azure firmament, like coals of actual fire. Again a louder splash aroused me; and, as I turned,
there floated on a glassy basin, into which the ripples of a tiny fall subsided, three
wood-ducks, with a noble drake, that loveliest in plumage of all aquatic fowl, perfectly undisturbed and fearless, although within ten yards of their most dreaded
enemy.

How beautiful are all their motions! There! one has reared herself half way out
of the water; another stretches forth a delicate web foot to scratch her ear, as hand-
ily as a dog on dry land; and now the drake reflects his purple neck to preen his
ruffled wing, and now--bad luck to you, Peacock, why did you snort and stamp?--
they are off like a bullet, and out of sight in an instant.

And now out comes the sun himself, and with him the accursed hum of a
musquitoe--and hark! hush!--what was that?--was it? By Heavens! it was the deep
note of a fox-hound! Aye! there comes Harry's cheer, faintly heard, swelling up the
breeze.

"Have at him, there! Ha-a-ve at him, good lads!"

Again! again! those are the musical deep voices of the slow hounds! They have
a dash in them of the old Southern breed! And now! there goes the yell! the quick
sharp yelping rally of those two high-bred bitches. By heaven! they must be viewing him! How the woods ring and crash!

"Together hark! Together hark! Together! For-ra-ard, good lads, get for-a-ard!
Hya-a-araway!"

Well halloaed, Harry! I could swear to that last screech, out of ten thousand,
though it is near ten years since I last heard it! But heavens! how they press him!
Hang it! there goes a shot--the squire has fired at him, as he tried the earths! Now,
if he have but missed him, and Pan, the god of hunters, send it so, he has no chance
but to try the open.

By Jove he has! he must have missed! for Bonny Belle and Blossom are raving
half a mile this side of him already. And now Tom sees him--how quietly he steals
up to the fence. There! he has fired! and all our sport is up! No! no! he waves his hat
and points this way! Can he have missed? No! he has got a fox!--he lifts it out by the
brush--there must have been two, then, on foot together. He has done it well to get
that he has killed away, or they would have stopped on him!

Hush! the leaves rustle here beside me, with a quick patter--the twigs crackle--it is he! Move not! not for your life, Peacock! There! he has broken cover fairly! Now he is half across the field! he stops to listen! Ah! he will head again. No! no! that crash, when they came upon the warm blood, has decided him--away he goes, with his brush high, and its white tag brandished in the sunshine--now I may halloa him away.

"Whoop! gone awa-ay! whoop!"

I was answered on the instant by Harry's quick--"Hark holloa! get awa-ay! to him hark! to him hark! hark holloa!"

Most glorious Artemis, what heaven-stirring music! And yet there are but poor six couple; the scent must be as hot as fire, for every hound seems to have twenty tongues, and every leaf an hundred echoes! How the boughs crash again! Lo! they are here! Bonny Belle leading--head and stern up, with a quick panting yelp! Blossom, and Dangerous, and Dauntless scarcely a length behind her, striving together, neck and neck; and, by St. Hubert, it must be a scent of twenty thousand, for here these heavy Southrons are scarcely two rods behind them.

But fidget not, good Peacock! fret not, most excellent Pythagoras! one moment more, and I am not the boy to baulk you. And here comes Harry on the gray; by George! he makes the brushwood crackle! Now for a nasty leap out of the tangled swamp! a high six-barred fence of rough trees, leaning toward him, and up hill! surely he will not try it!

Will he not though?

See!--his rein is tight yet easy! his seat, how beautiful, how firm, yet how relaxed and graceful! Well done, indeed! He slacks his rein one instant as the gray rises! the rugged rails are cleared, and the firm pull supports him! but Harry moves not in the saddle--no! not one hair's breadth! A five foot fence to him is nothing! You shall not see the slightest variation between his attitude in that strong effort, and in the easy gallop. If Tom Draw saw him now, he could have some excuse for calling him "half horse"--and he does see him! hark to that most unearthly knell! like unto nothing, either heavenly or human! He waves his hat and hurries back as fast as he is able to the horses, well knowing that for pedestrians at least, the morning's sport is ended.

Harry and I were now almost abreast, riding in parallel lines, down the rich valley, very nearly at the top speed of our horses; taking fence after fence in our stroke, and keeping well up with the hounds, which were running almost mute, such was the furious speed to which the blazing scent excited them.

We had already passed above two-thirds of the whole distance that divides the range of woods, wherein we found him, and the pretty village which we had constituted our head quarters, a distance of at least three miles; and now a very difficult and awkward obstacle presented itself to our farther progress, in the shape of a wide yawning brook between sheer banks of several feet in height, broken, with rough and pointed stones, the whole being at least five yards across. The gallant hounds dashed over it; and, when we reached it, were half way across the grass field next beyond it.

"Hold him hard, Frank," Harry shouted; "hold him hard, man, and cram him at it!"

And so I did, though I had little hope of clearing it. I lifted him a little on the snaffle, gave him the spur just as he reached the brink, and with a long and swinging leap, so easy that its motion was in truth scarce perceptible, he swept across it; before I had the time to think, we were again going at our best pace almost among the hounds.

Over myself, I cast a quick glance back toward Harry, who, by a short turn of the chase had been thrown a few yards behind me. He charged it gallantly; but on the very verge, cowed by the brightness of the rippling water, the gray made a half stop, but leaped immediately, beneath the application of the galling spur; he made a noble effort, but it was scarce a thing to be effected by a standing leap, and it was with far less pleasure than surprise, that I saw him drop his hind legs down the steep bank, having just landed with fore-feet in the meadow.

I was afraid, indeed, he must have had an ugly fall, but, picked up quickly by the delicate and steady finger of his rider, the good horse found some slight projection of the bank, whereby to make a second spring. After a heavy flounder, however, which must have dismounted any less perfect horseman, he recovered himself well, and before many minutes was again abreast of me.

Thus far the course of the hunted fox had lain directly homeward, down the valley; but now the turnpike road making a sudden turn crossed his line at right angles, while another narrower road coming in at a tangent, went off to the south-westward in the direction of the bold projection, which I had learned to recognize as Rocky Hill; over the high fence into the road; well performed, gallant horses! And now they check for a moment, puzzling about on the dry sandy turnpike.

"Dangerous feathers on it now! Speak to it! speak to it, good hound!"

How beautiful that flourish of the stern with which he darts away on the recovered scent; with what a yell they open it once again! Harry was right, he makes for Rocky Hill, but up this plaguey lane, where the scent lies but faintly. Now! now! the road turns off again far westward of his point! He may, by Jove! And he has left it!

"Have at him then, lads; he is ours!"

And lo! the pace increases. Ha! what a sudden turn, and in the middle too of a clear pasture.

"Has he been headed, Harry?"

"No, no; his strength is failing."

And see! he makes his point again toward the hill; it is within a quarter of a mile, and if he gain it we can do nothing with him, for it is full of earths. But he will never reach it. See! he turns once again; how exquisitely well those bitches run it; three times he has doubled, now almost as short as a hare, and they, running breast-high, have turned with him each time, not over-running it a yard.

See how the sheep have drawn together into phalanx yonder, in that bare pasture to the eastward; he has crossed that field for a thousand! Yes, I am right. See! they turn once again. What a delicious rally! An outspread towel would cover those four leading hounds--now Dauntless has it; has it by half a neck.

"He always goes up when a fox is sinking," Harry exclaimed, pointing toward him with his hunting whip.

Aye! he has given up his point entirely; he knew he could not face the hill. Look! look at those carrion crows! how low they stoop over that woody bank. That is his line. Here is the road again. Over it once more merrily! and now we view him.

"Whoop! Forra-ard, lads, forra-ard!"

He cannot hold five minutes; and see, there comes fat Tom pounding that mare along the road as if her fore-feet were of hammered iron; he has come up along the turnpike, at an infernal pace, while that turn favored him; but he will only see us kill him, and that, too, at a respectful distance.

Another brook stretches across our course, hurrying to join the greater stream along the banks of which we have so long been speeding; but this is a little one; there! we have cleared it cleverly. Now! now! the hounds are viewing him. Poor brute! his day is come. See how he twists and doubles, Ah! now they have him! No! that short turn has saved him, and he gains the fence--he will lie down there! No! he stretches gallantly across the next field--game to the last, poor devil! There!

"Who-whoop! Dead! dead! who-whoop!"

And in another instant Harry had snatched him from the hounds, and holding him aloft displayed him to the rest, as they came up along the road.

"A pretty burst," he said to me, "a pretty burst, Frank, and a good kill; but they can't stand before the hounds, the foxes here, like our stout islanders; they are not forced to work so hard to gain their living. But now let us get homeward; I want my breakfast, I can tell you, and then a rattle at the quail. I mean to get full forty brace to-day, I promise you."

"And we," said I, "have marked down fifteen brace already toward it; right in the line of our beat, Tom says."

"That's right; well, let us go on."

And in a short half hour we were all once again assembled about Tom's hospitable board, and making such a breakfast, on every sort of eatable that can be crowded on a breakfast table, as sportsmen only have a right to make; nor they, unless they have walked ten, or galloped half as many miles, before it.

Before we had been in an hour, Harry once again roused us out. All had been, during our absence, fully prepared by the indefatigable Tim; who, as the day before, accoutered with spare shot and lots of provender, seemed to grudge us each morsel that we ate, so eager was he to see us take the field in season.

Off we went then; but what boots it to repeat a thrice told tale; suffice it, that the dogs worked as well as dogs can work; that birds were plentiful, and lying good; that we fagged hard, and shot on the whole passably, so that by sunset we had exceeded Harry's forty brace by fifteen birds, and got beside nine couple and a half of woodcock; which we found, most unexpectedly, basking themselves in the open meadow, along the grassy banks of a small rill, without a bush or tree within five hundred yards of them.

Evening had closed before we reached the well known tavern-stand, and the merry blaze of the fire, and many candles, showed us, while yet far distant, that due preparations were in course for our entertainment.

"What have we here?" cried Harry, as we reached the door--"Race horses? Why, Tom, by heaven! we've got the Flying Dutchman here again; now for a night of it."

And so in truth it was, a most wet, and most jovial one, seasoned with no small wit; but of that, more anon.

DAY THE FOURTH

When we had entered Tom's hospitable dwelling, and delivered over our guns to be duly cleaned, and the dogs to be suppered, by Tim Matlock, I passed through the parlor, on my way to my own crib, where I found Archer in close confabulation with a tall rawboned Dutchman, with a keen freckled face, small 'cute gray eyes, looking suspiciously about from under the shade of a pair of straggling sandy eyebrows, small reddish whiskers, and a head of carroty hair as rough and tangled as a fox's back.

His aspect was a wondrous mixture of sneakingness and smartness, and his expression did most villainously belie him, if he were not as sharp a customer as ever wagged an elbow, or betted on a horse-race.

"Frank," exclaimed Harry, as I entered, "I make you know Mr. McTaggart, better known hereabouts as the Flying Dutchman, though how he came by a Scotch name I can't pretend to say; he keeps the best quarter horses, and plays the best hand of whist in the country; and now, get yourself clean as quick as possible, for Tom never gives one five minutes wherein to dress himself; so bustle."

And off he went as he had finished speaking, and I shaking my new friend cordially by an exceeding bony unwashed paw, incontinently followed his example--and in good time I did so; for I had scarcely changed my shooting boots and wet worsteds for slippers and silk socks, before my door, as usual, was lounged open by Tom's massy foot, and I was thus exhorted.

"Come, come, your supper's gittin' cold; I never see such men as you and Archer is; you're wash, wash, wash--all day. It's little water enough that you use any other ways."

"Why, is there any other use for water, Tom?" I asked, simply enough.

"It's lucky if there aint, any how--leastwise, where you and Archer is-- else you'd leave none for the rest of us. It's a good thing you han't thought of washing your darned stinking hides in rum--you will be at it some of these odd days, I warrant me--why now, McTaggart, it's only yesterday I caught Archer up stairs, a fiddling away up there at his teeth with a little ivory brush; brushing them with cold water--cleaning them he calls it. Cuss all such trash, says I."

While I was listening in mute astonishment, wondering whether in truth the old savage never cleaned his teeth, Archer made his appearance, and to a better supper never did I sit down, than was spread at the old round table, in such profusion as might have well sufficed to feed a troop of horse.

"What have we got here, Tom?" cried Harry, as he took the head of the social board; "quail-pie, by George--are there any peppers in it, Tom?"

"Sartain there is," replied that worthy, "and a prime rump-steak in the bottom, and some first-best salt pork, chopped fine, and three small onions; like little Waxskin used to fix them, when he was up here last fall."

"Take some of this pie, Frank;" said Archer, as he handed me a huge plate of leafy reeking pie-crust, with a slice of fat steak, and a plump hen quail, and gravy, and etceteras, that might have made an alderman's mouth water; "and if you don't say it's the very best thing you ever tasted, you are not half so good a judge as I used to hold you. It took little Johnny and myself three wet days to concoct it. Pie, Tom, or roast pig?" he continued; "or broiled woodcock? Here they are, all of them?"

"Why, I reckon I'll take cock; briled meat wants to be ate right stret away as soon as it comes off the griddle; and of all darned nice ways of cooking, to brile a thing, quick now, over hot hickory ashes, is the best for me!"

"I believe you're right about eating the cock first, for they will not be worth a farthing if they get cold. So you stick to the pig, do you-- hey, McTaggart? Well, there is no reckoning on taste--holloa, Tim, look sharp! the champagne all 'round--I'm choking!"

And for some time no sound was heard, but the continuous clatter of knives and forks, the occasional popping of a cork succeeded by the gurgling of the generous wine as it flowed into the tall rummers; and every now and then a loud and rattling eructation from Tom Draw, who, as he said, could never half enjoy a meal if he could not stop now and then to blow off steam.

At last, however--for supper, alas! like all other earthly pleasures, must come to an end--"The fairest still the fleetest"--our appetites waned gradually; and notwithstanding Harry's earnest exhortations, and the production of a broiled ham-bone, devilled to the very utmost pitch of English mustard, soy, oil of Aix, and cayenne pepper, by no hands, as may be guessed, but those of that universal genius, Timothy; one by one, we gave over our labors edacious, to betake us to potations of no small depth or frequency.

"It is directly contrary to my rule, Frank, to drink before a good day's shooting--and a good day I mean to have to-morrow!--but I am thirsty, and the least thought chilly; so here goes for a debauch! Tim, look in my box with the clothes, and you will find two flasks of Curacao; bring them down, and a dozen lemons, and some lump sugar--look alive! and you, Tom, out with your best brandy; I'll make a jorum that will open your eyes tight before you've done with it. That's right, Tim; now get the soup-tureen, the biggest one, and see that it's clean. The old villain has got a punch-bowl--bring half a dozen of champagne, a bucket full of ice, and then go down into the kitchen, and make two quarts of green tea, as strong as possible; and when it's made, set it to cool in the ice-house!"

In a few minutes all the ingredients were at hand; the rind, peeled carefully from all the lemons, was deposited with two tumblers full of finely powdered sugar in the bottom of the tureen; thereupon were poured instantly three pints of pale old Cognac; and these were left to steep, without admixture, until Tim Matlock made his entrance with the cold, strong, green tea; two quarts of this, strained clear, were added to the brandy, and then two flasks of curacoa!

Into this mixture a dozen lumps of clear ice were thrown, and the whole stirred up 'till the sugar was entirely suspended; then pop! pop! went the long necks, and their creaming nectar was discharged into the bowl; and by the body of Bacchus--as the Italians swear--and by his soul, too, which he never steeped in such delicious nectar, what a drink that was, when it was completed.

Even Tom Draw, who ever was much disposed to look upon strange potables as trash, and who had eyed the whole proceedings with ill-concealed suspicion and disdain, when he had quaffed off a pint-beaker full, which he did without once moving the vessel from his head, smacked his lips with a report which might have been heard half a mile off, and which resembled very nearly the crack of a first-rate huntsman's whip.

"That's not slow, now!" he said, half dubiously, "to tell the truth now, that's first rate; I reckon, though, it would be better if there wasn't that tea into it--it makes it weak and trashy-like!"

"You be hanged!" answered Harry, "that's mere affectation--that smack of your lips told the story; did you ever hear such an infernal sound? I never did, by George!"

"Begging your pardon, Measter Archer," interposed Timothy, pulling his fore-lock, with an expression of profound respect, mingled with a ludicrous air of regret, at being forced to differ in the least degree from his master; "begging your pardon, Measter Archer, that was a roommer noise, and by a vary gre-at de-al too, when Measter McTavish sneezed me clean oot o' t' wagon!"

"What's that?--what the devil's that?" cried I; "this McTavish must be a queer genius; one day I hear of his frightening a bull out of a meadow, and the next of his sneezing a man out of a phaeton."

"It's simply true! both are simply true! We were driving very slowly on an immensely hot day in the middle of August, between Lebanon Springs and Claverack; McTavish and I on the front seat, and Tim behind. Well! we were creeping at a foot's pace, upon a long, steep hill, just at the very hottest time of day; not a word had been spoken for above an hour, for we were all tired and languid--except once, when McTavish asked for his third tumbler, since breakfast, of Starke's Ferintosh, of which we had three two-quart bottles in the liquor case--when suddenly, without any sign or warning, McTavish gave a sneeze which, on my honor, was scarcely inferior in loudness to a pistol shot! The horses started almost off the road, I jumped about half a foot off my seat, and positively without exaggeration, Timothy tumbled slap out of the wagon into the road, and lay there sprawling in the dust, while Mac sat perfectly unmoved, without a smile upon his face, looking straight before him, exactly as if nothing had happened."

"Nonsense, Harry," exclaimed I; "that positively won't go down."

"That's an etarnal lie, now, Archer!" Tom chimed in; "leastwise I don't know why I should say so neither, for I never saw no deviltry goin' on yet, that didn't come as nat'ral to McTavish, as lying to a minister, or..."

"Rum to Tom Draw!" responded Harry. "But it's as true as the gospel, ask Timothy there!"

"Nay it's all true; only it's scarce so bad i' t' story, as it was i' right airnest! Ay

cooped oot o' t' drag--loike ivry thing--my hinder eend was sair a moanth and better!"

"Now then," said I, "it's Tom's turn; let us hear about the bull."

"Oh, the bull!" answered Tom. "Well you see, Archer there, and little Wax-
skin--you know little Waxskin, I guess, Mister Forester--and old McTavish, had
gone down to shoot to Hellhole--where we was yesterday, you see!--well now! it
was hot--hot, worst kind; I tell you--and I was sort o' tired out--so Waxskin, in he
goes into the thick, and Archer arter him, and up the old crick side--thinkin, you
see, that we was goin up, where you and I walked yesterday--but not a bit of it; we
never thought of no such thing, not we! We sot ourselves down underneath the
haystacks, and made ourselves two good stiff horns of toddy; and cooled off there,
all in the shade, as slick as silk.

"Well, arter we'd been there quite a piece, bang! we hears, in the very thick of
the swamp--bang! bang!--and then I heerd Harry Archer roar out 'mark! mark!--
Tom, mark!--you old fat rascal,'--and sure enough, right where I should have been,
if I'd been a doin right, out came two woodcock--big ones--they looked like hens,
and I kind o' thought it was a shame, so I got up to go to them, and called McTavish
to go with me; but torights, jest as he was a gitting up, a heap of critters comes all
chasin up, scart by a dog, I reckon, kickin their darned heels up, and bellowin like
mad--and there was one young bull amongst them, quite a lump of a bull now I tell
you; and the bull he came up pretty nigh to us, and stood, and stawmped, and sort
o' snorted, as if he didn't know right what he would be arter, and McTavish, he gits
up, and turns right round with his back to the critter; he got a bit of a round jacket
on, and he stoops down till his head came right atween his legs, kind o' straddlin
like, so that the bull could see nothing of him but his t'other eend, and his head
right under it, chin uppermost, with his big black whiskers, lookin as fierce as all
h-ll, and fiercer; well! the bull he stawmped agin, and pawed, and bellowed, and
I was in hopes, I swon, that he would have hooked him; but just then McTavish,
starts to run, going along as I have told you, hind eend foremost--bo-oo went the
bull, a-boooo, and off he starts like a strick, with his tail stret on eend, and his eyes
starin and all the critters arter him, and then they kind o' circled round--and all
stood still and stared--and stawmped, 'till he got nigh to them, and then they all
stricks off agin; and so they went on--runnin and then standin still,--and so they

went on the hull of an hour, I'll be bound; and I lay there upon my back laughin 'till I was stiff and sore all over; and then came Waxskin and all Archer, wrathy as h-ll and swearin'--Lord how they did swear!

"They'd been a slavin there through the darned thorns and briers, and the old stinkin mud holes, and flushed a most almighty sight of cock, where the brush was too thick to shoot them, and every one they flushed, he came stret out into the open field, where Archer knew we should have been, and where we should have killed a thunderin mess, and no mistake; and they went on dam-min, and wonderin, and sweatin through the brush, till they got out to the far eend, and there they had to make tracks back to us through the bog meadow, under a brilin sun, and when they did get back, the bull was jest a goin through the bars--and every d--d drop o' the rum was drinked up; and the sun was settin, and the day's shootin--that was spoiled!--and then McTavish tantalized them the worst sort. But I did laugh to kill; it was the best I ever did see, was that spree--Ha! ha! ha!"

And, as he finished, he burst out into his first horse laugh, in which I chorused him most heartily, having in truth been in convulsions, between the queerness of his lingo, and the absurdly grotesque attitudes into which he threw himself, in imitating the persons concerning whom his story ran. After this, jest succeeded jest! and story, story! 'till, in good truth, the glass circling the while with most portentous speed, I began to feel bees in my head, and till in truth no one, I believe, of the party, was entirely collected in his thoughts, except Tom Draw, whom it is as impossible for liquor to affect, as it would be for brandy to make a hogshead drunk, and who stalked off to bed with an air of solemn gravity that would have well become a Spanish grandee of the olden time, telling us, as he left the room, that we were all as drunk as thunder, and that we should be stinkin in our beds till noon to-morrow.

A prediction, by the way, which he took right good care to defeat in his own person; for in less than five hours after we retired, which was about the first of the small hours, he rushed into my room, and finding that the awful noises which he made, had no effect in waking me, dragged me bodily out of bed, and clapping my wet sponge in my face, walked off, as he said, to fetch the bitters, which were to make me as fine as silk upon the instant.

This time, I must confess that I did not look with quite so much disgust on the old apple-jack; and in fact, after a moderate horn, I completed my ablutions, and found myself perfectly fresh and ready for the field. Breakfast was soon despatched, and on this occasion as soon as we had got through the broiled ham and eggs, the wagon made its appearance at the door.

"What's this, Harry?" I exclaimed; "where are we bound for, now?"

"Why, Master Frank," he answered, "to tell you the plain truth, while you were sleeping off the effects of the last night's regent's punch, I was on foot inquiring into the state of matters and things; and since we have pretty well exhausted our home beats, and I have heard that some ground, about ten miles distant, is in prime order, I have determined to take a try there; but we must look pretty lively, for it is seven now, and we have got a drive of ten stiff miles before us. Now, old Grampus, are you ready?"

"Aye, aye!" responded Tom, and mounted up, a work of no small toil for him, into the back seat of the wagon, where I soon took my seat beside him, with the two well-broke setters crouching at our feet, and the three guns strapped neatly to the side rails of the wagons. Harry next mounted the box. Tim touched his hat and jumped up to his side, and off we rattled at a merry trot, wheeling around the rival tavern which stood in close propinquity to Tom's; then turning short again to the left hand, along a broken stony road, with several high and long hills, and very awkward bridges in the valleys, to the north-westward of the village.

Five miles brought us into a pretty little village lying at the base of another ridge of what might almost be denominated mountains, save that they were cultivated to the very top. As we paused on the brow of this, another glorious valley spread out to our view, with the broad sluggish waters of the Wallkill winding away, with hardly any visible motion, toward the north-east, through a vast tract of meadow-land covered with high, rank grass, dotted with clumps of willows and alder brakes, and interspersed with large, deep swamps, thick-set with high grown timber; while far beyond these, to the west, lay the tall variegated chain of the Shawangunk mountains.

Rattling briskly down the hill, we passed another thriving village, built on the mountain side; made two or three sharp ugly turns, still going at a smashing pace, and coming on the level ground, entered an extensive cedar swamp, impenetrable above with the dark boughs of the evergreen colossi, and below with half a dozen varieties of rhododendron, calmia, and azalia. Through this dark, dreary track, the road ran straight as the bird flies, supported on the trunks of trees, constituting what is here called a corduroy road; an article which, praise be to all the gods, is disappearing now so rapidly, that this is the only bit to be found in the civilized regions of New York--and bordered to the right and left by ditches of black tenacious mire. Beyond this we scaled another sandy hillock, and pulled up at a little wayside tavern, at the door of which Harry set himself lustily to halloa.

"Why, John; hilloa, hillo; John Riker!"

Whereon, out came, stooping low to pass under the lintel of a very fair sized door, one of the tallest men I ever looked upon; his height, too, was exaggerated by the narrowness of his chest and shoulders, which would have been rather small for a man of five foot seven; but to make up for this, his legs were monstrous, his arms muscular, and his whole frame evidently powerful and athletic, though his gait was slouching, and his air singularly awkward and unhandy.

"Why, how do, Mr. Archer? I hadn't heerd you was in these pairts--arter woodcock, I reckon?"

"Yes, John, as usual; and you must go along with us, and show us the best ground."

"Well, you see, I carn't go to-day--for Squire Breawn, and Dan Faushea, and a whole grist of Goshen boys is comin' over to the island here to fish; but you carn't well go wrong."

"Why not; are birds plenty?"

"Well! I guess they be! Plentier than ever yet I see them here."

"By Jove! that's good news," Harry answered; "where shall we find the first?"

"Why, amost anywheres--but here, jist down by the first bridge, there's a hull heap--leastwise there was a Friday--and then you'd best go on to the second bridge, and keep the edge of the hill right up and down to Merrit's Island; and then beat down here home to the first bridge again. But won't you liquor?"

"No, not this morning, John; we did our liquoring last night. Tom, do you hear what John says?"

"I hear, I hear," growled out old Tom; "but the critter lies like nauthen. He always does lie, cuss him."

"Well, here goes, and we'll soon see!"

And away we went again, spinning down a little descent, to a flat space between the hill-foot and the river, having a thick tangled swamp on the right, and a small boggy meadow full of grass, breast-high, with a thin open alder grove beyond it on the left. Just as we reached the bridge Harry pulled up.

"Jump out, boys, jump out! Here's the spot."

"I tell you there aint none; darn you! There aint none never here, nor haint been these six years; you know that now, yourself, Archer."

"We'll try it, all the same," said Harry, who was coolly loading his gun. "The season has been wetter than common, and this ground is generally too dry. Drive on, Tim, over the bridge, into the hollow; you'll be out of shot there; and wait till we come. Holloa! mark, Tom."

For, as the wagon wheels rattled upon the bridge, up jumped a cock out of the ditch by the road side, from under a willow brush, and skimmed past all of us within five yards. Tom Draw and I, who had got out after Harry, were but in the act of ramming down our first barrels; but Harry, who had loaded one, and was at that moment putting down the wad upon the second, dropped his ramrod with the most perfect sang-froid I ever witnessed, took a cap out of his right-hand pocket, applied it to the cone, and pitching up his gun, knocked down the bird as it wheeled to cross the road behind us, by the cleverest shot possible.

"That's pretty well for no birds, anyhow, Tom," he exclaimed, dropping his butt to load. "Go and gather that bird, Frank, to save time; he lies in the wagon rut, there. How now? down charge, you Chase, sir! what are you about?"

The bird was quickly bagged, and Harry loaded. We stepped across a dry ditch, and both dogs made game at the same instant.

"Follow the red dog, Frank!" cried Archer, "and go very slow; there are birds here!"

And as he spoke, while the dogs were crawling along, cat-like, pointing at every step, and then again creeping onward, up skirred two birds under the very nose of the white setter, and crossed quite to the left of Harry. I saw him raise his gun, but that was all; for at the self-same moment one rose to me, and my ear caught the flap of yet another to my right; five barrels were discharged so quickly, that they made but three reports; I cut my bird well down, and looking quickly to the left, saw nothing but a stream of feathers drifting along the wind. At the same time, old

Tom shouted on the right,

"I have killed two, by George! What have you done, boys?"

"Two, I!" said Archer. "Wait, Frank, don't you begin to load till one of us is ready; there'll be another cock up, like enough. Keep your barrel; I'll be ready in a jiffy!"

And well it was that I obeyed him, for at the squeak of the card, in its descent down his barrel, another bird did rise, and was making off for the open alders, when my whole charge riddled him; and instantly at the report three more flapped up, and of course went off unharmed; but we marked them, one by one, down in the grass at the wood edge. Harry loaded again. We set off to pick up our dead birds. Shot drew, as I thought, on my first, and pointed dead within a yard of where he fell. I walked up carelessly, with my gun under my arm, and was actually stooping to bag him, as I thought, when whiz! one rose almost in my face; and, bothered by seeing us all around him, towered straight up into the air. Taken completely by surprise, I blazed away in a hurry, and missed clean; but not five yards did he go, before Tom cut him down.

"Aha, boy! whose eye's wiped now?"

"Mine, Tom, very fairly; but can that be the same cock I knocked down, Archer?"

"Not a bit of it; I saw your's fall dead as a stone; he lies half a yard farther in that tussock."

"How the deuce did you see him? Why, you were shooting your own at the same moment."

"All knack, Frank; I marked both my own and yours, and one of Tom's besides. Are you ready? Hold up, Shot! There; he has got your dead bird. Was I not right? And look to! for, by Jove! he is standing on another, with the dead bird in his mouth! That's pretty, is it not?"

Again two rose, and both were killed; one by Tom, and one by Archer; my gun hanging fire.

"That's nine birds down before we have bagged one," said Archer; "I hope no more will rise, or we'll be losing these."

But this time his hopes were not destined to meet accomplishment, for seven more woodcock got up, five of which were scattered in the grass around us, wing-broken or dead, before we had even bagged the bird which Shot was gently mouthing.

"I never saw anything like this in my life, Tom. Did you?" cried Harry.

"I never did, by George!" responded Tom. "Now do you think there's any three men to be found in York, such darned etarnal fools as to be willing to shoot a match agin us?"

"To be sure I do, lots of them; and to beat us too, to boot, you stupid old porpoise. Why, there's Harry T--- and Nick L---, and a dozen more of them, that you and I would have no more chance with, than a gallon of brandy would have of escaping from you at a single sitting. But we have shot pretty well, to-day. Now do, for heaven's sake, let us try to bag them!"

And scattered though they were in all directions, among the most infernal tangled grass I ever stood on, those excellent dogs retrieved them one by one, till every bird was pocketed. We then beat on and swept the rest of the meadow, and the outer verge of the alders, picking up three more birds, making a total of seventeen brought to bag in less than half an hour. We then proceeded to the wagon, took a good pull of water from a beautiful clear spring by the road-side, properly qualified with whiskey, and rattled on about one mile farther to the second bridge. Here we again got out.

"Now, Tim," said Harry. "mark me well! Drive gently to the old barrack yonder under the west-end of that wood-side, unhitch the horses and tie them in the shade; you can give them a bite of meadow hay at the same time; and then get luncheon ready. We shall be with you by two o'clock at farthest."

"Ay, ay, sur!"

And off he drove at a steady pace, while we, striking into the meadow, to the left hand of the road, went along getting sport such as I never beheld, or even dreamed of before. For about five hundred yards in width from the stream, the ground was soft and miry to the depth of some four inches, with long sword-grass quite knee-deep, and at every fifty yards a bunch of willows or swamp alders. In every clump of bushes we found from three to five birds, and as the shooting was for the most part very open, we rendered on the whole a good account of them. The dogs throughout behaved superbly, and Tom was altogether frantic with the excitement of the sport. The time seemed short indeed, and I could not for a moment have imagined that it was even noon, when we reached the barrack.

This was a hut of rude, unplaned boards, which had been put up formerly with the intent of furnishing a permanent abode for some laboring men, but which, having been long deserted, was now used only as a temporary shelter by charcoal burners, haymakers, or like ourselves, stray sportsmen. It was, however, though rudely built, and fallen considerably into decay, perfectly beautiful from its romantic site; for it stood just at the end of a long tangled covert, with a huge pin oak-tree, leaning abruptly out from an almost precipitous bank of yellow sand, completely canopying it; while from a crevice in the sand-stone there welled out a little source of crystal water, which expanded into as sweet a basin as ever served a Dryad for her bath in Arcady, of old.

Before it stretched the wide sweep of meadow land, with the broad blue Wallkill gliding through it, fringed by a skirt of coppice, and the high mountains, veiled with a soft autumnal mist, sleeping beyond, robed in their many-colored garb of crimson, gold, and green. Besides the spring the indefatigable Tim had kindled a bright glancing fire, while in the basin were cooling two long-necked bottles of the Baron's best; a clean white cloth was spread in the shade before the barrack door, with plates and cups, and bread cut duly, and a traveling case of cruets, with all the other appurtenances needful.

On our appearance he commenced rooting in a heap of embers, and soon produced six nondescript looking articles enclosed--as they dress maintenon cutlets or red mullet--in double sheets of greasy letter paper--these he incontinently dished, and to my huge astonishment they turned out to be three couple of our woodcock, which that indefatigable varlet had picked, and baked under the ashes, according to some strange idea, whether original, or borrowed at second hand from his master, I never was enabled to ascertain.

The man, be he whom he may, who invented that plat, is second neither to Caramel nor to Ude--the exquisite juicy tenderness of the meat, the preservation of the gravy, the richness of the trail--by heaven! they were inimitable.

In that sweet spot we loitered a full hour--then counted our bag, which amounted already to fifty-nine cock, not including those with which Tim's gastronomic art had spread for us a table in the wilderness--then leaving him to pack up and meet us at the spot where we first started, we struck down the stream homeward, shooting our way along a strip of coppice about ten yards in breadth, bounded on one side by a dry bare bank of the river, and on the other by the open meadows. We of course kept the verges of this covert, our dogs working down the middle, and so well did we manage it, that when we reached the wagon, just as the sun was setting, we numbered a hundred and twenty-five birds bagged, besides two which were so cut by the shot as to be useless, six which we had devoured, and four or five which we lost in spite of the excellence of our retrievers. When we got home again, although the Dutchman was on the spot, promising us a quarter race upon the morrow, and pressing earnestly for a rubber to-night, we were too much used up to think of anything but a good supper and an early bed.

DAY THE FIFTH

Our last day's shooting in the vale of Sugar-loaf was over; and, something contrary to Harry's first intention, we had decided, instead of striking westward into Sullivan or Ulster, to drive five miles upon our homeward route, and beat the Longpond mountain--not now for such small game as woodcock, quail, or partridge; but for a herd of deer, which, although now but rarely found along the western hills, was said to have been seen already several times, to the number of six or seven head, in a small cove, or hollow basin, close to the summit of the Bellevale ridge.

As it was not of course our plan to return again to Tom Draw's, everything was now carefully and neatly packed away; the game, of which we had indeed a goodly stock, was produced from Tom's ice-house, where, suspended from the rafters, it had been kept as sound and fresh as though it had been all killed only on the preceding day.

A long deep box, fitting beneath the gun-case under the front seat, was now produced, and proved to be another of Harry's notable inventions; for it was lined throughout, lid, bottom, sides and all, with zinc, and in the centre had a well or small compartment of the same material, with a raised grating in the bottom. This well was forthwith lined with a square yard, or rather more, of flannel, into which was heaped a quantity of ice pounded as fine as possible, sufficient to cram it absolutely to the top; the rest of the box was then filled with the birds, displayed in regular rows, with heads and tails alternating, and a thin coat of clean dry wheaten straw between each layer, until but a few inches' depth remained between the noble pile and the lid of this extempore refrigerator; this space being filled in with flannel packed close and folded tightly, the box was locked and thrust into the accurately fitting boot by dint of the exertion of Timothy's whole strength.

"There, Frank," cried Harry, who had superintended the storage of the whole with nice scrutiny, "those chaps will keep there as sound as roaches, till we get to young Tom's at Ramapo; you cannot think what work I had, trying in vain to save them, before I hit upon this method; I tried hops, which I have known in England to keep birds in an extraordinary manner--for, what you'll scarce believe, I once ate a Ptarmigan, the day year after it was killed, which had been packed with hops, in perfect preservation, at Farnley, Mr. Fawke's place in Yorkshire!--and I tried prepared charcoal, and got my woodcock down to New York, looking like chimney sweeps, and smelling--"

"What the devil difference does it make to you now, Archer, I'd be pleased to know!" interposed Tom; "what under heaven they smells like--a man that eats cock with their guts in, like you does, needn't stick now, I reckon, for a leetle mite of a stink!"

"Shut up, you old villain," answered Harry, laughing, "bring the milk punch, and get your great coat on, if you mean to go with us; for it's quite keen this morning, I can tell you; and we must be stirring too, for the sun will be up before we get to Teachman's. Now, Jem, get out the hounds; how do you take them, Tom?"

"Why, that darned Injun, Jem, he'll take them in my lumber wagon--and, I say, Jem, see that you don't over-drive old roan--away with you, and rouse up Garry, he means to go, I guess!"

After a mighty round of punch, in which, as we were now departing, one half at least of the village joined, we all got under Way; Tom, buttoned up to the throat in a huge white lion skin wrap-rascal, looking for all the world like a polar bear erect on its hind legs; and all of us muffled up pretty snugly, a proceeding which was rendered necessary by a brisk bracing north-west breeze. The sky, though it was scarcely the first twilight of an autumnal dawn, was beautifully clear, and as transparent--though still somewhat dusky--as a wide sheet of crystal; a few pale stars were twinkling here and there; but in the east a broad gray streak changing on the horizon's edge to a faint straw color, announced the sun's approach.

The whole face of the country, hill, vale, and woodland, was overspread by an universal coat of silvery hoar-frost; thin wreaths of snowy mist rising above the tops of the sere woodlands, throughout the whole length of the lovely vale, indicated as clearly as though it were traced on a map, the direction of the stream that watered it; and as we paused upon the brow of the first hillock, and looked back toward the village, with its white steeples and neat cottage dwellings buried in the still repose of that early hour, with only one or two faint columns of blue smoke worming their way up lazily into the cloudless atmosphere, a feeling of regret--such as has often crossed my mind before, when leaving any place wherein I have spent a few days happily, and which I never may see more --rendered me somewhat indisposed to talk.

Something or other--it might with Harry, perhaps, have been a similar train of thought--caused both my comrades to be more taciturn by far than was their wont; and we had rattled over five miles of our route, and scaled the first ridge of the hills, and dived into the wide ravine; midway the depth of this the pretty village of Bellevale lies on the brink of the dammed rivulet, which, a few yards below the neat stone bridge, takes a precipitous leap of fifty feet, over a rustic wier, and rushes onward, bounding from ledge to ledge of rifted rocks, chafing and fretting as if it were doing a match against time, and were in danger of losing its race.

Thus we had passed the heavy lumber wagon, with Jem and Garry perched on a board laid across it, and the four couple of stanch hounds nestling in the straw which Tom had provided in abundance for their comfort, before the silence was broken by any sounds except the rattle of the wheels, the occasional interjectional whistle of Harry to his horses, or the flip of the well handled whip.

Just, however, as we were shooting ahead of the lumber wain, an exclamation from Tom Draw, which should have been a sentence, had it not been very abruptly terminated in a long rattling eructation, arrested Archer's progress.

Pulling short up where a jog across the road, constructed--after the damnable mode adopted in all the hilly portions of the interior--in order to prevent the heavy rains from channelling the descent, afforded him a chance of stopping on the hill, so as to slack his traces. "How now," he exclaimed; "what the deuce ails you now, you old rhinoceros?"

"Oh, Archer, I feels bad; worst sort, by Judas! It's that milk punch, I reckon; it keeps a raising--raising, all the time like..."

"And you want to lay it, I suppose, like a ghost, in a sea of whiskey; well, I've no especial objection! Here, Tim, hand the case bottle, and the dram cup! No! no! confound you, pass it this way first, for if Tom once gets hold of it, we may say good-bye to it altogether. There," he continued, after we had both taken a moderate sip at the superb old Ferintosh, "there, now take your chance at it, and for Heaven's sake do leave a drop for Jem and Garry; by George now, you shall not drink it all!" as Tom poured down the third cup full, each being as big as an ordinary beer-glass. "There was above a pint and a half in it when you began, and now there's barely one cup-full between the two of them. An't you ashamed of yourself now, you greedy old devil?"

"It doos go right, I swon!" was the only reply that could be got out of him.

"That's more a plaguy sight than the bullets will do, out of your old tower musket; you're so drunk now, I fancy, that you couldn't hold it straight enough to hit a deer at three rods, let alone thirty, which you are so fond of chattering about."

"Do tell now," replied Tom, "did you, or any other feller, ever see me shoot the worser for a mite of liquor, and as for deer, that's all a no sich thing; there arnt no deer a this side of Duckseedar's. It's all a lie of Teachman's and that Deckering son of a gun."

"Holloa! hold up, Tom--recollect yesterday!--I thought there had been no cock down by the first bridge there, these six years; why you're getting quite stupid, and a croaker too, in your old age."

"Mayhap I be," he answered rather gruffly; "mayhap I be, but you won't git no deer to-day, I'll stand drinks for the company; and if we doos start one, I'll lay on my own musket agin your rifle."

"Well! we'll soon see, for here we are," Harry replied, as after leaving the high-road just at the summit of the Bellevale mountain, he rattled down a very broken rutty bye-road at the rate of at least eight miles an hour, vastly to the discomfiture of our fat host, whose fleshy sides were jolted almost out of their skin by the concussion of the wheels against the many stones and jogs which opposed their progress.

"Here we are, or at least soon will be. It is but a short half mile through these woods to Teachman's cottage. Is there a gun loaded, Tim? It's ten to one we shall have a partridge fluttering up and treeing here directly; I'll let the dogs out--get away, Flash! get away, Dan! you little rascals. Jump out, good dogs, Shot, Chase--hie up with you!" and out they went rattling and scrambling through the brush-wood all four abreast!

At the same moment Tim, leaning over into the body of the wagon, lugged out a brace of guns from their leathern cases; Harry's short ounce ball rifle, and the long single barreled duck gun.

"'T roifle is loaden wi' a single ball, and 't single goon wi' yan of them green cartridges!"

"Much good ball and buck-shot will do us against partridge; nevertheless, if one trees, I'll try if I can't cut his head off for him," said Archer, laughing.

"Nay! nay! it be-ant book-shot; it's no but noomber three; tak' haud on't, Measter Draa, tak' haud on't. It's no hoort thee, mon, and 't horses boath stand foire cannily!"

Scarce had Fat Tom obeyed his imperative solicitations, and scarce had Tim taken hold of the ribbands which Harry relinquished the moment he got the rifle into his hands, before a most extraordinary hubbub arose in the little skirt of coppice to our left; the spaniels quested for a second's space at the utmost, when a tremendous crash of the branches arose, and both the setters gave tongue furiously with a quick savage yell.

The road at this point of the wood made a short and very sudden angle, so as to enclose a small point of extremely dense thicket between its two branches; on one of these was our wagon, and down the other the lumber-wain was rumbling, at the moment when this strange and most unexpected outcry started us all.

"What in t' fient's neam is yon?" cried Timothy.

"And what the devil's that?" responded I and Archer in a breath.

But whatever it was that had aroused the dogs to such an most unusual pitch of fury, it went crashing through the brush-wood for some five or six strokes at a fearful rate toward the other wagon; before, however it had reached the road, a most appalling shout from Jem, followed upon the instant by the blended voices of all the hounds opening at once, as on a view, excited us yet farther!

I was still tugging at my double gun, in the vain hope of getting it out time enough for action. Tom had scrambled out of the wagon on the first alarm, and stood eye, ear, and heart erect, by the off side of the horses, which were very restless, pawing, and plunging violently, and almost defying Timothy best skill to hold them; while Harry, having cast off his box-coat, stood firm and upright on the foot board as a carved statue, with his rifle cocked and ready; when, headed back upon us by the yell of Lyn and the loud clamor of his fresh foes, the first buck I had seen in America, and the largest I had seen any where, dashed at a single plunge into the round, clearing the green head of a fallen hemlock, apparently without an effort, his splendid antlers laid back on his neck, and his white flag lashing his fair round haunch as the fleet bitches Bonny Belle and Blossom yelled with their shrill fierce trebles close behind him.

Seeing that it was useless to persist in my endeavor to extricate my gun, and satisfied that the matter was in good hands, I was content to look on, an inactive but most eager witness.

Tom, who from his position at the head of the off horse, commanded the first view of the splendid creature, pitched his gun to his shoulder hastily and fired; the smoke drifted across my face, but through its vapory folds I could distinguish the dim figure of the noble hart still bounding unhurt onward; but, before the first echo of the round ringing report of Tom's shot-gun reached my ear, the sharp flat crack of Harry's rifle followed it, and at the self-same instant the buck sprang six feet into the air, and pitched head foremost on the ground; it was but for a moment, however, for with the speed of light he struggled to his feet, and though sore wounded, was yet toiling onward when the two English foxhounds dashed at his throat and pulled him down again.

"Run in, Tom, run in! quick," shouted Harry, "he's not clean killed, and may gore the dogs sadly!"

"I've got no knife," responded Tom, but dauntlessly he dashed in, all the same, to the rescue of the bitches--which I believe he loved almost as well as his own children--and though, encumbered by his ponderous white top-coat, not to say by his two hundred and fifty weight of solid flesh, seized the fierce animal by the brow-antlers, and bore him to the ground, before Harry, who had leaped out of the wagon, with his first words, could reach him.

The next moment the keen short hunting knife, without which Archer never takes the field, had severed at a single stroke the weasand of the gallant brute; the black blood streamed out on the smoking hoar-frost, the full eyes glazed, and, after one sharp fluttering struggle, the life departed from those graceful limbs, which had been but a few short instants previous so full of glorious energy--of fiery vigor.

"Well, that's the strangest thing I ever heard of, let alone seeing," exclaimed Archer, "fancy a buck like that lying in such a mere fringe of coppice, and so near to the road-side, too! and why the deuce did he lay here till we almost passed him!"

"I know how it's been, any heaw," said Jem, who had by this time come up, and was looking on with much exultation flashing in his keen small eye. "Bill Speer up on the hill there told me jist now, that they druv a big deer down from the back-bone clear down to this here hollow jist above, last night arter dark. Bill shot at him, and kind o' reckoned he hot him--but I guess he's mistaken--leastwise he jumped strong enough jist neaw!--but which on you was 't 'at killed him?"

"I did," exclaimed Tom, "I did by--!"

"Why you most impudent of all old liars," replied Harry--while at the same time, with a most prodigious chuckle, Tim Matlock pointed to the white bark of a birch sapling, about the thickness of a man's thigh, standing at somewhat less than fifteen paces' distance, wherein the large shot contained by the wire cartridge--the best sporting invention by the way, that has been made since percussion caps--had bedded themselves in a black circle, cut an inch at least into the solid wood, and about two inches in diameter!

"I ken gay and fairly," exclaimed Tim, "'at Ay rammed an Eley's patent cartridge into 't single goon this morning; and yonder is 't i' t' birk tree, and Ay ken a load o' shot fra an unce bullet!"

The laugh was general now against fat Tom; especially as the small wound made by the heavy ball of Harry's rifle was plainly visible, about a hand's breadth behind the heart, on the side toward which he had aimed; while the lead had passed directly through, in an oblique direction forward, breaking the left shoulder blade, and lodging just beneath the skin, whence a touch of the knife dislodged it.

"What now--what now, boys?" cried the old sinner, no whit disconcerted by the general mirth against him. "I say, by gin! I killed him, and I say so yet. Which on ye all--which on ye all daared to go in on him, without a knife nor nothen. I killed him, I say, anyhow, and so let's drink!"

"Well, I believe we must wet him," Harry answered, "so get out another flask of whiskey, Tim; and you Jem and Garry lend me a hand to lift this fine chap into the wagon. By Jove! but this will make the Teachmans open their eyes; and now look sharp! You sent the Teachmans word that we were coming, Tom?"

"Sartin! and they've got breakfast ready long enough before this, anyways."

With no more of delay, but with lots more of merriment and shouting, on we drove; and in five minutes' space, just as the sun was rising, reached the small rude enclosure around two or three log huts, lying just on the verge of the beautiful clear lake. Two long sharp boats, and a canoe scooped out of a whole tree, were drawn up on the sandy beach; a fishing net of many yards in length was drying on the rails; a brace of large, strong, black and tan foxhounds were lying on the step before the door; a dozen mongrel geese, with one wing-tipped wild one among them, were sauntering and gabbling about the narrow yard; and a glorious white-headed fishing eagle, with a clipped wing, but otherwise at large, was perched upon the roof hard by the chimney.

At the rattle of our arrival, out came from the larger of the cottages, three tall rough-looking countrymen to greet us, not one of whom stood less than six foot in his stockings, while two were several inches taller.

Great was their wonder, and loud were their congratulations when they beheld the unexpected prize which we had gained, while on our route; but little space was given at that time to either; for the coffee, which, by the way, was poor enough, and the hot cakes and fried perch, which were capital, and the grilled salt pork, swimming in fat, and the large mealy potatoes bursting through their brown skins, were ready smoking upon a rough wooden board, covered, however, by a clean white table cloth, beside a sparkling fire of wood, which our drive through the brisk mountain air had rendered by no means unacceptable.

We breakfasted like hungry men and hunters, both rapidly and well; and before half an hour elapsed, Archer, with Jem and one of our bold hosts, started away, well provided with powder and ball, and whiskey, and accompanied by all the hounds, to make a circuit of the western hill, on the summit of which they expected to be joined by two or three more of the neighbors, whence they proposed to drive the whole sweep of the forest-clad descent down to the water's edge.

Tim was enjoined to see to the provisions, and to provide as good a dinner as his best gastronomic skill and the contents of our portable larder might afford, and I was put under the charge of Tom, who seemed, for about an hour, disposed to do nothing but to lie dozing with a cigar in his mouth, stretched upon the broad of his back, on a bank facing the early sunshine just without the door; while our hosts were collecting bait, preparing fishing tackle, and cleaning or repairing their huge clumsy muskets. At length, when the drivers had been gone already for considerably more than an hour, he got up and shook himself.

"Now, then, boys," he exclaimed, "we'll be a movin. You Joe Teachman, what are you lazin there about, cuss you? You go with Mr. Forester and Garry in the big boat, and pull as fast as you can put your oars to water, till you git opposite the white-stone pint--and there lie still as fishes! You may fish, though, if you will, Forester," he added, turning to me, "and I do reckon the big yellow pearch will bite the darndest, this cold morning, arter the sun gits fairly up--but soon as ever you hear the hounds holler, or one of them chaps shoot, then look you out right stret away for business! Cale, here, and I'll take the small boat, and keep in sight of you; and so we can kiver all this eend of the pond like, if the deer tries to cross hereaways. How long is't, Cale, since we had six on them all at once in the water--six--seven-- eight! well, I swon, it's ten years agone now! But come, we mus'nt stand here talkin, else we'll get a dammin when they drives down a buck into the pond, and none of us in there to tackle with him!"

So without more ado, we got into our boats, disposed our guns, with the stocks towards us in the bows, laid in our stock of tinder, pipes, and liquor, and rowed off merrily to our appointed stations.

Never, in the whole course of my life, has it been my fortune to look upon more lovely scenery than I beheld that morning. The long narrow winding lake, lying as pure as crystal beneath the liquid skies, reflecting, with the correctness of the most perfect mirror, the abrupt and broken hills, which sank down so precipitously into it--clad as they were in foliage of every gorgeous dye, with which the autumn of America loves to enhance the beauty of her forest pictures--that, could they find their way into its mountain-girdled basin, ships of large burthen might lie afloat within a stone's throw of the shore--the slopes of the wood-covered knolls, here brown, or golden, and interspersed with the rich crimson of the faded maples, there verdant with the evergreen leaves of the pine and cedar--and the far azure summits of the most distant peaks, all steeped in the serene and glowing sunshine of an October morning.

For hours we lay there, our little vessel floating as the occasional breath of a sudden breeze, curling the lake into sparkling wavelets, chose to direct our course, smoking our cigars, and chatting cozily, and now and then pulling up a great broad-backed yellow bass, whose flapping would for a time disturb the peaceful silence, which reigned over wood, and dale, and water, quite unbroken save by the chance clamor of a passing crow; yet not a sound betokening the approach of our drivers had reached our ears.

Suddenly, when the sun had long passed his meridian height, and was declining rapidly toward the horizon, the full round shot of a musket rang from the mountain top, followed immediately by a sharp yell, and in an instant the whole basin of the lake was filled with the harmonious discord of the hounds.

I could distinguish on the moment the clear sharp challenge of Harry's high-bred foxhounds, the deep bass voices of the Southern dogs, and the untamable and cur-like yelping of the dogs which the Teachmans had taken with them.

Ten minutes passed full of anxiety, almost of fear.

We knew not as yet whither to turn our boat's head, for every second the course of the hounds seemed to vary, at one instant they would appear to be rushing directly down to us, and the next instant they would turn as though they were going up the hill again. Meantime our beaters were not idle--their stirring shouts, serving alike to animate the hounds, and to force the deer to water, made rock and wood reply in cheery echoes; but, to my wonder, I caught not for a long time one note of Harry's gladsome voice.

At length, as I strained my eyes against the broad hill-side, gilt by the rays of the declining sun, I caught a glimpse of his form running at a tremendous pace, bounding over stock and stone, and plunging through dense thickets, on a portion of the declivity where the tall trees had a few years before been destroyed by accidental fire.

At this moment the hounds were running, to judge from their tongues, parallel to the lake and to the line which he was running--the next minute, with a redoubled clamor, they turned directly down to him. I lost sight of him. But half a minute afterward, the sharp crack of his rifle again rang upon the air, followed by a triumphant "Whoop! who-whoop!" and then, I knew, another stag had fallen.

The beaters on the hill shouted again louder and louder than before--and the hounds still raved on. By heaven! but there must be a herd of them a-foot! And now the pack divides! The English hounds are bringing their game down--here--by the Lord! just here--right in our very faces! The Southrons have borne away over the shoulder of the hill, still running hot and hard in Jolly Tom's direction.

"By heaven!" I cried, "look, Teachman! Garry, look! There! See you not that noble buck?--he leaped that sumac bush like a race-horse! and see! see! now he will take the water. Bad luck on it! he sees us, and heads back!"

Again the fleet hounds rally in his rear, and chide till earth and air are vocal and harmonious. Hark! hark! how Archer's cheers ring on the wind! Now he turns once again--he nears the edge--how glorious! with what a beautiful bold bound he leaped from that high bluff into the flashing wave! with what a majesty he tossed his antlered head above the spray! with how magnificent and brave a stroke he breasts the curling billows!"

"Give way! my men, give way!"

How the frail bark creaks and groans as we ply the long oars in the rullocks--how the ash bends in our sturdy grasp--how the boat springs beneath their impulse.

"Together, boys! together! now--now we gain--now, Garry, lay your oar aside--up with your musket--now you are near enough--give it to him, in heaven's name! a good shot, too! the bullet ricocheted from the lake scarcely six inches from his nose! Give way again--it's my shot now!"

And lifting my Joe Manton, each barrel loaded with a bullet carefully wadded with greased buckskin, I took a careful aim and fired.

"That's it," cried Garry; "well done, Forester--right through the head, by George!"

And, as he spoke, I fancied for a moment he was right. The noble buck plunged half his height out of the bright blue water, shaking his head as if in the death agony, but the next instant he stretched out again with vigor unimpaired, and I could see that my ball had only knocked a tine off his left antler.

My second barrel still remained, and without lowering the gun, I drew my second trigger. Again, a fierce plunge told that the ball had not erred widely; and this time, when he again sank into his wonted posture, the deep crimson dye that tinged the foam which curled about his graceful neck, as he still struggled, feebly fleet, before his unrelenting foes, gave token of a deadly wound.

Six more strokes of the bending oars--we shot alongside--a noose of rope was cast across his branching tines, the keen knife flashed across his throat, and all was over! We towed him to the shore, where Harry and his comrades were awaiting us with another victim to his unerring aim. We took both bucks and all hands on board, pulled stoutly homeward, and found Tom lamenting.

Two deer, a buck of the first head, and a doe, had taken water close beside him--he had missed his first shot, and in toiling over-hard to recover lost ground, had broken his oar, and been compelled inactively to witness their escape.

Three fat bucks made the total of the day's sport--not one of which had fallen to Tom's boasted musket.

It needed all that Tim's best dinner, with lots of champagne and Ferintosh, could do to restore the fat chap's equanimity; but he at last consoled himself, as we threw ourselves on the lowly beds of the log hut, by swearing that by the etarnal devil he'd bea us both at partridges to-morrow.

DAY THE SIXTH

The sun rose broad and bright in a firmament of that most brilliant and transparent blue, which I have witnessed in no other country than America, so pure, so cloudless, so immeasurably distant as it seems from the beholder's eye! There was not a speck of cloud from east to west, from zenith to horizon; not a fleece of vapor on the mountain sides; not a breath of air to ruffle the calm basin of the Greenwood lake.

The rock-crowned, forest-mantled ridge, on the farther side of the narrow sheet, was visible almost as distinctly through the medium of the pure fresh atmosphere, as though it had been gazed at through a telescope--the hues of the innumerable maples, in their various stages of decay, purple, and crimson, and bright gorgeous scarlet, were contrasted with the rich chrome yellow of the birch and poplars, the sere red leaves of the gigantic oaks, and with the ever verdant plumage of the junipers, clustered in massy patches on every rocky promontory, and the tall spires of the dark pines and hemlock.

Over this mass of many-colored foliage, the pale thin yellow light of the new-risen sun was pouring down a flood of chaste illumination; while, exhaled from the waters by his first beams, a silvery gauze-like haze floated along the shores, not rising to the height of ten feet from the limped surface, which lay unbroken by the smallest ripple, undisturbed by the slightest splash of fish or insect, as still and tranquil to the eye as though it had been one huge plate of beaten burnished silver; with the tall cones of the gorgeous hills in all their rich variety, in all their clear minuteness, reflected, summit downward, palpable as their reality, in that most perfect mirror.

Such was the scene on which I gazed, as on the last day of our sojourn in the Woodlands of fair Orange, I issued from the little cabin, under the roof of which I had slept so dreamlessly and deep, after the fierce excitement of our deer hunt, that while I was yet slumbering, all save myself had risen, donned their accoutrements, and sallied forth, I knew not whither, leaving me certainly alone, although as certainly not so much to my glory.

From the other cottage, as I stood upon the threshold, I might hear the voices of the females, busy at their culinary labors, the speedily approaching term of which was obviously denoted by the rich savory steams which tainted--not, I confess, unpleasantly--the fragrant morning air.

As I looked out upon this lovely morning, I did not, I acknowledge it, regret the absence of my excellent though boisterous companions; for there was something which I cannot define in the deep stillness, in the sweet harmonious quiet of the whole scene before me, that disposed my spirit to meditation far more than to mirth; the very smoke which rose from the low chimneys of the Teachmans' colony--not surging to and fro, obedient to the fickle winds--but soaring straight, tall, unbroken, upward, like Corinthian columns, each with its curled capital--seemed to invite the soul of the spectator to mount with it toward the sunny heavens.

By-and-by I strayed downward to the beach, a narrow strip of silvery sand and variegated pebbles, and stood there long, silently watching the unknown sports, the seemingly--to us at least--unmeaning movements, and strange groupings of the small fry, which darted to and fro in the clear shallows within two yards of my feet; or marking the brief circling ripples, wrought by the morning swallow's wing, and momently subsiding into the wonted rest of the calm lake.

How long I stood there musing I know not, for I had fallen into a train of thought so deep that I was utterly unconscious of everything around me, when I was suddenly aroused from my reverie by the quick dash of oars, and by a volley of some seven barrels discharged in quick succession. As I looked up with an air, I presume somewhat bewildered, I heard the loud and bellowing laugh of Tom and saw the whole of our stout company gliding up in two boats, the skiff and the canoe, toward the landing place, perhaps a hundred yards from the spot where I stood.

"Come here, darn you," were the first words I heard, from the mouth of what speaker it need not be said--"come here, you lazy, snortin, snoozin Decker--lend a hand here right stret away, will you? We've got more perch than all of us can carry--and Archer's got six wood-duck."

Hurrying down in obedience to this unceremonious mandate, I perceived that indeed their time had not been misemployed, for the whole bottom of the larger boat was heaped with fish--the small and delicate green perch, the cat-fish, hideous in its natural, but most delicious in its artificial shape, and, above all, the large and broad-backed yellow bass, from two to four pounds weight. While Archer, who had gone forth with Garry only in the canoe, had picked up half a dozen wood-duck, two or three of the large yellow-legs, a little bittern, known by a far less elegant appellative throughout the country, and thirteen English snipe.

"By Jove!" cried I, "but this is something like--where the deuce did you pick the snipe up, Harry--and, above all, why the deuce did you let me lie wallowing in bed this lovely morning?"

"One question at a time," responded he, "good Master Frank; one question at a time. For the snipe, I found them very unexpectedly, I tell you, in a bit of marshy meadow just at the outlet of the pond. Garry was paddling me along at the top of his pace, after a wing-tipped wood-duck, when up jumped one of the long-billed rascals, and had the impudence to skim across the creek under my very nose--'skeap! skeap!' Well, I dropped him, you may be sure, with a charge, too, of duck shot; and he fell some ten yards over on the meadow; so leaving Garry to pursue the drake, I landed, loaded my gun with No. 9, and went to work--the result as you see; but I cleared the meadow--devil a bird is left there, except one I cut to pieces, and could not find for want of Chase--two went away without a shot, over the hills and far away. As for letting you lie in bed, you must talk to Tom about it; I bid him call you, and the fat rascal never did so, and never said a word about you, till we were ready for a start, and then no Master Frank was to the fore."

"Well, Tom," cried I, "what have you got to say to this?"

"Now, cuss you, don't come foolin' about me," replied that worthy, aiming a blow at me, which, had it taken place, might well have felled Goliah; but which, as I sprang aside, wasting its energies on the impassive air, had well nigh floored the striker. "Don't you come foolin' about me--you knows right well I called you, and you knows, too, you almost cried, and told me to clear out, and let you git an hour's sleep; for by the Lord you thought Archer and I was made of steel!--you couldn't and you wouldn't--and now you wants to know the reason why you warn't along with us!"

"Never mind the old thief, Frank," said Archer, seeing that I was on the point of answering, "even his own aunt says he is the most notorious liar in all Orange county--and Heaven forbid we should gainsay that most respectable old lady!"

Into what violent asseveration our host would have plunged at this declaration, remains, like the tale of Cambuscan bold, veiled in deep mystery; for as he started from the log on which he had been reposing while in the act of unsplicing his bamboo fishing pole, the elder of the Teachmans thrust his head out of the cabin nearest to us--"Come, boys, to breakfast! "--and at the first word of his welcome voice, Tom made, as he would have himself defined it, stret tracks for the table. And a mighty different table it was from that to which we had sat down on the preceding morning. Timothy--unscared by the wonder of the mountain nymphs, who deemed a being of the masculine gender as an intruder, scarce to be tolerated, on the mysteries of the culinary art--had exerted his whole skill, and brought forth all the contents of his canteen! We had a superb steak of the fattest venison, graced by cranberries stewed with cayenne pepper, and sliced lemons. A pot of excellent black tea, almost as strong as the cognac which flanked it; a dish of beautiful fried perch, with cream as thick as porridge, our own loaf sugar, and Teachman's new laid eggs, hot wheaten cakes, and hissing rashers of right tender pork, furnished a breakfast forth that might have vied successfully with those which called forth, in the Hebrides, such raptures from the lexicographer.

Breakfast despatched--for which, to say the truth, Harry gave us but little time--we mustered our array and started; Harry and Tom and I making one party, with the spaniels--Garry, the Teachmans, and Timothy, with the setters, which would hunt very willingly for him in Archer's absence, forming a second. It was scarce eight o'clock when we went out, each on a separate beat, having arranged our routes so as to meet at one o'clock in the great swamp, said to abound, beyond all other places, in the ruffed grouse or partridge, to the pursuit of which especially we had devoted our last day.

"Now, Frank," said Harry, "you have done right well throughout the week; and if you can stand this day's tramp, I will say for you that you are a sportsman, aye, every inch of one. We have got seven miles right hard walking over the roughest hills you ever saw--the hardest moors of Yorkshire are nothing to them--before we reach the swamp, and that you'll find a settler! Tom, here, will keep along the bottoms, working his way as best he can; while we make good the uplands! Are your flasks full?"

"Sartain, they are!" cried Tom--"and I've got a rousin big black bottle, too--but not a drop of the old cider sperrits do you git this day, boys; not if your thirsty throats were cracking for it!"

"Well, well! we won't bother you--you'll need it all, old porpoise, before you get to the far end. Here, take a hard boiled egg or two, Frank, and some salt, and I'll pocket a few biscuits--we must depend on ourselves to-day."

"Ay, ay, Sur," chuckled Timothy, "there's naw Tim Matlock to mak looncheon ready for ye 'a the day. See thee, measter Frank. Ay'se gotten 't measter's single barrel; and gin I dunna ootshoot measter Draa--whoy Ay'se deny my coontry!"

"Most certainly you will deny it then, Tim," answered I, "for Mr. Draw shoots excellently well, and you--"

"And Ay'se shot mony a hare by 't braw moon, doon i' bonny Cawoods. Ay'se beat, Ay'se oophaud[4] it!" So saying, he shouldered the long single barrel, and paddled off with the most extraordinary expedition after the Teachmans, who had already started, leading the setters in a leash, till they were out of sight of Archer.

"They have the longest way to go," said Harry, "by a mile at the least; so we have time for a cheroot before we three get under way."

Cigars were instantly produced and lighted, and we lounged about the little court for the best part of half an hour, till the report of a distant gunshot, ringing with almost innumerable reverberations along the woodland shores, announced to us that our companions had already got into their work.

"Here goes," cried Harry, springing to his feet at once, and grasping his good gun; "here goes--they have got into the long hollow, Tom, and by the time we've crossed the ridge, and got upon our ground, they'll be abreast of us."

"Hold on! hold on!" Tom bellowed, "you are the darndest critter, when you do git goin--now hold on, do--I wants some rum, and Forester here looks a kind of white about the gills, his what-d'ye-call, cheeroot, has made him sick, I reckon!"

Of course, with such an exhortation in our ears as this, it was impossible to do otherwise than wet our whistles with one drop of the old Ferintosh; and then, Tom having once again recovered his good humor, away we went, and "clombe the high

---

4 Oophaud, Yorkshire. Anglice, uphold

hill," though we "swam not the deep river," as merrily as ever sportsman did, from the days of Arbalast and Longbow, down to these times of Westley Richards' caps and Eley's wire cartridges.

A tramp of fifteen minutes through some scrubby brushwood, brought us to the base of a steep stony ridge covered with tall and thrifty hickories and a few oaks and maples intermixed, rising so steeply from the shore that it was necessary not only to strain every nerve of the leg, but to swing our bodies up from tree to tree, by dint of hand. It was indeed a hard and heavy tug; and I had pretty tough work, what between the exertion of the ascent, and the incessant fits of laughter into which I was thrown by the grotesquely agile movements of fat Tom; who, grunting, panting, sputtering, and launching forth from time to time the strangest and most blasphemously horrid oaths, contrived to make way to the summit faster than either of us--crashing through the dense underwood of juniper and sumac, uprooting the oak saplings as he swung from this to that, and spurning down huge stones upon us, as we followed at a cautious distance. When we at last crowned the ridge, we found him, just as Harry had predicted, stretched in a half recumbent attitude, leaning against a huge gray stone, with his fur cap and double-barrel lying upon the withered leaves beside him, puffing, as Archer told him, to his mighty indignation, like a great grampus in shoal water.

After a little rest, however, Falstaff revived, though not before he had imbibed about a pint of applejack, an occupation in which he could not persuade either of us, this time, to join him. Descending from our elevated perch, we now got into a deep glen, with a small brooklet winding along the bottom, bordered on either hand by a stripe of marshy bog earth, bearing a low growth of alder bushes, mixed with stunted willows. On the side opposite to that by which we had descended, the hill rose long and lofty, covered with mighty timber-trees standing in open ranks and overshadowing a rugged and unequal surface, covered with whortleberry, wintergreen, and cranberries, the latter growing only along the courses of the little runnels, which channeled the whole slope. Here, stony ledges and gray broken crags peered through the underwood, among the crevices of which the stunted cedars stood thick set, and matted with a thousand creeping vines and brambles; while there, from some small marshy basin, the giant Rhododendron Maximum rose almost to the height of a timber tree.

"Here, Tom," said Harry, "keep you along this run--you'll have a woodcock every here and there, and look sharp when you hear them fire over the ridge, for they can't shoot to speak of, and the ruffed grouse will cross--you know. You, master Frank, stretch your long legs and get three parts of the way up this hill--over the second mound--there, do you see that great blue stone with a thunder-splintered tree beside it? just beyond that! then turn due west, and mark the trending of the valley, keeping a little way ahead of me, which you will find quite easy, for I shall have to beat across you both. Go very slow, Tom--now, hurrah!"

Exhorted thus, I bounded up the hill and soon reached my appointed station; but not before I heard the cheery voice of Archer encouraging the eager spaniels--"Hie cock! hie cock! pu-r-r-h!"--till the woods rang to the clear shout.

Scarce had I reached the top, before, as I looked down into the glen below me, a puff of white smoke, instantly succeeded by a second, and the loud full reports of both his barrels from among the green-leafed alders, showed me that Tom had sprung game. The next second I heard the sharp questing of the spaniel Dan, followed by Harry's "Charge!--down Cha-arge, you little thief--down to cha-arge, will you!"

But it was all in vain--for on he went furious and fast, and the next moment the thick whirring of a grouse reached my excited ears. Carefully, eagerly, I gazed out to mark the wary bird; but the discharge of Harry's piece assured me, as I thought, that further watch was needless; and stupidly enough I dropped the muzzle of my gun.

Just at the self-same point of time--"Mark! mark, Frank!" shouted Archer, "mark! there are a brace of them!"--and as he spoke, gliding with speed scarcely inferior to a bullet's flight upon their balanced pinions, the noble birds swept past me, so close that I could have struck them with a riding whip.

Awfully fluttered was I--I confess--but by a species of involuntary and instinctive consideration I rallied instantly, and became cool. The grouse had seen me, and wheeled diverse; one darting to the right, through a small opening between a cedar bush and a tall hemlock--the other skimming through the open oak woods a little toward the left.

At such a crisis thought comes in a second's space; and I have often fancied that in times of emergency or great surprise, a man deliberates more promptly, and more prudently withal, than when he has full time to let his second thought trench on his first and mar it. So was it in this case with me. At half a glance I saw, that if I meant to get both birds, the right-hand fugitive must be the first, and that with all due speed; for but a few yards further he would have gained a brake which would have laughed to scorn Lord Kennedy or Harry T--r.

Pitching my gun up to my shoulder, both barrels loaded with Eley's red wire cartridge No. 6, I gave him a snap shot, and had the satisfaction of seeing him keeled well over, not wing-tipped or leg-broken, but fairly riddled by the concentrated charge of something within thirty yards. Turning as quick as light, I caught a fleet sight of the other, which by a rapid zig-zag was now flying full across my front, certainly over forty-five yards distant, among a growth of thick-set saplings--the hardest shot, in my opinion, that can be selected to test a quick and steady sportsman. I gave it him, and down he came too--killed dead--that I knew, for I had shot full half a yard before him. Just as I dropped my butt to load, the hill began to echo with the vociferous yells of master Dan, the quick redoubled cracks of Harry's heavy dog-whip, and his incessant rating--"Down, cha-arge! For sha-ame! Dan! Dan! down cha-arge! for sha-ame! "--broken at times by the impatient oaths of Tom Draw, in the gulley, who had, it seems, knocked down two woodcock, neither of which he could bag, owing to the depth and instability of the wet bog.

"Quit! quit! cuss you, quit there, leatherin that brute! Quit, I say, or I'll send a shot at you! Come here, Archer--I say, come here!--there be the darndest lot of droppins here, I ever see--full twenty cock, I swon!"

But still the scourge continued to resound, and still the raving of the spaniel excited Tom's hot ire.

"Frank Forester!" exclaimed he once again. "Do see now--Harry missed them partridge, and so he licks the poor dumb brute for it. I wish I were a spannel, and he'd try it on with me!"

"I will, too," answered Archer, with a laugh; "I will, too, if you go wish it, though you are not a spaniel, nor any thing else half so good. And why, pray, should I not scourge this wild little imp? he ran slap into the best pack of ruffed grouse I have seen this two years--fifteen or sixteen birds. I wonder they're not scattered--it's full late to find them packed!"

"Did you kill ere a one?" Tom holloaed; "not one, either of you!"

"I did," answered Harry, "I nailed the old cock bird, and a rare dog he is!--two pounds, good weight, I warrant him," he added, weighing him as he spoke. "Look at the crimson round his eye, Frank, like a cock pheasant's, and his black ruff or tippet--by George! but he's a beauty! And what did you do?" he continued.

"I bagged a brace--the only two that crossed me."

"Did you, though?" exclaimed Archer, with no small expression of surprise; "did you, though?--that's prime work--it takes a thorough workmen to bag a double shot upon October grouse. But come, we must go down to Tom; hark how the old hound keeps bawling."

Well, down we went. The spaniels quickly retrieved his dead birds, and flushed some fifteen more, of which we gave a clean account--Harry making up for lost time by killing six cock, right and left, almost before they topped the bushes--seven more fell to me, but single birds all of them--and but one brace to Tom, who now began to wax indignant; for Archer, as I saw, for fun's sake, was making it a point to cut down every bird that rose to him, before he could get up his gun; and then laughed at him for being fat and slow. But the laugh was on Tom's side before long--for while we were yet in the valley, the report of a gun came faintly down the wind from beyond the hill, and as we all looked out attentively, a grouse skimmed the brow, flying before the wind at a tremendous pace, and skated across the valley without stooping from his altitude. I stood the first, and fired, a yard at least ahead of him--on he went, unharmed and undaunted; bang went my second barrel--still on he went, the faster, as it seemed, for the weak insult.

Harry came next, and he too fired twice, and--tell it not in Gath-- missed twice! "Now, Fat-Guts!" shouted Archer, not altogether in his most amiable or pleasing tones; and sure enough up went the old man's piece--roundly it echoed with its mighty charge--a cloud of feathers drifted away in a long line from the slaughtered victim--which fell not direct, so rapid was its previous flight, but darted onward in a long declining tangent, and struck the rocky soil with a thud clearly audible where we stood, full a hundred yards from the spot where it fell.

He bagged, amid Tom's mighty exultation, forward again we went and in a short half hour got into the remainder of the pack which we had flushed before, in some low tangled thorn cover, among which they lay well, and we made havoc of them. And here the oddest accident I ever witnessed in the field took place--so odd, that I am half ashamed to write to it--but where's the odds, for it is true.

A fine cock bird was flushed close at Tom's feet, and went off to the left, Harry and I both standing to the right; he blazed away, and at the shot the bird sprung up six or eight feet into the air, with a sharp staggering flutter. "Killed dead!" cried I; "well done again, Fat Tom." But to my great surprise the grouse gathered wing, and flew on, feebly at first, and dizzily, but gaining strength more and more as he went on the farther. At the last, after a long flight, he treed in a tall leafless pine.

"Run after him, Frank," Archer called to me, "you are the lightest; and we'll beat up the swale till you return. You saw the tree he took?"

"Aye, aye!" said I preparing to make off.

"Well! he sits near the top--now mind me! no chivalry Frank! give him no second chance--a ruffed grouse, darting downward from a tall pine tree, is a shot to balk the devil--it's full five to one that you shoot over and behind him--give him no mercy!"

Off I went, and after a brisk trot, five or six minutes long, reached my tree, saw my bird perched on a broken limb close to the time-blanched trunk, cocked my Joe Manton, and was in the very act of taking aim, when something so peculiar in the motion of the bird attracted me, that I paused. He was nodding like a sleepy man, and seemed with difficulty to retain his foot-hold. While I was gazing, he let go, pitched headlong, fluttered his wings in the death-struggle, yet in air, and struck the ground close at my feet, stone-dead. Tom's first shot had cut off the whole crown of the head, with half the brain and the right eye; and after that the bird had power to fly five or six hundred yards, and then to cling upon its perch for at least ten minutes.

Rejoining my companions, we again went onward, slaying and bagging as we went, till when the sun was at meridian we sat down beside the brook to make our frugal meal--not to-day of grilled woodcock and champagne, but of hard eggs, salt, biscuit, and Scotch whiskey--not so bad either--nor were we disinclined to profit by it. We were still smoking on the marge, when a shot right ahead told us that our out-skirting party was at hand.

All in an instant were on the alert; in twenty minutes we joined forces, and compared results. We had twelve grouse, five rabbits, seventeen woodcock; they, six gray squirrels, seven grouse, and one solitary cock --Tim, proud as Lucifer at having led the field. But his joy now was at an end--for to his charge the setters were committed to be led in leash, while we shot on, over the spaniels. Another dozen grouse, and eighteen rabbits, completed our last bag in the Woodlands.

Late was it when we reached the Teachmans' hut--and long and deep was the carouse that followed; and when the moon had sunk and we were turning in, Tom Draw swore with a mighty oath of deepest emphasis--that since we had passed a week with him, he'd take a seat down in the wagon, and see the Beacon Races. So we filled round once more, and clinked our glasses to bind the joyous contract, and turned in happy.

DAY THE SEVENTH

Once more we were compelled to change our purpose.

When we left Tom Draw's it had been, as we thought, finally decided that we were for this bout to visit that fair village no more, but when that worthy announced his own determination to accompany us on our homeward route, and when we had taken into consideration the fact, that, that, independent of Tom's two hundred and fifty weight of solid flesh, we had two noble bucks, beside quail, ruffed grouse, woodcock, and rabbit almost innumerable to transport, in addition to our two selves and Timothy, with the four dogs, and lots of luggage--when we, I say, considered all this, it became apparent that another vehicle must be provided for our return. So during the last jorum, it had been put to the vote and unanimously carried that we should start for Tom's, by a retrograde movement, at four o'clock in the morning, breakfast with him, and rig up some drag or other wherein Timothy might get the two deer and the dogs, as best he might, into the city.

"As for us," said Harry, "we will go down the other road, Tom, over the backbone of the mountain, dine with old Colonel Beams, stop at Paterson, and take a taste at the Holy Father's poteen--you may look at the Falls if you like it, Frank, while we're looking at the Innishowen-- and so get home to supper. I'll give you both beds for one night--but not an hour longer--my little cellar would be broken, past all doubt, if old Tom were to get two nights out of it!"

"Ay'se sure it would," responded Timothy, who had been listening, all attention, mixing meanwhile some strange compound of eggs and rum and sugar. "Whoy, measter Draa did pratty nigh drink 't out yance--that noight 'at eight chaps, measter Frank, drank oop two baskets o' champagne, and fifteen bottles o' 't breawn sherry--Ay carried six on 'em to bed, Ay'se warrant it--and yan o' them, young measter

Clark, he spoilt me a new suit o' liveries, wi' vomiting a top on me."

"That'll do, Timothy," interposed Archer, unwilling, as I thought, that the secret mysteries of his establishment should be revealed any further to the profane ears which were gaping round about us--"that'll do for the present--give Mr. Draw that flip--he's looking at it very angrily, I see! and then turn in, or you'll be late in the morning; and, by George, we must be away by four o'clock at latest, for we have all of sixty miles to make to-morrow, and Tom's fat carcase will try the springs most consumedly, down hill."

Matters thus settled, in we turned, and--as it seemed to me, within five minutes, I was awakened by Harry Archer, who stood beside my bed full dressed, with a candle in his hand.

"Get up," he whispered, "get up, Frank, very quietly; slip on your great-coat and your slippers--we have a chance to serve Tom out--he's not awake for once! and Timothy will have the horses ready in five minutes!"

Up I jumped on the instant, hauled on a rough-frieze pea-jacket, thrust my unstockinged feet into their contrary slippers, and followed Harry, on the tips of my toes, along a creaking passage, guided by the portentous ruckling snorts, which varied the ilk profundity of the fat man's slumbers. When I reached his door, there stood Harry, laughing to himself, with a small quiet chuckle, perfectly inaudible at three feet distance, the intensity of which could, however, be judged by the manner in which it shook his whole person. Two huge horse-buckets, filled to the brim, were set beside him; and he had cut a piece of an old broomstick so as to fit exactly to the width of the passage, across which he had fastened it, at about two feet from the ground, so that it must most indubitably trip up any person, who should attempt to run along that dark and narrow thoroughfare.

"Now, Frank," said he, "see here! I'll set this bucket here behind the door--we'll heave the other slap into his face--there he lies, full on the broad of his fat back, with his mouth wide open--and when he jumps up full of fight, which he is sure to do, run you with the candle, which blow out the moment he appears, straight down the passage. I'll stand back here, and as he trips over that broomstick, which he is certain to do, I'll pitch the other bucket on his back--and if he does not think he's bewitched, I'll promise not to laugh. I owe him two or three practical jokes, and now I've got a chance, so I'll pay him all at once."

Well! we peeped in, aided by the glare of the streaming tallow candle, and there, sure enough, with all the clothes kicked off him, and his immense rotundity protected only from the cold by an exceeding scanty shirt of most ancient cotton, lay Tom, flat on his back, like a stranded porpoise, with his mouth wide open, through which he was puffing and breathing like a broken-winded cab-horse, while through his expanded nostrils he was snoring loudly enough to have awaked the seven sleepers. Neither of us could well stand up for laughing. One bucket was deposited behind the door, and back stood Harry ready to slip behind it also at half a moment's warning--the candlestick was placed upon the floor, which I was to kick over in my flight.

"Stand by to heave!" whispered my trusty comrade--"heave!" and with the word--flash!--slush!--out went the whole contents of the full pail, two gallons at the least of ice-cold water, slap in the chaps, neck, breast, and stomach of the sound sleeper. With the most wondrous noise that ears of mine have ever witnessed--a mixture of sob, snort, and groan, concluding in the longest and most portentous howl that mouth of man ever uttered--Tom started out of bed; but, at the very instant I discharged my bucket, I put my foot upon the light, flung down the empty pail, and bolted. Poor devil!--as he got upon his feet the bucket rolled up with its iron handles full against his shins, the oath he swore at which encounter, while he dashed headlong after me, directed by the noise I made on purpose, is most unmentionable. Well knowing where it was, I easily jumped over the stick which barred the passage. Not so Tom--for going at the very top of his pace, swearing like forty troopers all the time, he caught it with both legs just below the knees, and went down with a squelch that shook the whole hut to the rooftree, while at the self-same instant Harry once again soused him with the contents of the second pail, and made his escape unobserved by the window of Tom's own chamber. Meanwhile I had reached my room, and flinging off my jacket, came running out with nothing but my shirt and a lighted candle, to Tom's assistance, in which the next moment I was joined by Harry, who rushed in from out of doors with the stable lanthorn.

"What's the row now?" he said, with his face admirably cool and quiet. "What the devil's in the wind?"

"Oh! Archer!" grunted poor Tom, in most piteous accents--"them darned etarnal Teachmans--they've murdered me right out! I'll never get over this--ugh! ugh!

ugh! Half drowned and smashed up the darndest! Now aint it an etarnal shame! Cuss them, if I doos n't sarve them out for it, my name's not Thomas Draw!"

"Well, it is not," rejoined Harry, "who in the name of wonder ever called you Thomas? Christened you never were at all, that's evident enough, you barbarous old heathen--but you were certainly named Tom."

Swearing, and vowing vengeance on Jem Lyn, and Garry, and the Teachmans --each one of whom, by the way, was sound asleep during this pleasant interlude-- and shaking with the cold, and sputtering with uncontrollable fury, the fat man did at length get dressed, and after two or three libations of milk punch, recovered his temper somewhat, and his spirits altogether.

Although, however, Harry and I told him very frankly that we were not merely the sole planners, but the sole executors, of the trick--it was in vain we spoke. Tom would not have it.

"No--he knew--he knew well enough; did we go for to think he was such an old etarnal fool as not to know Jem's voice--a bloody Decker--he would be the death of him."

And direful, in good truth, I do believe, were the jokes practical, and to him no jokes at all, which poor Jem had to undergo, in expiation of his fancied share in this our misdemeanor.

Scarce had the row subsided, before the horses were announced. Harry and I, and Tom and Timothy, mounted the old green drag; and, with our cheroots lighted- -the only lights, by the way, that were visible at all --off we went at a rattling trot, the horses in prime condition, full of fire, biting and snapping at each other, and making their bits clash and jingle every moment. Up the long hill, and through the shadowy wood, they strained, at full ten miles an hour, without a touch of the whip, or even a word of Harry's well-known voice.

We reached the brow of the mountain, where there are four cleared fields- -whereon I once saw snow lie five feet deep on the tenth day of April--and an old barn; and thence we looked back through the cold gray gloom of an autumnal morning, three hours at least before the rising of the sun, while the stars were waning in the dull sky, and the moon had long since set, toward the Greenwood lake.

Never was there a stronger contrast, than between that lovely sheet of limpid water, as it lay now--cold, dun, and dismal, like a huge plate of pewter, without one glittering ripple, without one clear reflection, surrounded by the wooded hills which, swathed in a dim mist, hung grim and gloomy over its silent bosom--and its bright sunny aspect on the previous day.

Adieu! fair Greenwood Lake! adieu! Many and blithe have been the hours which I have spent around, and in, and on you--and it may well be I shall never see you more--whether reflecting the full fresh greenery of summer; or the rich tints of cisatlantic autumn; or sheeted with the treacherous ice; but never, thou sweet lake, never will thy remembrance fade from my bosom, while one drop of life-blood warms it; so art thou intertwined with memories of happy careless days, that never can return --of friends, truer, perhaps, though rude and humble, than all of prouder seeming. Farewell to thee, fair lake! Long may it be before thy rugged hills be stripped of their green garniture, or thy bright waters marred by the unpictur-esque improvements of man's avarice!--for truly thou, in this utilitarian age, and at brief distance from America's metropolis, art young, and innocent, and unpolluted, as when the red man drank of thy pure waters, long centuries ere he dreamed of the pale-faced oppressors, who have already rooted out his race from half its native continent.[5]

Another half hour brought us down at a rattling pace to the village, and once again we pulled up at Tom's well-known dwelling, just as the day was breaking. A crowd of loiterers, as usual, was gathered even at that untimely season in the large bar-room; and when the clatter of our hoofs and wheels announced us, we found no lack of ready-handed and quick tongued assistants.

"Take out the horses, Timothy," cried Harry, "unharness them, and rub them down as quickly and as thoroughly as may be--let them have four quarts each, and mind that all is ready for a start before an hour. Meantime, Frank, we will overhaul the game, get breakfast, and hunt up a wagon for the deer and setters."

---

5   Marred it has been long ago. A huge dam has been drawn across its outlet, in order to supply a feeder to the Morris Canal--a gigantic piece of unprofitable improvement, made, I believe, merely as a basis on which for brokers, stock-jobbers--et id genus omne of men too utilitarian and ambitious to be content with earning money honestly--to exercise their prodigious 'cuteness. The effect of this has been to change the bold shores into pestilential submerged swamps, whereon the dead trees still stand, tall, gray and ghostly; to convert a number of acres of beautiful meadow-land into stagnant grassy shallows; to back up the waters at the lake's head, to the utter destruction of several fine farms; and, last not least, to create fever and ague in abundance, where no such thing had ever been heard tell of before. Certainly! your well devised improvement is a great thing for a country!

"Don't bother yourself about no wagon," interposed Tom, "but come you in and liquor, else we shall have you gruntin half the day; and if old roan and my long pig-box wont carry down the deer, why I'll stand treat."

A jorum was prepared, and discussed accordingly, fresh ice produced, the quail and woodcock carefully unpacked, and instantly re-stowed with clean straw, a measure which, however, seemed almost supererogatory, since so completely had the external air been excluded from the game-box, that we found not only the lumps of ice in the bottom unthawed, but the flannel which lay over it stiff frozen; the birds were of course perfectly fresh, cool, and in good condition. Our last day's batch, which it was found impossible to get into the box, with all the ruffed grouse, fifty at least in number, were tied up by the feet, two brace and two brace, and hung in festoons round the inside rails of the front seat and body, while about thirty hares dangled by their hind legs, with their long ears flapping to and fro, from the back seat and baggage rack. The wagon looked, I scarce know how, something between an English stage-coach when the merry days of Christmas are at hand, and a game-hunter's taxed cart.

The business of re-packing had been scarce accomplished, and Harry and myself had just retired to change our shooting-jackets and coarse fustians for habiliments more suitable for the day and our destination-- New York, to-wit, and Sunday-- when forth came Tom, bedizened from top to toe in his most new and knowing rig, and looking now, to do him justice, a most respectable and portly yeoman.

A broad-brimmed, low-crowned, and long-napped white hat, set forth assuredly to the best advantage his rotund, rubicund, good-humored phiz; a clean white handkerchief circled his sturdy neck, on the voluminous folds of which reposed in placid dignity the mighty collops of his double chin. A bright canary waistcoat of imported kerseymere, with vast mother-of-pearl buttons, and a broad-skirted coat of bright blue cloth, with glittering brass buttons half the size of dollars, covered his upper man, while loose drab trousers of stout double-milled, and a pair of well-blacked boots, completed his attire; so that he looked as different an animal as possible, from the unwashed, uncombed, half-naked creature he presented, when lounging in his bar-room in his every-day apparel.

"Why, halloa, Guts!" cried Archer, as he entered, "you've broken out here in a new place altogether."

"Now quit, you, callin' of me Guts," responded Tom, more testily than I had ever heard him speak to Harry, whose every whim and frolic he seemed religiously to venerate and humor; "a fellow doesn't want to have it 'Guts' here, and 'Guts' there, over half a county. Why, now, it was but a week since, while 'lections was a goin' on, I got a letter from some d--d chaps to Newburg--'Rouse about now, old Guts, you'll need it this election?'"

"Ha! ha! ha!" shouted Harry and I almost simultaneously, delighted at Tom's evident annoyance.

"Who wrote it, Tom?"

"That's what I'd jist give fifty dollars to know now," replied mine host, clinching his mighty paw.

"Why, what would you do," said I, "if you did know?"

"Lick him, by George! Lick him, in the first place, till he was as nigh dead as I daared lick him--and then I'd make him eat up every darned line of it! But come, come--breakfast's ready; and while we're getting through with it, Timothy and Jem Lyn will fix the pig-box, and make the deer all right and tight for traveling!"

No sooner said than done--an ample meal was speedily despatched--and when that worthy came in to announce all ready, for the saving of time, master Timothy was accommodated with a seat at a side-table, which he occupied with becoming dignity, abstaining, as it were, in consciousness of his honorable promotion, from any of the quaint and curious witticisms, in which he was wont to indulge; but manducating, with vast energy, the various good things which were set before him.

It was a clear, bright Sabbath morning, as ever shone down on a sinful world, on which we started homeward--and, though I fear there was not quite so much solemnity in our demeanor as might have best accorded with the notions of over strict professors, I can still answer that, with much mirth, much merriment, and much good feeling in our hearts, there was no touch of irreverence, or any taint of what could be called sinful thought. The sun had risen fairly, but the hour was still too early for the sweet peaceful music of the church-going bells to have made their echoes tunable through the rich valley. A merry cavalcade, indeed, we started-- Harry leading the way at his usual slap-dash pace, so that one, less a workman than himself, would have said he went up hill and down at the same break-neck pace, and would take all the grit out of his team before he had gone ten miles--while a more accurate observer would have seen, at a glance, that he varied his rate at almost every inequality of road, that he quartered every rut, avoided every jog or mud-hole, husbanded for the very best his horses' strength, never making them either pull or hold a moment longer than was absolutely necessary from the abruptness of the ground.

At his left hand sat I, while Tom, in honor of his superior bulk and weight, occupied with his magnificent and portly person the whole of the back seat, keeping his countenance as sanctified as possible, and nodding, with some quaint and characteristic observation, to each one of the scattered groups of country-people, which we encountered every quarter of a mile for the first hour of our route, wending their way toward the village church--but, when we reached the forest-mantled road which clombe the mountain, making the arched woods resound to many a jovial catch or merry hunting chorus.

Mounted sublime on an arm-chair lashed to the forepart of the pig-box, sat Timothy in state--his legs well muffled in a noble scarlet-fringed buffalo skin, and his body encased in his livery top-coat--the setters and the spaniels crouching most meekly at his feet, and the two noble bucks--the fellow on whose steaks we had already made an inroad, having been left as fat Tom's portion--securely corded down upon a pile of straw, with their sublime and antlered crests drooping all spiritless and humble over the backboard, toward the frozen soil which crashed and rattled under the ponderous hoofs of the magnificent roan horse--Tom's special favorite-- which, though full seventeen hands high, and heavy in proportion; yet showing a good strain of blood, trotted away with his huge load at full ten miles an hour.

Plunging into the deep recesses of the Greenwoods, hill after hill we scaled, a toilsome length of stony steep ascents, almost precipitous, until we reached the back-bone of the mountain ridge--a rugged, bare, sharp edge of granite rock, without a particle of soil upon it, diving down at an angle not much less than forty-five degrees into a deep ravine, through which thundered and roared a flashing torrent. This fearful descent overpast, and that in perfect safety, we rolled merrily away down hill, till we reached Colonel Beam's tavern, a neat, low-browed, Dutch, stone farmhouse, situate in an angle scooped out of a green hill-side, with half a dozen tall and shadowy elms before it--a bright crystal stream purling along into the horse-trough through a miniature aqueduct of hollowed logs, and a clear cold spring in front of it, with half a score of fat and lazy trout floating in its transparent waters.

A hearty welcome, and a no less hearty meal having been here encountered and despatched, we rattled off again, through laden orchards and rich meadows; passed the confluence of the three bright rivers which issue from their three mountain gorges, to form, by their junction, the fairest of New Jersey's rivers, the broad Passaic; reached the small village noted for rum-drinking and quarter racing--high Pompton--thence by the Preakness mountain, and Mose Canouze's tavern--whereat, in honor of Tom's friend, a worthy of the self-same kidney with himself, we paused awhile--to Paterson, the filthiest town, situate on one of the loveliest rivers in the world, and famous only for the possession, in the person of its Catholic priest, of the finest scholar and best fellow in America, whom we unluckily found not at home, and therefore tasted not, according to friend Harry's promise, the splendid Innishowen which graces at all times his hospitable board.

Eight o'clock brought us to Hoboken, where, by good luck, the ferry boat lay ready--and nine o'clock had not struck when we three sat down once again about a neat small supper-table, before a bright coal fire, in Archer's snuggery--Tom glorying in the prospect of the races on the morrow, and I regretting that I had brought to its conclusion--MY FIRST WEEK IN THE WOODLANDS

THE WARWICK WOODLANDS:
ON A SECOND VISIT

THE WAYSIDE INN

On a still evening in October, Frank Forester and Harry Archer were sitting at the open window of a neat country tavern, in a sequestered nook of Rockland County, looking out upon as beautiful a view as ever gladdened the eyes of wandering amateur or artist.

The house was a large old-fashioned stone mansion, certainly not of later date than the commencement of the revolution; and probably had been, in its better days, the manor-house of some considerable proprietor--the windows were of a form very unusual in the States, opening like doors, with heavy wooden mullions and small lattices, while the walls were so thick as to form a deep embrasure, provided with a cushioned windowseat; the parlor, in which the friends had taken up their temporary domicile, contained two of these pleasant lounges, the larger looking out due south upon the little garden, with the road before it, and, beyond the road, a prospect, of which more anon--the other commanding a space of smooth green turf in front of the stables, whereon our old acquaintance, Timothy, was leading to and fro a pair of smoking horses. The dark green drag, with all its winter furniture of gaily decorated bearskins, stood half-seen beneath the low-arched wagon-shed.

The walls of the room--the best room of the tavern--were paneled with the dark glossy wood of the black cherry, and a huge mantel-piece of the same material, took up at least one-half of the side opposite the larger window, while on the hearth below reposed a glowing bed of red-hot hickory ashes, a foot at least in depth, a huge log of that glorious fuel blazing upon the massive andirons. Two large, deep gun-cases, a leathern magazine of shot, and sundry canisters of diamond gunpowder, Brough's, were displayed on a long table under the end window--a four-horse whip, and two fly-rods in India-rubber cases, stood in the chimney-corner; while reveling in the luxurious warmth of the piled hearth lay basking on the rug, three exquisitely formed Blenheim spaniels of the large breed--short-legged and bony, with ears that almost swept the ground as they stood upright, and coats as soft and lustrous as floss silk.

On a round table, which should have occupied the centre of the parlor, now pulled up to the window-seat, whereon reclined the worthies, stood a large pitcher of iced water; a square case-bottle of cut crystal filled, as the flavor which pervaded the whole room sufficiently demonstrated, with superb old Antigua Shrub; several large rummers corresponding to the fashion of the bottle; a twisted taper of green wax, and a small silver plate with six or eight cheroots, real manillas.

Supper was evidently over, and the friends, amply feasted, were now luxuriating in the delicious indolence, half-dozing, half-daydreaming, of a calm sleepy smoke, modestly lubricated by an occasional sip of the cool beverage before them. If we except a pile of box-coats, capes, and mackintoshes of every cut and color--a traveling liquor-case which, standing open, displayed the tops of three more bottles similar to that on the table, and spaces lined with velvet for all the glass in use--and another little leathern box, which, like the liquor-case, showed its contents of several silver plates, knives, forks, spoons, flasks of sauce, and condiments of different kinds--the whole interior, as a painter would have called it, has been depicted with all accuracy.

Without, the view on which the windows opened was indeed most lovely. The day had been very bright and calm; there was not a single cloud in the pale transparent heaven, and the sun, which had shone cheerfully all day from his first rising in the east, till now when he was hanging like a ball of bloody fire in the thin filmy haze which curtained the horizon, was still shooting his long rays, and casting many a shadow over the slopes and hollows which diversified the scene.

Immediately across the road lay a rich velvet meadow, luxuriant still and green--for the preceding month had been rather wet, and frost had not set in to nip its verdure--sloping down southerly to a broad shallow trout-stream, which rippled all glittering and bright over a pebbly bed, although the margin on the hither side was somewhat swampy, with tufts of willows and bushes of dark alder fringing it here and there, and dipping their branches in its waters--the farther bank was skirted by a tall grove of maple, hickory, and oak, with a thick undergrowth of sumac arrayed in all the gorgeous garniture of autumn, purples and brilliant scarlets and chrome yellows, mixed up and harmonized with the dark copper foliage of a few sere beeches, and the gray trunks apparent here and there through the thin screen of the fast falling leaves.

Beyond this grove, the bank rose bold and rich in swelling curves, with a fine corn-field, topped already to admit every sunbeam to the ripening ears. A buckwheat stubble, conspicuous by its deep ruddy hue, and two or three brown pastures divided by high fences, along the lines of which flourished a copious growth of catbriers and sumacs, with here and there a goodly tree waving above them, made up the centre of the picture. Beyond this cultured knoll there seemed to be a deep pitch of the land clothed with a hanging wood of heavy timber; and, above this again, the soil surged upward into a huge and round-topped hill, with several golden stubbles, shining out from the frame-work of primeval forest, which, dark with many a mighty pine, covered the mountain to the top, except where at its western edge it showed a huge and rifted precipice of rock.

To the right, looking down the stream, the hills closed in quite to the water's brink on the far side, rough and uncultivated, with many a blue and misty peak discovered through the gaps in their bold, broken outline, and a broad, lake-like sheet, as calm and brightly pictured as a mirror, reflecting their inverted beauties so wondrously distinct and vivid, that the amazed eye might not recognize the parting between reality and shadow. An old gray mill, deeply embosomed in a clump of weeping willows, still verdant, though the woods were sere and waxing leafless, explained the nature of that tranquil pool, while, beyond that, the hills swept down from the rear of the building, which contained the parlor whence the two sportsmen gazed, and seemed entirely to bar the valley, so suddenly, and in so short a curve, did it wind round their western shoulder. To the left hand, the view was closed by a thick belt of second growth, through which the sandy road and glittering stream wandered away together on their mazy path, and over which the summits of yet loftier and more rugged steeps towered heavenward.

Over this valley they had for some time gazed in silence, till now the broad sun sank behind the mountains, and the shrill whistle of the quail, which had been momently audible during the whole afternoon, ceased suddenly; four or five night-hawks might be seen wheeling high in pursuit of their insect prey through the thin atmosphere, and the sharp chirrup of a solitary katydid, the last of its summer tribe, was the only sound that interrupted the faint rush of the rapid stream, which came more clearly on the ear now that the louder noises of busy babbling daylight had yielded to the stillness of approaching night. Before long a bright gleam shot through the tufted outline of a dark wooded hill, and shortly after, just when a gray and misty shadow had settled down upon the half-seen landscape, the broad full moon came soaring up above the tree-tops, pouring her soft and silver radiance over the lovely valley, and investing its rare beauties with something of romance--a sentiment which belongs not to the gay, gaudy sunshine.

Just at this moment, while neither of the friends felt much inclined to talk, the door opened suddenly, and Timothy's black head was thrust in, with a query if "they didn't need t' waax candles?"

"Not yet, Tim," answered Archer, "not yet for an hour or so--but hold a min-ute--how have the horses fed?"

"T' ould gray drayed off directly, and he's gane tull t' loike bricks-- but t' bay's no but sillyish--he keeps a breaking oot again for iver-- and sae Ay'se give him a hot maash enow!"

"That's right. I saw he wasn't quite up to the mark the last ten miles or so. If he don't dry off now, give him a cordial ball out of the tool-chest--one of the number 3--camphire and cardamums and ginger; a clove of garlic, and treacle quantum sic, hey, Frank, that will set him to rights, I warrant it. Now have you dined yourself, or supped, as the good people here insist on calling it?"

"Weel Ay wot, have I, sur," responded Timothy; "an hour agone and better."

"Exactly; then step out yourself into the kitchen, and make us a good cup of our own coffee, strong and hot, do you see? and when that's done, bring it in with the candles; and, hark you, run up to the bed-room and bring my netting needles down, and the ball of silk twist, and the front of that new game-bag, I began the other night. If you were not as lazy as possible, friend Frank, you would bring your fly-book out, when the light comes, and tie some hackles."

"Perhaps I may, when the light comes," Forester answered; "but I'm in no hurry for it; I like of all things to look out, and watch the changes of the night over a landscape even less beautiful than this. One-half the pleasures of field sports to me, is other than the mere excitement. If there were nothing but the eagerness of the pursuit, and the gratification of successful vanity, fond as I am of shooting, I should, I believe, have long since wearied of it; but there are so many other things connected with it--the wandering among the loveliest scenery--the full enjoyment of the sweetest weather--the learning the innumerable and all-wondrous attributes and instincts of animated nature--all these are what make up to me the rapture I derive from woodcraft! Why, such a scene as this--a scene which how few, save the vagrant sportsman, or the countryman who but rarely appreciates the picturesque, have ever witnessed--is enough, with the pure and tranquil thoughts it calls up in the heart, to plead a trumpet-tongued apology, for all the vanity, and uselessness, and cruelty, and what not, so constantly alleged against our field sports."

"Oh! yes," cried Harry; "yes, indeed, Frank, I perfectly agree with you. But all that last is mere humbug--humbug, too, of the lowest and most foolish order--I never hear a man droning about the cruelty of field sports, but I set him down, on the spot, either as a hypocrite or a fool, and probably a glorious union of the two. When man can exist without killing myriads of animals with every breath of vital air he draws, with every draught of water he imbibes, with every footstep he prints upon the turf or gravel of his garden--when he abstains from every sort of animal food--and, above all, when he abstains from his great pursuit of torturing his fellow men--then let him prate, if he will, of sportsmen's cruelty.

"For show me one trade, one profession, wherein one man's success is not based upon another's failure; all rivalry, all competition, triumph and rapture to the winner, disgrace and anguish to the loser! And then these fellows, fattened on widows' tears and orphans' misery, preach you pure homilies about the cruelty of taking life. But you are quite right about the combination of pleasures--the excitement, too, of quick motion through the fresh air--the sense of liberty amid wide plains, or tangled woods, or on the wild hill tops--this, surely, to the reflective sportsman--and who can be a true sportsman, and not reflective--is the great charm of his pursuit."

"And do you not think that this pleasure exists in a higher degree here in America than in our own England?"

"As how, Frank?--I don't take."

"Why, in the greater, I will not say beauty--for I don't think there is greater natural beauty in the general landscape of the States--but novelty and wildness of the scenery! Even the richest and most cultivated tracts of America, that I have seen, except the Western part of New York, which is unquestionably the ugliest, and dullest, and most unpoetical region on earth, have a young untamed freshness about them, which you do not find in England.

"In the middle of the high-tilled and fertile cornfield you come upon some sudden hollow, tangled with brake and bush, which hedge in some small pool where float the brilliant cups and smooth leaves of the water lily, and whence, on your approach, up springs the blue-winged teal or gorgeous wood-duck. Then the long sweeping woodlands, embracing in themselves every variety of ground, deep marshy swamp, and fertile level thick-set with giant timber, and sandy barrens with their scrubby undergrowth, and difficult rocky steeps; and, above all, the seeming and comparative solitude--the dinner carried along with you and eaten under the shady tree, beside the bubbling basin of some spring--all this is vastly more exciting, than walking through trim stubbles and rich turnip fields, and lunching on bread and cheese and home-brewed, in a snug farmhouse. In short, field sports here have a richer range, are much more various, wilder--"

"Hold there, Frank; hold hard there; I cannot concede the wilder, not the really wilder--seemingly they are wilder; for, as you say, the scenery is wilder--and all the game, with the exception of the English snipe, being wood-haunters, you are led into rougher districts. But oh! no, no!--the field sports are not really wilder--in the Atlantic States at least--nor half so wild as those of England!"

"I should like to hear you prove that, Archer," answered Frank, "for I am constantly beset with the superiority of American field sports to tame English preserve shooting!"

"Pooh! pooh! that is only by people who know nothing about either; by people who fancy that a preserve means a park full of tame birds, instead of a range, perhaps, of many thousand acres, of the very wildest, barest moorland, stocked with the wariest and shyest of the feathered race, the red grouse. But what I mean to say, is this, that every English game-bird--to use an American phrase--is warier and wilder than its compeer in the United States. Who, for instance, ever saw in

England, Ireland, or Scotland, eighteen or twenty snipe or woodcock, lying within a space of twelve yards square, two or three dogs pointing in the midst of them, and the birds rising one by one, the gunshots rattling over them, till ten or twelve are on the ground before there is time to bag one.

"English partridge will, I grant, do this sometimes, on very warm days in September; but let a man go out with his heavy gun and steady dog late in December, or the month preceding it, let him see thirty or more covies--as on good ground he may--let him see every covey rise at a hundred yards, and fly a mile; let him be proud and glad to bag his three or four brace; and then tell me that there is any sport in these Atlantic States so wild as English winter field-shooting.

"Of grouse shooting on the bare hills, which, by the way, are wilder, more solitary far, and more aloof from the abodes of men, than any thing between Boston and the Green Bay, I do not of course speak; as it confessedly is the most wild and difficult kind of shooting.

"Still less of deer stalking--for Scrope's book has been read largely even here; and no man, how prejudiced soever, can compare with the standing at a deer-path all day long waiting till a great timid beast is driven up within ten yards of your muzzle, with that extraordinary sport on bald and barren mountains, where nothing but vast and muscular exertion, the eye of the eagle, and the cunning of the serpent, can bring you within range of the wild cattle of the hills.

"Battue shooting, I grant, is tame work; but partridge shooting, after the middle of October, is infinitely wilder, requiring more exertion and more toil than quail shooting. Even the pheasant--the tamest of our English game--is infinitely bolder on the wing than the ruffed grouse, or New York partridge; while about snipe and woodcock there exists no comparison--since by my own observation, confirmed by the opinion of old sportsmen, I am convinced that nine-tenths of the snipe and cock bagged in the States, are killed between fifteen and twenty paces; while I can safely say, I never saw a full snipe rise in England within that average distance. Quail even, the hardest bird to kill, the swiftest and the boldest on the wing, are very rarely killed further than twenty-five to thirty, whereas you may shoot from daylight to sunset in England, after October, and not pick up a single partridge within the farthest, as a minimum distance."

"Well! that's all true, I grant," said Forester, "yet even you allow that it is harder to kill game here than at home; and if I do not err, I have heard you admit that the best shot in all England could be beat easily by the crack shots on this side; how does all this agree!"

"Why very easily, I think," Harry replied, "though to the last remark, I added in his first season here! Now that American field sports are wilder in one sense, I grant readily; with the exception of snipe-shooting here, and grouse-shooting in Scotland, the former being tamer, in all senses, than any English--the latter wilder in all senses than any American--field-sport.

"American sporting, however, is certainly wilder, in so much as it is pursued on much wilder ground; in so much as we have a greater variety of game--and in so much as we have many more snap shots, and fewer fair dead points.

"Harder it is, I grant; for it is all, with scarcely an exception, followed in very thick and heavy covert--covert to which the thickest woods I ever saw in England are but as open ground. Moreover, the woods are so very large that the gun must be close up with the dog; and consequently the shots must, half of them, be fired in attitudes most awkward, and in ground which would, I think, at home, be generally styled impracticable; thirdly, all the summer shooting here is made with the leaf on--with these thick tangled matted swamps clad in the thickest foliage.

"Your dogs must beat within twenty yards at farthest, and when they stand you are aware of the fact rather by ceasing to hear their motion, than by seeing them at point; I am satisfied that of six pointed shots in summer shooting, three at the least must be treated as snap shots! Many birds must be shot at--and many are killed-- which are never seen at all, till they are bagged; and many men here will kill three out of four summer woodcock, day in and day out, where an English sportsman, however crack a shot he might be, would give the thing up in despair in half an hour.

"Practice, however, soon brings this all to rights. The first season I shot here--I was a very fair, indeed a good, young shot, when I came out hither--not at all crack, but decidedly better than the common run!--the first day I shot was on 4th of July, 1832, the place Seer's swamp, the open end of it; the witness old Tom Draw--and there I missed, in what we now call open covert, fourteen birds running; and left the place in despair--I could not, though I missed at home by shooting too quick- -I could not, for the life of me, shoot quick enough. Even you, Frank, shoot three times as well as you did, when you began here; yet you began in autumn, which is decidedly a great advantage, and came on by degrees, so that the following summer you were not so much nonplussed, though I remember the first day or two, you bitched it badly."

"Well, I believe I must knock under, Harry," Forester answered; "and here comes Timothy with the coffee, and so we will to bed, that taken, though I do want to argufy with you, on some of your other notions about dogs, scent, and so forth. But do you think the Commodore will join us here to-morrow?"

"No! I don't think so," Harry said, "I know it! Did not he arrive in New York last first of July, from a yachting tour at four o'clock in the afternoon; receive my note saying that I was off to Tom's that morning; and start by the Highlander at five that evening? Did he not get a team at Whited's and travel all night through, and find me just sitting down to breakfast, and change his toggery, and out, and walk all day--like a trump as he is? And did not we, by the same token, bag--besides twenty-five more killed that we could not find--one hundred and fifteen cock between ten o'clock and sunset; while you, you false deceiver, were kicking up your heels in Buffalo? Is not all this a true bill, and have you now the impudence to ask me whether I think the Commodore will come? I only wish I was as sure of a day's sport tomorrow, as I am of his being to the fore at luncheon time!"

"At luncheon time, hey? I did not know that you looked for him so early! Will he be in time, then, for the afternoon's shooting?"

"Why, certainly he will," returned Archer. "The wind has been fair up the river all day long, though it has been but light; and the Ianthe will run up before it like a race-horse. I should not be much surprised if he were here to breakfast." "And that we may be up in time for him, if perchance he should let us to bed forthwith," said Frank with a heavy yawn.

"I am content," answered Harry, finishing his cup of coffee, and flinging the stump of his cheroot into the fire. "Good-night! Timothy will call you in the morning."

"Goodnight, old fellow."

And the friends parted merrily, in prospect of a pleasant day's sport on the morrow.

THE MORNING'S SPORT

It was not yet broad daylight when Harry Archer, who had, as was usual with him on his sporting tour, arisen with the lark, was sitting in the little parlor I have before described, close to the chimney corner, where a bright lively fire was already burning, and spreading a warm cheerful glow through the apartment. The large round table, drawn up close to the hearth, was covered with a clean though coarse white cloth, and laid for breakfast, with two cups and saucers, flanked by as many plates and egg-cups, although as yet no further preparations for the morning meal, except the presence of a huge home-made loaf and a large roll of rich golden-hued butter, had been made by the neat-handed Phillis of the country inn. Two candles were lighted, for though the day had broken, the sun was not yet high enough to cast his rays into that deep and rock-walled valley, and by their light Archer was busy with the game-bag, the front of which he had finished netting on the previous night.

Frank Forester had not as yet made his appearance; and still, while the gigantic copper kettle bubbled and steamed away upon the hearth, discoursing eloquent music, and servant after servant bustled in, one with a cold quail-pie, another with a quart jug of cream, and fresh eggs ready to be boiled by the fastidious epicures in person, he steadily worked on, housewife and saddler's silk, and wax and scissors ready to his hand; and when at last the door flew open, and the delinquent comrade entered, he flung his finished job upon the chair, and gathered up his implements, with:

"Now, Frank, let's lose no time, but get our breakfasts. Halloa! Tim, bring the rockingham and the tea-chest; do you hear?"

"Well, Harry, so you've done the game-bag," exclaimed the other, as he lifted it up and eyed it somewhat superciliously--"Well, it is a good one certainly; but you are the queerest fellow I ever met, to give yourself unnecessary trouble. Here you have been three days about this bag, hard all; and when it's done, it is not half as good a one as you can buy at Cooper's for a dollar, with all this new-fangled machinery of loops and buttons, and I don't know what."

"And you, Master Frank," retorted Harry, nothing daunted, "to be a good shot and a good sportsman--which, with some few exceptions, I must confess you are--are the most culpably and wilfully careless about your appointments I ever met. I don't call a man half a sportsman, who has not every thing he wants at hand for an emergency, at half a minute's notice. Now it so happens that you cannot get, in New York at all, anything like a decent game-bag--a little fancy-worked French or German jigmaree machine you can get anywhere, I grant, that will do well enough for a fellow to carry on his shoulders, who goes out robin-gunning, but nothing for your man to carry, wherein to keep your birds cool, fresh, and unmutilated. Now, these loops and buttons, at which you laugh, will make the difference of a week at least in the bird's keeping, if every hour or so you empty your pockets--wherein I take it for granted you put your birds as fast as you bag them--smooth down their plumage gently, stretch their legs out, and hang them by the heads, running the button down close to the neck of each. In this way this bag, which is, as you see, half a yard long, by a quarter and a half a quarter deep, made double, one hag of fustian, with a net front, which makes two pockets-- will carry fifty-one quail or woodcock, no one of them pressing upon, or interfering with, another, and it would carry sixty-eight if I had put another row of loops in the inner bag; which I did not, that I might have the bottom vacant to carry a few spare articles, such as a bag of Westley Richards' caps, and a couple of dozen of Ely's cartridges."

"Oh! that's all very well," said Frank, "but who the deuce can be at the bore of it?"

"Why be at the bore of shooting at all, for that matter?" replied Harry --"I, for one, think that if a thing is worth doing at all, it is worth doing well--and I can't bear to kill a hundred or a hundred and fifty birds, as our party almost always do out here, and then be obliged to throw them away, just for want of a little care. Why, I was shooting summer cock one July day two years ago--there had been heavy rain in the early morning, and the grass and bushes were very wet--Jem Blake was with me, and we had great sport, and he laughed at me like the deuce for taking my birds out of my pocket at the end of every hour's sport, and making Timothy smooth them down carefully, and bag them all after my fashion. Egad I had the laugh though, when we got home at night!"

"How so," asked Frank, "in what way had you the laugh?"

"Simply in this--a good many of the birds were very hard shot, as is always the case in summer shooting, and all of them got more or less wet, as did the pockets of Jem's shooting jacket, wherein he persisted in carrying his birds all day--the end was, that when we got home at night, it having been a close, hot, steamy day, he had not one bird which was not more or less tainted--and, as you know of course, when taint has once begun, nothing can check it."

"Ay! ay! well that indeed's a reason; if you can't buy such a bag, especially!"

"Well, you cannot then, I can tell you! and I'm glad you're convinced for once; and here comes breakfast--so now let us to work, that we may get on our ground as early as may be. For quail you cannot be too early; for if you don't find them while they are rambling on their feeding ground, it is a great chance if you find them at all."

"But, after all, you can only use up one or two bevies or so; and, that done, you must hunt for them in the basking time of day, after all's done and said," replied Frank, who seemed to have got up somewhat paradoxically given that morning.

"Not at all, Frank, not at all," answered Harry--"that is if you know your ground; and know it to be well stocked; and have a good marker with you."

"Oh! this is something new of yours--some strange device fantastical-- let's have it, pray."

"Certainly you shall; you shall have it now in precept, and in an hour or two in practice. You see those stubbles on the hill--in those seven or eight fields there are, or at least should be, some five bevies; there is good covert, good easy covert all about, and we can mark our birds down easily; now, when I find one bevy, I shall get as many barrels into it as I can, mark it down as correctly as possible, and then go and look for another."

"What! and not follow it up? Now, Harry, that's mere stuff; wait till the scent's gone cold, and till the dogs can't find them? 'Gad, that's clever, any way!"

"Exactly the reverse, friend Frank; exactly the reverse. If you follow up a bevy, of quail mark you, on the instant, it's ten to one almost that you don't spring them.

If, on the contrary, you wait for half an hour, you are sure of them. How it is, I cannot precisely tell you. I have sometimes thought that quail have the power of holding in their scent, whether purposely or naturally--from the effect of fear perhaps contracting the pores, and hindering the escape of the effluvia--I know not, but I am far from being convinced even now that it is not so. A very good sportsman, and true friend of mine, insists upon it that birds give out no scent except from the feet, and that, consequently, if they squat without running they cannot be found. I do not, however, believe the theory, and hold it to be disproved by the fact that dead birds do give out scent. I have generally observed that there is no difficulty in retrieving dead quail, but that, wounded, they are constantly lost. But, be that as it may, the birds pitch down, each into the best bit of covert he can find, and squat there like so many stones, leaving no trail or taint upon the grass or bushes, and being of course proportionally hard to find; in half an hour they will begin, if not disturbed, to call and travel, and you can hunt them up, without the slightest trouble. If you have a very large tract of country to beat, and birds are very scarce, of course it would not answer to pass on; nor ever, even if they are plentiful, in wild or windy weather, or in large open woods; but where you have a fair ground, lots of birds, and fine weather, I would always beat on in a circuit, for the reason I have given you. In the first place, every bevy you flush flies from its feeding to its basking ground, so that you get over all the first early, and know where to look afterward; instead of killing off one bevy, and then going blundering on, at blind guess work, and finding nothing. In the second place, you have a chance of driving two or three bevies into one brake, and of getting sport proportionate; and in the third place, as I have told you, you are much surer of finding marked birds after an hour's lapse, than on the moment."

"I will do you the justice to say," Forester replied, "that you always make a tolerably good fight in support of your opinions; and so you have done now, but I want to hear something more about this matter of holding scent--facts! facts! and let me judge for myself."

"Well, Frank, give me a bit more of that pie in the mean time, and I will tell you the strongest case in point I ever witnessed. I was shooting near Stamford, in Connecticut, three years ago, with C--- K---, and another friend; we had three as good dogs out, as ever had a trigger drawn over them. My little imported yellow and white setter, Chase, after which this old rascal is called--which Mike Sandford considered the best-nosed dog he had ever broken--a capital young pointer dog of K---'s, which has since turned out, as I hear, superlative, and P---'s old and stanch setter Count. It was the middle of a fine autumn day, and the scenting was very uncommonly good. One of our beaters flushed a bevy of quail very wide of us, and they came over our heads down a steep hillside, and all lighted in a small circular hollow, without a bit of underbrush or even grass, full of tall thrifty oak trees, of perhaps twenty-five years' growth. They were not much out of gun-shot, and we all three distinctly saw them light; and I observed them flap and fold their wings as they settled. We walked straight to the spot, and beat it five or six times over, not one of our dogs ever drawing, and not one bird rising. We could not make it out; my friends thought they had treed, and laughed at me when I expressed my belief that they were still before us, under our very noses. The ground was covered only by a deep bed of sere decaying oak leaves. Well, we went on, and beat all round the neighborhood within a quarter of a mile, and did not find a bird, when lo! at the end of perhaps half an hour, we heard them calling-- followed the cry back to that very hollow; the instant we entered it, all the three dogs made game, drawing upon three several birds, roaded them up, and pointed steady, and we had half an hour's good sport, and we were all convinced that the birds had been there all the time. I have seen many instances of the same kind, and more particularly with wing-tipped birds, but none I think so tangible as this!"

"Well, I am not a convert, Harry; but, as the Chancellor said, I doubt."

"And that I consider not a little, from such a positive wretch as you are; but come, we have done breakfast, and it's broad daylight. Come, Timothy, on with the bag and belts; he breakfasted before we had got up, and gave the dogs a bite."

"Which dogs do you take, Harry; and do you use cartridge?"

"Oh! the setters for the morning; they are the only fellows for the stubble; we should be all day with the cockers; even setters, as we must break them here for wood shooting, have not enough of speed or dash for the open. Cartridges? yes! I shall use a loose charge in my right, and a blue cartridge in my left; later in the season I use a blue in my right and a red in my left. It just makes the difference between killing with both, or with one barrel. The blue kills all of twenty, and the red all of thirty-five yards further than loose shot; and they kill clean!"

"Yet many good sportsmen dislike them," Frank replied; "they say they ball!"

"They do not now, if you load with them properly; formerly they would do so at times, but that defect is now rectified--with the blue and red cartridges at least-- the green, which are only fit for wild-fowl, or deer-shooting, will do so sometimes, but very rarely; and they will execute surprisingly. For a bad or uncertain rifle-shot, the green cartridge, with SG shot is the thing--twelve good-sized slugs, propelled with force enough to go through an inch plank, at eighty yards, within a compass of three feet--but no wad must be used, either upon the cartridge or between that and the powder; the small end must be inserted downward, and the cartridge must be chosen so that the wad at the top shall fit the gun, the case being two sizes less than the caliber. With these directions no man need make a mistake; and, if he can cover a bird fairly, and is cool enough not to fire within twenty yards, he will never complain of cartridges, after a single trial. Remember, too, that vice versa to the rule of a loose charge, the heavier you load with powder, the closer will your cartridge carry. The men who do not like cartridges are--you may rely upon it--of the class which prefers scattering guns. I always use them, except in July shooting, and I shall even put a few red in my pockets, in case the wind should get up in the afternoon. Besides which, I always take along two buckshot cartridges, in case of happening, as Timothy would say, on some big varmint. I have four pockets in my shooting waistcoat, each stitched off into four compartments--each of which holds, erect, one cartridge--you cannot carry them loose in your pocket, as they are very apt to break. Another advantage of this is, that in no way can you carry shot with so little inconvenience, as to weight; besides which, you load one-third quicker, and your gun never leads!"

"Well! I believe I will take some to-day--but don't you wait for the Commodore?"

"No! He drives up, as I told you, from Nyack, where he lands from his yacht, and will be here at twelve o'clock to luncheon; if he had been coming for the morning shooting, he would have been here ere this. By that time we shall have bagged twenty-five or thirty quail, and a ruffed grouse or two; besides driving two or three bevies down into the meadows and the alder bushes by the stream, which are quite full of woodcock. After luncheon, with the Commodore's aid, we will pick up these stragglers, and all the timber-doodles!"

In another moment the setters were unchained, and came careering, at the top of their speed, into the breakfast room, where Harry stood before the fire, loading his double gun, while Timothy was buttoning on his left leggin. Frank, meanwhile, had taken up his gun, and quietly sneaked out of the door, two flat irregular reports explaining, half a moment after, the purport of his absence.

"Well, now, Frank, that is"--expostulated Harry--"that is just the most snobbish thing I ever saw you do; aint you ashamed of yourself now, you genuine cockney!"

"Not a bit--my gun has not been used these three months, and something might have got into the chamber!"

"Something might not, if when you cleaned it last you had laid a wad in the centre of a bit of greased rag three inches square and rammed it about an inch down the barrel, leaving the ends of the linen hanging out. And by running your rod down you could have ascertained the fact, without unnecessarily fouling your piece. A gun has no right ever to miss fire now; and never does, if you use Westley Richards' caps, and diamond gunpowder--putting the caps on the last thing--which has the further advantage of being much the safer plan, and seeing that the powder is up to the cones before you do so. If it is not so, let your hammer down, and give a smart tap to the under side of the breech, holding it uppermost, and you will never need a picker; or at least almost never. Remember, too, that the best picker in the world is a strong needle headed with sealing wax. And now that you have finished loading, and I lecturing, just jump over the fence to your right; and that footpath will bring us to the stepping-stones across the Ramapo. By Jove, but we shall have a lovely morning."

He did so, and away they went, with the dogs following steadily at the heel, crossed the small river dry-shod, climbed up the wooded bank by dint of hand and foot, and reached the broad brown corn stubble. Harry, however, did not wave his dogs to the right-hand and left, but calling them in, quietly plodded along the headland, and climbed another fence, and crossed a buckwheat stubble, still without beating or disturbing any ground, and then another field full of long bents and ragwort, an old deserted pasture, and Frank began to grumble, but just then a pair of bars gave access to a wide fifty acre lot, which had been wheat, the stubble standing still knee deep, and yielding a rare covert.

"Now we are at the far end of our beat, and we have got the wind too in the dogs' noses, Master Frank--and so hold up good lads," said Harry. And off the setters shot like lightning, crossing and quartering their ground superbly.

"There! there! well done, old Chase--a dead stiff point already, and Shot backing him as steady as a rail. Step up, Frank, step up quietly, and let us keep the hill of them."

They came up close, quite close to the stanch dog, and then, but not till then, he feathered and drew on, and Shot came crawling up till his nose was but a few inches in the rear of Chase's, whose point he never thought of taking from him. Now they are both upon the game. See how they frown and slaver, the birds are close below their noses.

Whirr--r--r! "There they go--a glorious bevy!" exclaimed Harry, as he cocked his right barrel and cut down the old cock bird, which had risen rather to his right hand, with his loose charge--"blaze away, Frank!" Bang--bang!--and two more birds came fluttering down, and then he pitched his gun up to his eye again, and sent the cartridge after the now distant bevy, and to Frank's admiration a fourth bird was keeled over most beautifully, and clean killed, while crossing to the right, at forty-six yards, as they paced it afterward.

"Now mark! mark, Timothy--mark, Frank!" And shading their eyes from the level sunbeams, the three stood gazing steadily after the rapid bevy. They cross the pasture, skim very low over the brush fence of the cornfield--they disappear behind it they are down! no! no! not yet--they are just skirting the summit of the topped maize stalks--now they are down indeed, just by that old ruined hovel, where the cat-briers and sumac have overspread its cellar and foundation with thick underwood. And all the while the sturdy dogs are crouching at their feet unmoving.

"Will you not follow those, Harry?" Forester inquired--"there are at least sixteen of them!"

"Not I," said Archer, "not I, indeed, till I have beat this field--I expect to put up another bevy among those little crags there in the corner, where the red cedars grow--and if we do, they will strike down the fence of the buckwheat stubble--that stubble we must make good, and the rye beside it, and drive, if possible, all that we find before us to the corn field. Don't be impatient, and you'll see in time that I am in the right."

No more words were now wasted; the four birds were bagged without trouble, and the sportsmen being in the open, were handed over on the spot to Tim; who stroked their freckled breasts, and beautifully mottled wing-coverts and backs, with a caressing touch, as though he loved them; and finally, in true Jack Ketch style, tucked them up severally by the neck. Archer was not mistaken in his prognostics--another bevy had run into the dwarf cedars from the stubble at the sound of the firing, and were roaded up in right good style, first one dog, and then the other, leading; but without any jealousy or haste.

They had, however, run so far, that they had got wild, and as there was no bottom covert on the crags, had traversed them quite over to the open, on the far side--and, just as Archer was in the act of warning Forester to hurry softly round and head them, they flushed at thirty yards, and had flown some five more before they were in sight, the feathery evergreens for a while cutting off the view--the dogs stood dead at the sound of their wings. Then, as they came in sight, Harry discharged both barrels very quickly--the loose shot first, which evidently took effect, for one bird cowered and seemed about to fall, but gathered wing again, and went on for the present--the cartridge, which went next, although the bevy had flown ten yards further, did its work clean, and stopped its bird. Frank fired but once, and killed, using his cartridge first, and thinking it in vain to fire the loose shot. The remaining birds skimmed down the hill, and lighted in the thick bushy hedge-row, as Archer had foreseen.

"So much for Ely!" exclaimed Harry--"had we both used two of them, we should have bagged four then. As it is, I have killed one which we shall not get; a thing that I most particularly hate."

"That bird will rise again," said Frank.

"Never!" replied the other, "he has one, if not two, shot in him, well forward--if I am not much mistaken, before the wing--he is dead now! but let us on. These we must follow, for they are on our line; you keep this side the fence, and I will cross it with the dogs--come with me, Timothy."

In a few minutes more there was a dead point at the hedge-row. "Look to, Frank!" "Ay! ay! Poke them out, Tim;" then followed sundry bumps and threshings of the briers, and out with a noisy flutter burst two birds under Forester's nose. Bang! bang!

"The first shot too quick, altogether," muttered Archer; "Ay, he has missed one; mark it, Tim--there he goes down in the corn, by jingo-- you've got that bird, Frank! That's well! Hold up, Shot"--another point within five yards. "Look out again, Frank."

But this time vainly did Tim poke, and thrash, and peer into the bushes --yet still Shot stood, stiff as a marble statue--then Chase drew up and snuffed about, and pushed his head and forelegs into the matted briers, and thereupon a muzzling noise ensued, and forthwith out he came, mouthing a dead bird, warm still, and bleeding from the neck and breast.

"Frank, he has got my bird--and shot, just as I told you, through the neck and near the great wing joint--good dog! good dog!"

"The devil!"

"Yes, the devil! but look out man, here is yet one more point;" and this time ten or twelve birds flushed upon Archer's side; he slew, as usual, his brace, and as they crossed, at long distance, Frank knocked down one more--the rest flew to the corn-field.

In the middle of the buckwheat they flushed another, and, in the rye, another bevy, both of which crossed the stream, and settled down among the alders. They reached the corn-field, and picked up their birds there, quite as fast as Frank himself desired--three ruffed grouse they had bagged, and four rabbits, in a small dingle full of thorns, before they reached the corn; and just as the tin horns were sounding for noon and dinner from many a neighboring farm, they bagged their thirty-fourth quail. At the same moment, the rattle of a distant wagon on the hard road, and a loud cheer replying to the last shot, announced the Commodore; who pulled up at the tavern door just as they crossed the stepping-stones, having made a right good morning's work, with a dead certainty of better sport in the afternoon, since they had marked two untouched bevies, thirty-five birds at least, beside some ten or twelve more stragglers into the alder brakes, which Harry knew to hold-- more-over, thirty woodcock, as he said, at the fewest.

"Well! Harry," exclaimed Frank, as he set down his gun, and sat down to the table, "I must for once knock under--your practice has borne out your precepts."

THE WOODCOCK

Luncheon was soon discussed, a noble cold quail pie and a spiced round of beef, which formed the most essential parts thereof, displaying in their rapidly diminished bulk ocular evidence of the extent of sportmen's appetites; a single glass of shrub and water followed, cheroots were lighted, and forth the comrades sallied, the Commodore inquiring as they went what were the prospects of success.

"You fellows," he concluded, "have, I suppose, swept the ground completely."

"That you shall see directly," answered Archer; "I shall make you no promises. But see how evidently Grouse recollects those dogs of mine, though it is nearly a year since they have met; don't you think so, A---?"

"To be sure I do," replied the Commodore; "I saw it the first moment you came up--had they been strangers he would have tackled them upon the instant; and instead of that he began wagging his tail, and wriggling about, and playing with them. Oh! depend upon it, dogs think, and remember, and reflect far more than we imagine--"

"Oh! run back, Timothy--run back!" here Archer interrupted him--"we don't want you this afternoon. Harness the nags and pack the wagon, and put them to, at five--we shall be at home by then, for we intend to be at Tom's to-night. Now look out, Frank, those three last quail we marked in from the hill dropped in the next field, where the ragwort stands so thick; and five to one, as there is a thin growth of brushwood all down this wall side, they will have run down hither. Why, man alive! you've got no copper caps on!"

"By George! no more I have--I took them off when I laid down my gun in the house, and forgot to replace them."

"And a very dangerous thing you did in taking them off, permit me to assure you. Any one but a fool, or a very young child, knows at once that a gun with caps on is loaded. You leave yours on the table without caps, and in comes some meddling chap or other, puts on one to try the locks, or to frighten his sweetheart, or for some other no less sapient purpose, and off it goes! and if it kill no one, it's God's mercy! Never do that again, Frank!"

Meanwhile they had arrived within ten yards of the low rickety stone wall, skirted by a thin fringe of saplings, in which Archer expected to find game--Grouse, never in what might be called exact command, had disappeared beyond it.

"Hold up, good dogs!" cried Harry, and as he spoke away went Shot and Chase--the red dog, some three yards ahead, jumped on the wall, and, in the act of bounding over it, saw Grouse at point beyond. Rigid as stone he stood upon that tottering ridge, one hind foot drawn up in the act of pointing, for both the fore were occupied in clinging to some trivial inequalities of the rough coping, his feathery flag erect, his black eye fixed, and his lip slavering; for so hot was the scent that it reached his exquisitely fashioned organs, though Grouse was many feet advanced between him and the game. Shot backed at the wall-foot, seeing the red dog only, and utterly unconscious that the pointer had made the game beyond.

"By Jove! but that is beautiful!" exclaimed the Commodore. "That is a perfect picture!--the very perfection of steadiness and breaking."

They crossed the wall, and poor Shot, in the rear, saw them no more; his instinct strongly, aye! naturally, tempted him to break in, but second nature, in the shape of discipline, prevailed; and, though he trembled with excitement, he moved not an inch. Grouse was as firm as iron, his nose within six inches of a bunch of wintergreen, pointed directly downward, and his head cocked a little on one side--they stepped up to him, and still on the wall-top, Chase held to his uneasy attitude.

"Now, then," said Harry, "look out, till I kick him up."

No sooner said than done--the toe of his thick shooting-boot crushed the slight evergreen, and out whirred, with his white chaps and speckled breast conspicuous, an old cock quail. He rose to Forester, but ere that worthy had even cocked his gun--for he had now adopted Archer's plan, and carried his piece always at half cock, till needed--flew to the right across the Commodore; so Frank released his hammer and brought down his Manton, while A--- deliberately covered, and handsomely cut down the bird at five-and-twenty yards.

Grouse made a movement to run in, but came back instantly when called.

"Just look back, if you please, one moment, before loading," said Harry, "for that down-charge is well worth looking at."

And so indeed it was--for there, upon the wall-top, where he had been balancing, Chase had contrived to lie down at the gunshot--wagging his stern slightly to and fro, with his white forepaws hanging down, and his head couched between them, his haunches propped up on the coping stone, and his whole attitude apparently untenable for half a minute.

"Now, load away for pity's sake, as quickly as you can; that posture must be any thing but pleasant."

This was soon done; inasmuch as the Commodore is not exactly one to dally in such matters; and when his locks ticked, as he drew the hammers to half-cock, Chase quietly dismounted from his perch, and Shot's head and fore-paws appeared above the barrier; but not till Archer's hand gave the expected signal did the stanch brutes move on.

"Come, Shot, good dog--it is but fair you should have some part of the fun! Seek dead! seek dead! that's it, sir! Toho! steady! Fetch him, good lad! Well done!"

In a few minutes' space, four or five more birds came to bag--they had run, at the near report, up the wall side among the bushes, and the dogs footed them along it, now one and now another taking the lead successively, but without any eagerness or raking looking round constantly, each to observe his comrades' or his master's movements, and pointing slightly, but not steadily, at every foot, till at the last all three, in different places, stood almost simultaneously--all three dead points.

One bird jumped up to Frank, which he knocked over. A double shot fell to the Commodore, who held the centre of the line, and dropped both cleverly--the second, a long shot, wing-tipped only. Harry flushed three and killed two dean, both within thirty paces, and then covered the third bird with his empty barrels--but, though no shot could follow from that quarter, he was not to escape scot free, for wheeling short to the left hand, and flying high, he crossed the Commodore in easy distance, and afterward gave Forester a chance.

"Try him, Frank," halloaed Archer--and "It's no use!" cried A---, almost together, just as he raised his gun, and levelled it a good two feet before the quail.

But it was use, and Harry's practiced eye had judged the distance more correctly than the short sight of the Commodore permitted--the bird quailed instantly as the shot struck, but flew on notwithstanding, slanting down wind, however, towards the ground, and falling on the hill-side at a full hundred yards.

"We shall not get him," Forester exclaimed; "and I am sorry for it, since it was a good shot."

"A right good shot," responded Harry, "and we shall get him. He fell quite dead; I saw him bounce up, like a ball, when he struck the hard ground. But A---'s second bird is only wing-tipped, and I don't think we shall get him; for the ground where he fell is very tussockky and full of grass, and if he creeps in, as they mostly will do, into some hole in the bog-ground, it is ten to one against the best dog in America!"

And so it came to pass, for they did bag Forester's, and all the other quail except the Commodore's which, though the dogs trailed him well, and worked like Trojans, they could not for their lives make out.

After this little rally they went down to the alders by the stream-side, and had enough to do, till it was growing rapidly too dark to shoot--for the woodcock were very plentiful--it was sweet ground, too, not for feeding only, but for lying, and that, as Harry pointed out, is a great thing in the autumn.

The grass was short and still rich under foot, although it froze hard every night; but all along the brook's marge there were many small oozy bubbling springlets, which it required a stinging night to congeal; and round these the ground was poached up by the cattle, and laid bare in spots of deep, soft, black loam; and the innumerable chalkings told the experienced eye at half a glance, that, where they laid up for the night soever, here was their feeding ground, and here it had been through the autumn.

But this was not all, for at every ten or twenty paces was a dense tuft of willow bushes, growing for the most part upon the higher knolls where it was dry and sunny, their roots heaped round with drift wood, from the decay of which had shot up a dense tangled growth of cat-briers. In these the birds were lying, all but some five or six which had run out to feed, and were flushed, fat and large, and lazy, quite in the open meadow.

"They stay here later," Harry said, as they bagged the last bird, which, be it observed, was the twenty-seventh, "than any where I know. Here I have killed them when there was ice thicker than a dollar on all the waters round about, and when you might see a thin and smoke-like mist boiling up from each springlet. Kill them all off to-day, and you will find a dozen fresh birds here to-morrow, and so on for a fortnight--they come down from the high ground as it gets too cold for them to endure their high and rarified atmosphere, and congregate hither!"

"And why not more in number at a time?" asked A---.

"Ay! there we are in the dark--we do not know sufficiently the habits of the bird to speak with certainty. I do not think they are pugnacious, and yet you never find more on a feeding ground than it will well accommodate for many days, nay weeks, together. One might imagine that their migrations would be made en masse, that all the birds upon these neighboring hills would crowd down to this spot together, and feed here till it was exhausted, and then on--but this is not so! I know fifty small spots like this, each a sure find in the summer for three or four broods, say from eight to twelve birds. During the summer, when you have killed the first lot, no more return--but the moment the frost begins, there you will find them--never exceeding the original eight or ten in number, but keeping up continually to that mark--and whether you kill none at all, or thirty birds a week, there you will always find about that number, and in no case any more. Those that are killed off are supplied, within two days at farthest, by new comers; yet, so far as I can judge, the original birds, if not killed, hold their own, unmolested by intruders. Whence the supplies come in--for they must be near neighbors by the rapidity of their succession--and why they abstain from their favorite grounds in worse locations, remains, and I fear we must remain, in the dark. All the habits of the woodcock are, indeed, very partially and slightly understood. They arrive here, and breed early in the spring--sometimes, indeed, before the snow is off the hills--get their young off in June, and with their young are most unmercifully, most unsportsmanly, thinned off, when they can hardly fly--such is the error, as I think it, of the law--but I could not convince my stanch friends, Philo, and J. Cypress, Jr., of the fact, when they bestirred themselves in favor of the progeny of their especial favorites, perdix virginiana and tetrao umbellus, and did defer the times for slaying them legitimately to such a period, that it is in fact next to impossible to kill the latter bird at all. But vainly did I plead, and a false advocate was Cypress after all, despite his nominal friendship, for that unhappy Scolopax, who in July at least deserves his nickname minor, or the infant. For, setting joke apart, what a burning shame it is to murder the poor little half-fledged younglings in July, when they will scarcely weigh six ounces; when they will drop again within ten paces of the dog that flushes, or the gun that misses them; and when the heat will not allow you even to enjoy the consummation of their slaughter. Look at these fellows now, with their gray foreheads, their plump ruddy breasts, their strong, well-feathered pinions, each one ten ounces at the least. Think how these jolly old cocks tower away, with their shrill whistle, through the tree-tops, and twist and dodge with an agility of wing and thought-like speed, scarcely inferior to the snipe's or swallow's, and fly a half mile if you miss them; and laugh to scorn the efforts of any one to bag them, who is not an out-and-outer! No chance shot, no stray pellet speaks for these--it must be the charge, the whole charge, and nothing but the charge, which will cut down the grown bird of October! The law should have said woodcock thou shalt not kill until September; quail thou shalt not kill till October, the twenty-fifth if you please; partridge thou shalt kill in all places, and at all times, when thou canst! and that, as we know, Frank, and A---, that is not everywhere or often."

"But, seriously," said the Commodore, "seriously, would you indeed abolish summer shooting?"

"Most seriously! most solemnly I would!" Archer responded. "In the first place because, as I have said, it is a perfect sin to shoot cock in July; and secondly, because no one would, I am convinced, shoot for his own pleasure at that season, if it were not a question of now or never. Between the intense heat, and the swarms of mosquitoes, and the unfitness of that season for the dogs, which can rarely scent their game half the proper distance, and the density of the leafy coverts; and lastly, the difficulty of keeping the game fresh till you can use it, render July shooting a toil, in my opinion, rather than a real pleasure; although we are such hunting creatures, that rather than not have our prey at all, we will pursue it in all times, and through all inconveniences. Fancy, my dear fellows, only fancy what superb shooting we should have if not a bird were killed till they were all full grown, and fit to kill; fancy bagging a hundred and twenty-five fall woodcock in a single autumn day, as we did this very year on a summer's day!"

"Oh! I agree with you completely," said Frank Forester, "but I am afraid such a law will never be brought to bear in this country--the very day on which cock shooting does not really begin, but is supposed by nine tenths of the people to begin--the fourth of July is against it.[6] Moreover, the amateur killers of game are so very few, in comparison with the amateur eaters thereof, that it is all but impossible to enforce the laws at all upon this subject. Woodcock even now are eaten in June--nay, I have heard, and believe it to be true, that many hotels in New York serve them up even in March and April; quail, this autumn, have been sold openly in the markets, many days previous to the expiration of close time. And, in fact, sorry I am to say it, as far as eating-houses are in question, the game laws are nearly a dead letter.

"In the country, also, I have universally found it to be the case, that although the penalty of a breach may be exacted from strangers, no farmer will differ with a neighbor, as they call it, for the sake of a bird. Whether time, and a greater diffusion of sporting propensities, and sporting feelings, may alter this for the better or no, I leave to sager and more politic pates than mine. And now I say, Harry, you surely do not intend to trundle us off to Tom Draw's to-night without a drink at starting? I see Timothy has got the drag up to the door, and the horses harnessed, and all ready for a start."

"Yes! yes! all that's true," answered Harry, "but take my word for it, the liquor case is not put in yet. Well, Timothy," he went on, as they reached the door, "that is right. Have you got everything put up?"

"All but t' gam' bag and t' liquor ca-ase, sur," Tim replied, touching his hat gnostically as he spoke; "Ay reckoned ple-ease sur, 'at you'd maybe want to fill t' yan oop, and empty t' oother!"

"Very well thought, indeed!" said Archer, winking to Forester the while. "Let that boy stand a few minutes to the horses' heads, and come into the house yourself and pack the birds up, and fetch us some water."

"T' watter is upon t' table, sur, and t' cigars, and a loight; but Ay'se be in wi' you directly. Coom hither, lad till Ay shew thee hoo to guide 'em; thou munna tooch t' bits for the loife o' thee, but joost stan' there anent them--if they stir loike, joost speak to 'em--Ayse hear thee!" and he left his charge and entered the small parlor, where the three friends were now assembled, with a cheroot apiece already lighted, and three tall brimming rummers on the table.

"Look sharp and put the birds up," said Harry, pitching, as he spoke, the fine

6   In the State of New York close time for woodcock expires on the last day of June--in New Jersey on the fourth of July--leaving the bird lawful prey on the 1st and the 5th, respectively.

fat fellows right and left out of his wide game pockets, "and when that's done fill yourself out a drink, and help us on with our great coats."

"What are you going to do with the guns?" inquired the Commodore.

"To carry them uncased and loaded; substituting in my own two buckshot cartridges for loose shot," replied Archer. "The Irish are playing the very devil through this part of the country--we are close to the line of the great Erie railroad--and they are murdering, and robbing, and I know not what, for miles around. The last time I was at old Tom's he told me that but ten days or a fortnight previously a poor Irish woman, who lived in his village, started to pay a visit to her mother by the self same road we shall pass to-night; and was found the next morning with her person brutally abused, kneeling against a fence stone dead, strangled with her own cambric handkerchief. He says, too, that not a week passes but some of them are found dead in the meadows, or in the ditches, killed in some lawless fray; and no one ever dreams of taking any notice, or making any inquiry about the matter!"

"Is it possible? then keep the guns at hand by all means!"

"Yes! but this time we will violate my rule about the copper caps--there is no rule, you are aware, but what has some exception--and the exception to this of mine is, always take off your copper caps before getting into a wagon; the jar will occasionally explode them, an upset will undoubtedly. So uncap, Messrs. Forester and A---, and put the bright little exploders into your pockets, where they will be both safe and handy! And now, birds are in, drinks are in, dogs and guns are in, and now let us be off!"

No more words were wasted; the landlord's bill was paid, Frank Forester and Timothy got up behind, the Commodore took the front seat, Harry sprang, reins in hand, to the box, and off they bowled, with lamps and cigars burning merrily, for it was now quite dark, along the well-known mountain road, which Archer boasted he could drive as safely in the most gloomy night of winter as in a summer noon. And so it proved this time, for though he piloted his horses with a cool head and delicate finger through every sort of difficulty that a road can offer, up long and toilsome hills without a rail between the narrow track and the deep precipice, down sharp and stony pitches, over loose clattering bridges, along wet marshy levels, he never seemed in doubt or trouble for a moment, but talked and laughed away, as if he were a mere spectator.

After they had gone a few miles on their way--"you broke off short, Archer," said the Commodore, "in the middle of your dissertation on the natural history and habits of the woodcock, turning a propos des bottes to the cruelty of killing them in midsummer. In all which, by the way, I quite agree with you. But I don't want to lose the rest of your lucubrations on this most interesting topic. What do you think becomes of the birds in August, after the moult begins?"

"Verily, Commodore, that is a positive poser. Many good sportsmen believe that they remain where they were before; getting into the thickest and wettest brakes, refusing to rise before the dog, and giving out little or no scent!"

"Do you believe this?"

"No; I believe there is a brief migration, but whither I cannot tell you with any certainty. Some birds do stay, as they assert; and that a few do stay, and do give out enough scent to enable dogs to find them, is a proof to me that all do not. A good sportsman can always find a few birds even during the moult, and I do not think that birds killed at that time are at all worse eating than others. But I am satisfied that the great bulk shift their quarters, whither I have not yet fully ascertained; but I believe to the small runnels and deep swales which are found throughout all the mountain tracts of the middle States; and in these, as I believe, they remain dispersed and scattered in such small parties that they are not worth looking after, till the frost drives them down to their old haunts. A gentleman, whom I can depend on, told me once that he climbed Bull Hill one year late in September--Bull Hill is one of the loftiest peaks in the Highlands of the Hudson--merely to show the prospect to a friend, and he found all the brushwood on the summit full of fine autumn cock, not a bird having been seen for weeks in the low woodlands at the base. They had no guns with them at the time, and some days elapsed before he could again spare a few hours to hunt them up; in the meantime frost came, the birds returned to their accustomed swamps and levels, and, when he did again scale the rough mountain, not a bird rewarded his trouble. This, if true, which I do not doubt, would go far to prove my theory correct; but it is not easy to arrive at absolute certainty, for if I am right, during that period birds are to be found no where in abundance, and a man must be a downright Audubon to be willing to go mountain-stalking--the hardest walking in the world, by the way--purely for the sake of learning the habits of friend Scolopax, with no hope of getting a good bag after all."

"How late have you ever killed a cock previous to their great southern flight?"

"Never myself beyond the fifteenth of November; but Tom Draw assures me, and his asseveration was accidentally corroborated by a man who walked along with him, that he killed thirty birds last year in Hell-hole, which both of you fellows know, on the thirteenth of December. There had been a very severe frost indeed, and the ice on that very morning was quite thick, and the mud frozen hard enough to bear in places. But the day was warm, bright, and genial, and, as he says, it came into his head to see 'if cock was all gone,' and he went to what he knew to be the latest ground, and found the very heaviest and finest birds he ever saw!"

"Oh! that of course," said A---, "if he found any! Did you ever hear of any other bird so late?"

"Yes! later--Mike Sandford, I think, but some Jerseyman or other--killed a couple the day after Christmas day, on a long southern slope covered with close dwarf cedars, and watered by some tepid springs, not far from Pine Brook; and I have been told that the rabbit shooters, who always go out in a party between Christmas and New Year's day, almost invariably flush a bird or two there in mid-winter. The same thing is told of a similar situation on the south-western slope of Staten Island; and I believe truly in both instances. These, however, must, I think, be looked upon not as cases of late emigration, but as rare instances of the bird wintering here to the northward; which I doubt not a few do annually. I should like much to know if there is any State of the Union where the cock is perennial. I do not see why he should not be so in Maryland or Delaware, though I have never heard it stated so to be. The great heat of the extreme southern summer drives them north, as surely as our northern winter sends them south; and the great emigrations of the main flight are northward in February and March, and southward in November, varying by a few days only according to the variations of the seasons!"

"Well, I trust they have not emigrated hence yet--ha! ha! ha!" laughed the Commodore, with his peculiar hearty, deep-toned merriment.

"Not they! not they! I warrant them," said Archer; "but that to-morrow must bring forth."

"Come, Harry," exclaimed Forester, after a little pause, "spin us a shooting yarn, to kill the time, till we get to fat Tom's."

"A yarn! well, what shall it be?"

"I don't know; oh! yes! yes! I do. You once told me something about a wolf-hunt, and then shut up your mouth all at once, and would give me no satisfaction."

"A wolf-hunt?" cried the Commodore, "were you ever at a wolf-hunt; and here in this country, Harry?"

"Indeed was I, and--"

"The story, then, the story; we must have it."

"Oh! as for story, there is not much--"

"The story! the story!" shouted Frank. "You may as well begin at once, for we will have it."

"Oh! very well. All is one to me, but you will be tired enough of it before I have got through, so here goes for: A WOLF HUNT ON THE WARWICK HILLS," said Archer, and without more ado, spun his yarn as follows:

"There are few wilder regions within the compass of the United States, much less in the vicinity of its most populous and cultivated districts, than that long line of rocky wood-crowned heights which--at times rising to an elevation and exhibiting a boldness of outline that justifies the application to them of the term 'mountains', while at others they would be more appropriately designated as hills or knolls--run all across the Eastern and the Midland States, from the White Mountains westward to the Alleghanies, between which mighty chains they form an intermediate and continuous link.

"Through this stern barrier, all the great rivers of the States, through which they run, have rent themselves a passage, exhibiting in every instance the most sublime and boldest scenery, while many of the minor, though still noble streams, come forth sparkling and bright and cold from the clear lakes and lonely springs embosomed in its dark recesses.

"Possessing, for the most part, a width of eight or ten miles, this chain of hills consists, at some points, of a single ridge, rude, forest-clad and lonely--at others, of two, three, or even four distinct and separate lines of heights, with valleys more or less highly cultured, long sheets of most translucent water, and wild mountain streams dividing them.

"With these hills--known as the Highlands--where the gigantic Hudson has cloven, at some distant day, a devious path for his eternal and resistless waters, and by a hundred other names, the Warwick Hills, the Greenwoods, and yet farther west, the Blue Ridge and the Kittatinny Mountains, as they trend southerly and west across New York and New Jersey--with these hills I have now to do.

"Not as the temples meet for the lonely muse, fit habitations for the poet's rich imaginings! not as they are most glorious in their natural scenery--whether the youthful May is covering their rugged brows with the bright tender verdure of the tasseled larch, and the yet brighter green of maple, mountain ash and willow--or the full flush of summer has clothed their forests with impervious and shadowy foliage, while carpeting their sides with the unnumbered blossoms of calmia, rhododendron and azalea!--whether the gorgeous hues of autumn gleam like the banners of ten thousand victor armies along their rugged slopes, or the frozen winds of winter have roofed their headlands with inviolate white snow! Not as their bowels teem with the wealth of mines which ages of man's avarice may vainly labor to exhaust! but as they are the loved abode of many a woodland denizen that has retreated, even from more remote and seemingly far wilder fastnesses, to these sequestered haunts. I love them, in that the graceful hind conceals her timid fawn among the ferns that wave on the lone banks of many a nameless rill, threading their hills, untrodden save by the miner, or the infrequent huntsman's foot--in that the noble stag frays oftentimes his antlers against their giant trees--in that the mighty bear lies hushed in grim repose amid their tangled swamps--in that their bushy dingles resound nightly to the long-drawn howl of the gaunt famished wolf--in that the lynx and wild-cat yet mark their prey from the pine branches--in that the ruffed grouse drums, the woodcock bleats, and the quail chirrups from every height or hollow--in that, more strange to tell, the noblest game of trans-atlantic fowl, the glorious turkey--although, like angels' visits, they be indeed but few and far between--yet spread their bronzed tails to the sun, and swell and gobble in their most secret wilds.

"I love those hills of Warwick--many a glorious day have I passed in their green recesses; many a wild tale have I heard of sylvan sport and forest warfare, and many, too, of patriot partisanship in the old revolutionary days--the days that tried men's souls--while sitting at my noontide meal by the secluded wellhead, under the canopy of some primeval oak, with implements of woodland sport, rifle or shot-gun by my side, and well-broke setter or stanch hound recumbent at my feet. And one of these tales will I now venture to record, though it will sound but weak and feeble from my lips, if compared to the rich, racy, quaint and humorous thing it was, when flowing from the nature-gifted tongue of our old friend Tom Draw."

"Hear! hear!" cried Frank, "the chap is eloquent!"

"It was the middle of the winter 1832--which was, as you will recollect, of most unusual severity--that I had gone up to Tom Draw's, with a view merely to quail shooting, though I had taken up, as usual, my rifle, hoping perhaps to get a chance shot at a deer. The very first night I arrived, the old bar-room was full of farmers, talking all very eagerly about the ravages which had been wrought among their flocks by a small pack of wolves, five or six, as they said, in number, headed by an old gaunt famished brute, which had for many years been known through the whole region, by the loss of one hind foot, which had been cut off in a steel trap.

"More than a hundred sheep had been destroyed during the winter, and several calves beside; and what had stirred especially the bile of the good yeomen, was that, with more than customary boldness, they had the previous night made a descent into the precincts of the village, and carried off a fat wether of Tom Draw's.

"A slight fall of snow had taken place the morning I arrived, and, this suggesting to Tom's mind a possibility of hunting up the felons, a party had gone out and tracked them to a small swamp on the Bellevale Mountain, wherein they had undoubtedly made their head-quarters. Arrangements had been made on all sides--forty or fifty stout and active men were mustered, well armed, though variously, with muskets, ducking-guns and rifles--some fifteen couple of strong hounds, of every height and color, were collected--some twenty horses saddled and bridled, and twice as many sleighs were ready; with provisions, ammunition, liquor and blankets, all prepared for a week's bivouac. The plan prescribed was in the first place to surround the swamp, as silently as possible, with all our forces, and then to force the pack out so as to face our volley. This, should the method be successful, would finish the whole hunt at once; but should the three-legged savage succeed in making his escape, we were to hunt him by relays, bivouacking upon the ground wherever night should find us, and taking up the chase again upon the following morning, until continual fatigue should wear out the fierce brute. I had two horses with me, and Tim Matlock; so I made up my mind at once, got a light one-horse sleigh up in the village, rigged it with all my bear-skins, good store of whiskey, eatables, and so forth, saddled the gray with my best Somerset, holsters and surcingle attached, and made one of the party on the instant.

"Before daylight we started, a dozen mounted men leading the way, with the intent to get quite round the ridge, and cut off the retreat of these most wily beasts of prey, before the coming of the rear-guard should alarm them--and the remainder of the party, sleighing it merrily along, with all the hounds attached to them. The dawn was yet in its first gray dimness when we got into line along the little ridge which bounds that small dense brake on the northeastern side--upon the southern side the hill rose almost inaccessibly in a succession of short limestone ledges-- westward the open woods, through which the hounds and footmen were approaching, sloped down in a long easy fall, into the deep secluded basin, filled with the densest and most thorny coverts, and in the summer time waist deep in water, and almost inaccessible, though now floored with a sheet of solid ice, firm as the rocks around it--due northward was an open field, dividing the wolf-dingle from the mountain road by which we always travel.

"Our plot had been well laid, and thus far had succeeded. I, with eleven horsemen, drawn up in easy pistol shot one of the other, had taken our ground in perfect silence; and, as we readily discovered, by the untrodden surface of the snow, our enemies were as yet undisturbed. My station was the extreme left of our line, as we faced westward, close to the first ridge of the southern hill; and there I sat in mute expectancy, my holsters thrown wide open, my Kuchenreuters loaded and cocked, and my good ounce-ball rifle lying prepared within the hollow of my arm.

"Within a short half hour I saw the second party, captained by our friend Garry, coming up one by one, and forming silently and promptly upon the hill side-- and directly after I heard the crash and shout of our beaters, as they plunged into the thicket at its westward end. So far as I could perceive, all had gone well. Two sides, my own eyes told me, were surrounded, and the continuous line in which the shouts ran all along the farther end, would have assured me, if assurance had been needful, for Tom himself commanded in that quarter, that all was perfectly secure on that side. A Jerseyman, a hunter of no small repute, had been detached with a fourth band to guard the open fields upon the north; due time had been allotted to him, and, as we judged, he was upon his ground. Scarce had the first yell echoed through the forest before the pattering of many feet might be heard, mingled with the rustling of the matted boughs throughout the covert--and as the beaters came on, a whole host of rabbits, with no less than seven foxes, two of them gray, came scampering through our line in mortal terror; but on they went unharmed, for strict had been the orders that no shot should be fired, save at the lawful objects of the chase. Just at this moment I saw Garry, who stood a hundred feet above me on the hill, commanding the whole basin of the swamp, bring up his rifle. This was enough for me--my thumb was on the cock, the nail of my forefinger pressed closely on the trigger-guard. He lowered it again, as though he had lost sight of his object--raised it again with great rapidity, and fired. My eye was on the muzzle of his piece, and just as the bright stream of flame glanced from it, distinctly visible in the dim of morning twilight, before my ear had caught the sound of the report, a sharp long snarl rose from the thicket, announcing that a wolf was wounded. Eagerly, keenly did I listen; but there came no further sound to tell me of his whereabouts.

"'I hit him,' shouted Garry, 'I hit him then, I swon; but I guess not so badly, but he can travel still. Look out you, Archer, he's squatted in the thick there, and won't stir 'till they get close a top on him.'

"While he was speaking yet, a loud and startling shout arose from the open field, announcing to my ear upon the instant that one or more had broken covert at some unguarded spot, as it was evident from the absence of any firing. The leader of our squad was clearly of the same opinion; for, motioning to us to spread our line a little wider, he galloped off at a tremendous rate, spurning the snowballs high into the air, accompanied by three of his best men, to stop the gap which had been left through the misapprehension of the Jerseyman.

"This he accomplished; but not until the great wolf, wilier than his comrades, had got off unharmed. He had not moved five minutes before a small dark bitch-wolf broke away through our line, at the angle furthest from my station, and drew a scattering volley from more than half our men--too rapid and too random to be deadly--though several of the balls struck close about her, I thought she had got off scot free; but Jem McDaniel--whom you know--a cool, old steady hand, had held his fire, and taking a long quiet aim, lodged his ball fairly in the centre of her shoulders--over she went, and over, tearing the snow with tooth and claw in her death agony; while fancying, I suppose, that all our guns were emptied--for, by my life, I think the crafty brutes can almost reason-- out popped two more! one between me and my right hand man--the other, a large dog, dragging a wounded leg behind him, under my horse's very feet. Bob made a curious demi-volte, I do assure you, as the dark brindled villain darted between his fore legs with an angry snarl; but at a single word and slight admonition of the curb, stood motionless as though he had been carved in marble. Quickly I brought my rifle up, though steadily enough, and--more, I fancy, by good luck than management--planted my bullet in the neck, just where the skull and spine unite, so that he bounced three feet at least above the frozen snow, and fell quite dead, within twelve paces of the covert. The other wolf, which had crept out to my right hand, was welcomed by the almost simultaneous fire of three pieces, one of which only lodged its bullet, a small one by the way-- eighty or ninety only to the pound--too light entirely to tell a story, in the brute's loins.

"He gave a savage yell enough as the shot told; and, for the first twenty or thirty yards, dragged his hind quarters heavily; but, as he went on, he recovered, gather- ing headway very rapidly over the little ridge, and through the open woodland, toward a clear field on the mountain's brow. Just as this passed, a dozen shots were fired, in a quick running volley, from the thicket, just where an old cart-way di- vides it; followed, after a moment's pause, by one full, round report, which I knew instantly to be the voice of old Tom's musket; nor did I err, for, while its echoes were yet vocal in the leafless forest, the owner's jovial shout was heard--

"'Wiped all your eyes, boys! all of them, by the Eternal!--Who-whoop for our side!--and I'll bet horns for all on us, old leather-breeches has killed his'n.'

"This passed so rapidly--in fact it was all nearly simultaneous--that the fourth wolf was yet in sight, when the last shot was fired. We all knew well enough that the main object of our chase had for the time escaped us!--the game was all afoot!- -three of them slain already; nor was there any longer aught to be gained by stick- ing to our stations. So, more for deviltry than from entertaining any real hope of overtaking him, I chucked my rifle to the nearest of the farmers, touched old Bob with the spur, and went away on a hard gallop after the wounded fugitive, who was now plodding onward at the usual long loping canter of his tribe. For about half a mile the wood was open, and sloped gently upward, until it joined the open coun- try, where it was bounded by a high rugged fence, made in the usual snake fashion, with a huge heavy top-rail. This we soon reached; the wolf, which was more hurt than I had fancied, beginning to lag grievously, crept through it scarcely a hundred yards ahead of me, and, by good luck, at a spot where the top rail had been partially dislodged, so that Bob swept over it, almost without an effort, in his gallop; though it presented an impenetrable rampart to some half dozen of the horsemen who had followed. I was now in a cleared lot of some ten acres, forming the summit of the hill, which, farther on, sunk steeply into a dark ravine full of thick brushwood, with a small verge of thinly growing coppice not more than twenty yards in width, on tolerably level ground, within the low stone-wall which parted it from the cultivated land. I felt that I was now upon my vantage ground; and you may be sure, Frank, that I spared not the spurs; but the wolf, conscious probably of the vicinity of some place of safety, strained every nerve and ran, in fact, as if he had been almost unwounded; so that he was still twelve or fourteen paces from me when he jumped on the wall.

"Once over this, I well knew he was safe; for I was thoroughly acquainted with the ground, and was of course aware that no horse could descend the banks of the precipitous ravine. In this predicament, I thought I might as well take a chance at him with one of my good pistols, though of course with faint hopes of touching him. However, I pulled out the right hand nine-inch barrel, took a quick sight, and let drive at him; and, much to my delight, the sound was answered by the long snarling howl, which I had that day heard too often to doubt any more its meaning. Over he jumped, however, and the wall covering him from my sight, I had no means of judging how badly he was hurt; so on I went, and charged the wall with a tight rein, and a steady pull; and lucky for me was it, that I had a steady pull; for under the lee of the wall there was a heap of rugged logs into which Bob plunged gallantly, and, in spite of my hard hold on him, floundered a moment, and went over. Had I been going at top speed, a very nasty fall must have been the immediate consequence--as it was, both of us rolled over; but with small violence, and on soft snow, so that no harm was done.

"As I came off, however, I found myself in a most unpleasant neighborhood; for my good friend the wolf, hurt pretty badly by the last shot, had, as it seemed, ensconced himself among the logs, whence Bob's assault and subsequent discomfiture had somewhat suddenly dislodged him; so that, as I rolled over on the snow, I found myself within six feet of my friend, seemingly very doubtful whether to fight or fly! But, by good luck, my bullet had struck him on the hip-bone, and being of a rather large calibre, had let his claret pretty freely loose, besides shattering the bone, so that he was but in poor fighting trim; and I had time to get back to the gray--who stood snorting and panting, up to his knees in snow and rubbish, but without offering to stir--to draw my second pistol, and to give Isegrin--as the Germans call him--the coup de grace, before he could attain the friendly shelter of the dingle, to which with all due speed he was retreating. By this time all our comrades had assembled. Loud was the glee--boisterous the applause, which fell especially to me, who had performed with my own hand the glorious feat of slaying two wolves in one morning; and deep the cups of applejack, Scotch whiskey, and Jamaica spirits, which flowed in rich libations, according to the tastes of the compotators, over the slaughtered quarry.

"Breakfast was produced on the spot; cold salt pork, onions, and hard biscuit forming the principal dishes, washed down by nothing weaker than the pure ardent! Not long, however, did fat Tom permit us to enjoy our ease.

"'Come, boys," he shouted, "no lazin' here; no gormandizin'--the worst part of our work's afore us; the old lame devil is afoot, and five miles off by now. We must get back, and lay the hounds on, right stret off-- and well if the scent an't cold now! He's tuk right off toward Duckcedars'--for so Tom ever calls Truxedo Pond--a lovely crescent-shaped lakelet deep in the bosom of the Greenwoods--'so off with you, Jem, down by the road, as hard as you can strick with ten of your boys in sleighs, and half the hounds; and if you find his tracks acrost the road, don't wait for us, but stick right arter him. You, Garry, keep stret down the old road with ten dogs and all the plunder-- we'll meet at night, I reckon.'

"No sooner said than done! the parties were sent off with the relays. This was on Monday morning--Tom and I, and some thirteen others, with eight couple of the best dogs, stuck to his slot on foot. It was two hours at least, so long had he been gone, before a single hound spoke to it, and I had begun well nigh to despair; but Tom's immense sagacity, which seemed almost to know instinctively the course of the wily savage, enabling us to cut off the angles of his course, at last brought us up somewhat nearer to him. At about noon, two or three of the hounds opened, but doubtfully and faintly. His slot, however, showed that they were right, and lustily we cheered them on! Tom, marvelling the while that we heard not the cry of Jem's relay.

"'For I'll be darned,' he said, 'if he hasn't crossed the road long enough since; and that dumb nigger, Jem's not had the sense to stick to him!'

"For once, however, the fat man was wrong; for, as it appeared when we neared the road, the wolf had headed back, scared doubtless by some injudicious noise of our companions, and making a wide ring, had crossed three miles below the spot where Jem was posted. This circuit we were forced to make, as at first sight we fancied he had headed altogether back, and it was four o'clock before we got upon his scent, hot, fresh, and breast-high; running toward the road, that is, due eastward from the covert whence he had bolted in the morning. Nor were our friends inactive; for, guided by the clamors of our pack, making the forest musical, they now held down the road; and, as the felon crossed, caught a long view of him as he limped over it, and laid the fresh hounds on.

"A brilliant rally followed--we calling off our wearied dogs, and hasting to the lower road, where we found Garry with the sleighs, and dashing off in our turn through all sorts of by-paths and wood-roads to head them once again! This, with much labor, we effected; but the full winter-moon had risen, and the innumerable stars were sparkling in the frosty skies, when we flogged off the hounds--kindled our night fires-- prepared our evening meal, feasted, and spread our blankets, and slept soundly under no warmer canopy than the blue firmament--secure that our lame friend would lie up for the night at no great distance. With the first peep of dawn we were again afoot, and, the snow still befriending us, we roused him from a cedar-brake at about nine o'clock, cut him off three times with fresh dogs and men, the second day, and passed the night, some sixteen miles from home, in the rude hovel of a charcoal burner.

"Greater excitement I cannot imagine, than that wild, independent chase!--sometimes on foot, cheering the hounds through swamp and dingle, over rough cliffs and ledges where foot of horse could avail nothing. Sometimes on horseback, galloping merrily through the more open woodlands. Sometimes careering in the flying sleigh, to the gay music of its bells, along the wild wood-paths! Well did we fare, too--ay, sumptuously!--for our outskirters, though they reserved their rifles for the appropriate game, were not so sparing with the shot-gun; so that, night after night, our chaldron reeked with the mingled steam of rabbit, quail, and partridge, seethed up a la Meg Merrilies, with fat pork, onions, and potatoes--by the Lord

Harry! Frank, a glorious and unmatched consummee.

"To make, however, a long tale short--for every day's work, although varied to the actors by thousands of minute but unnarratable particulars, would appear but as a repetition of the last, to the mere listener--to make a long tale short, on the third day he doubled back, took us directly over the same ground--and in the middle of the day, on Saturday, was roused in view by the leading hounds, from the same little swamp in which the five had harbored during the early winter. No man was near the hounds when he broke covert. But fat Tom, who had been detached from the party to bring up provisions from the village, was driving in his sleigh steadily along the road, when the sharp chorus of the hounds aroused him. A minute after, the lame scoundrel limped across the turnpike, scant thirty yards before him. Alas! Tom had but his double-barrel, one loaded with buck shot, the other merely pre-pared for partridge--he blazed away, however, but in vain! Out came ten couple on his track, hard after him; and old Tom, cursing his bad luck, stood to survey the chase across the open.

"Strange was the felon's fate! The first fence, after he had crossed the road, was full six feet in height, framed of huge split logs, piled so close together that, save between the two topmost rails, a small dog even could have found no passage. Full at this opening the wolf dashed, as fresh, Tom said, as though he had not run a yard; but as he struggled through it, his efforts shook the top rails from the yokes, and the huge piece of timber falling across his loins, pinned him completely! At a mile off I heard his howl myself, and the confused and savage hubbub, as the hounds front and rear, assailed him.

"Hampered although he was, he battled it out fiercely--ay, heroically-- as six of our best hounds maimed for life, and one slain outright, testified.

"Heavens! how the fat man scrambled across the fence! he reached the spot, and, far too much excited to reload his piece and quietly blow out the fierce brute's brains, fell to belaboring him about the head with his gun-stock, shouting the while and yelling; so that the din of his tongue, mixed with the snarls and long howls of the mangled savage, and the fierce baying of the dogs, fairly alarmed me, as I said before, at a mile's distance.

"As it chanced, Timothy was on the road close by, with Peacock; I caught sight of him, mounted, and spurred on fiercely to the rescue; but when I reached the hill's brow, all was over. Tom, puffing and panting like a grampus in shoal water, covered--garments and face and hands--with lupine gore, had finished his huge enemy, after he had destroyed his gun, with what he called a stick, but what you and I, Frank, should term a fair-sized tree; and with his foot upon the brindled monster's neck was quaffing copious rapture from the neck of a quart bottle--once full, but now well nigh exhausted--of his appropriate and cherished beverage.[7] Thus fell the last wolf on the Hills of Warwick!

"There, I have finished my yarn, and in good time," cried Harry, "for here we are at the bridge, and in five minutes more we shall be at old Tom's door."

"A right good yarn!" said Forester; "and right well spun, upon my word."

"But is it a yarn?" asked A---, "or is it intended to be the truth?"

"Oh! the truth," laughed Frank, "the truth, as much as Archer can tell the truth; embellished, you understand, embellished!"

"The truth, strictly," answered Harry, quietly--"the truth not embellished. When I tell personal adventures, I am not in the habit of decorating them with falsehood."

"I had no idea," responded the Commodore, "that there had been any wolves here so recently."

"There are wolves here now," said Archer, "though they are scarce and wary. It was but last year that I rode down over the back-bone of the mountain, on the Pompton road, in the nighttime, and that on the third of July, and one fellow followed me along the road till I got quite down into the cultivated country."

"The devil he did!"

"How did you know he was following you?" exclaimed Frank and the Commodore, almost in a breath.

"Did you see him?"

"Not I--but I heard him howl half a dozen times, and each time nearer than before. When I got out of the hills he was not six hundred yards behind me."

"Pleasant, that! Were you armed? What did you do?"

"It was not really so unpleasant, after all--for I knew that he would not attack me at that season of the year. I had my pistols in my holsters; and for the rest, I jogged steadily along, taking care to keep my nag in good wind for a spirt,

7   The facts and incidents of the lame wolf's death are strictly true, although they were not witnessed by the writer.

if it should be needed. I knew that for three or four miles I could outrun him, if it should come to the worst, though in the end a wolf can run down the fastest horse; and, as every mile brought me nearer to the settlement, I did not care much about it. Had it been winter, when the brutes are hard pressed for food, and the deep snows are against a horse's speed, it would be a very different thing. Hurrah! here we are! Hurrah! fat Tom! ahoy! a-ho-oy!"

THE SUPPER PARTY

Blithe, loud and hearty was the welcome of fat Tom, when by the clear view halloa with which Harry drove up to the door at a spanking trot, the horses stopping willingly at the high well-known stoop, he learned who were these his nocturnal visitors. There was a slight tinge of frostiness in the evening air, and a bright blazing fire filled the whole bar-room with a cheerful merry light, and cast a long stream of red lustre from the tall windows, and half-open doorway, but in an instant all that escaped from the last mentioned aperture was totally obstructed, as if the door had been pushed to, by the huge body of mine host.

"Why, darn it," he exclaimed, "if that beant Archer! and a hull grist of boys he's brought along with him, too, any how. How are you, Harry, who've you got along? It's so etarnal thunderin' dark as I carnt see 'em no how!"

"Frank and the Commodore, that's all," Archer replied, "and how are you, old Corporation?"

"Oh! oh! I'm most darned glad as you've brought A---; you might have left that other critter to home, though, jest as well--we doosn't want him blowin' out his little hide here; lazin' about, and doin' nothin' day nor night but eat and grumble; and drink, and drink, as if he'd got a meal-sack in his little guts. Why, Timothy, how be you?" he concluded, smiting him on the back a downright blow, that would have almost felled an ox, as he was getting out the baggage.

"Doant thee noo, Measter Draa," expostulated Tim, "behaave thyself, man, or Ay'se give thee soomat thou woant loike, I'm thinking. Noo! send oot yan o' t' nagers, joost to stand till t' nags till Ay lift oot t' boxes!"

"A nigger, is it? darn their black skins! there was a dozen here jest now, a blockin' up the fire-side, and stinkin' so no white man could come nearst it, till I got an axe-handle, half an hour or so since, and cleared out the heap of them! Niggers! they'll be here all of them torights, I warrant; where you sees Archer, there's never no scarceness of dogs and niggers. But come, walk in boys! walk in, anyhow--Jem'll be here to rights, and he's worth two niggers any day, though he's black-fleshed, I guess, if one was jest to skin the etarnal creatur."

Very few minutes passed before they were all drawn up round the fire, Captain Reade and two or three more making room for them, as they pulled up their chairs about the glowing hearth--having hung up their coats and capes against the wall.

"You'll be here best, boys," said Tom, "for a piece--the parlor fire's not been lit yet this fall, and it is quite cold nights now--but Brower'll kindle it up agin supper, for you'll be wantin' to eat, all of you, I reckon, you're sich darned everlastin' gormandizers."

"That most undoubtedly we shall," said Frank, "for it's past eight now, and the deuce a mouthful have we put into our heads since twelve."

"Barrin' the liquor, Frank! barrin' the liquor--now don't lie! don't lie, boy, so ridic'lous--as if I'd known you these six years, and then was a goin' to believe as you'd not drinked since noon!"

"Why, you old hogshead, you! who wants you to believe anything of the kind--we had one drink at Tom's, your cousin's, when we started, but deuce the drop since."

"That's just the reason why you're so snarlish, then, I reckon! Your coppers is got bilin', leastwise if they beant all biled out--you'd best drink stret away, I guess, afore the bottom of the biler gits left bare --for if it does, and it's red hot now, boy, you'll be a blowin' up, like an old steamboat, when you pumps in fresh water."

"Well, Tom," said Archer, "I do not think it would be a bad move to take a drop of something, and a cracker; for I suppose we shall not get supper much short of two hours; and I'm so deuced hungry, that if I don't get something just to take off the edge, I shall not be able to eat when it does come!"

"I'll make a pitcher of egg nog; A--- drinks egg nog, I guess, although he's the poorest drinkin' man I ever did see. Now, Brower, look alive-- the fire's lit, is it? Well, then, jump now and feed them poor starvin' bags-a-bones, as Archer calls dogs, and tell your mother to git supper. Have you brought anything along to eat or drink, boys--I guess we haven't nothin' in the house!"

"Oh! you be hanged," said Harry, "I've brought a round of cold spiced beef, but I'm not going to cut that up for supper; we shall want it to take along for luncheon--you must get something! Oh! by the way, you may let the girls pick half a dozen quail, and broil them, if you choose!"

"Quail! do you say? and where'll I git quail, I'd be pleased to know?"

"Out of that gamebag," answered Harry, deliberately, pointing to the well filled plump net which Timothy had just brought in and hung up on the pegs beside the box-coats. Without a word or syllable the old chap rushed to the wall, seized it, and scarcely pausing to sweep out of the way a large file of "The Spirit," and several numbers of "The Register," emptied it on the table.

"Where the plague, Archer, did you kill them?" he asked, "you didn't kill all them to-day, I guess! One, two, three--why, there's twenty-seven cock, and forty-nine quail! By gin! here's another; just fifty quail, three partridge, and six rabbits; well that's a most all-fired nice mess, I swon; if you killed them today you done right well, I tell you--you won't get no such mess of birds here now--but you was two days killing these, I guess!"

"Not we, Tom! Frank and I drove up from York last night, and slept at young Tom's, down the valley--we were out just as soon as it was light, and got the quail, all except fifteen or sixteen, the ruffed grouse and four hares, before twelve o'clock. At twelve the Commodore came up from Nyack, where he left his yacht, and joined us; we got some luncheon, went out again at one, and between that and five bagged all the cock, the balance, as you would call it, of the quail, and the other two bunnies."

"Well, then, you made good work of it, I tell you, and you won't do nothin' like that agin this winter--not in Warwick; but I won't touch them quail--it's a sin to break that bunch--but you don't never care to take the rabbits home, and the old woman's got some beautiful fresh onions--she'll make a stew of them--a smother, as you call it, in a little less than no time, Archer; and I've got half a dozen of them big gray snipe--English snipe--that I killed down by my little run'-side; you'll have them roasted with the guts in, I guess! and then there's a pork-steak and sassagers--and if you don't like that, you can jist go without. Here, Brower, take these to your mother, and tell her to git supper right stret off--and you tell Emma Jane to make some buckwheat cakes for A---! he can't sup no how without buckwheat cakes; and

I sets a great store by A---! I does, by G--! and you needn't laugh, boys, for I doos a darned sight more than what I doos by you."

"That's civil, at all events, and candid," replied Frank; "and it's consolatory, too, for I can fancy no greater reproach to a man, than to be set store on by you. I do not comprehend at all, how A--- bears up under it. But come, do make that egg-nog that you're chattering about."

"How will I make it, Harry--with beer, or milk, or cider?"

"All three! now be off, and don't jaw any more!" answered Archer-- "asking such silly questions, as if you did not know better than any of us."

In a few minutes the delicious compound was prepared, and, with a plate of toasted crackers and some right good Orange County butter, was set on a small round stand before the fire; while from the neighboring kitchen rich fumes began to load the air, indicative of the approaching supper. In the mean time, the wagon was unloaded; Timothy bustled to and fro; the parlor was arranged; the bed-rooms were selected by that worthy; and everything set out in its own place, so that they could not possibly have been more comfortable in their own houses. The horses had been duly cleaned, and clothed, and fed; the dogs provided with abundance of dry straw, and a hot mess of milk and meal; and now, in the far corner of the bar-room, the indefatigable varlet was cleaning the three double guns, as scientifically as though he had served his apprenticeship to a gunsmith.

Just at this moment a heavy foot was heard upon the stoop, succeeded by a whining and a great scratching at the door. "Here comes that Indian, Jem," cried Tom, and as he spoke the door flew open, and in rushed old Whino, the tall black and tan foxhound, and Bonnybelle, and Blossom, and another large blue-mottled bitch, of the Southern breed. It was a curious sight to observe by how sudden and intuitive an instinct the hounds rushed up to Archer, and fawned upon him, jumping up with their forepaws upon his knees, and thrusting their bland smiling faces almost into his face; as he, nothing loath, nor repelling their caresses, discoursed most eloquent dog-language to them, until, excited beyond all measure, old Whino seated himself deliberately on the floor, raised his nose toward the ceiling, and set up a long, protracted, and most melancholy howl, which, before it had attained, however, to its grand climax, was brought to a conclusion by being converted into a sharp and treble yell! a consummation brought about by a smart application of

Harry's double-thonged four-horse whip, wielded with all the power of Tom's right arm, and accompanied by a "Git out, now--the whole grist! Kennel! now, kennel! out with them, Jem, consarn you; out with them, and yourself, too! out of this, or I'll put the gad about you, you white Deckerin' nigger you!"

"Come back, when you have put them up, Jem; and mind you don't let them be where they can get at the setters, or they'll be fighting like the devil," interposed Archer--"I want to have a chat with you. By-the-by, Tom, where's Dash--you'd better look out, or the Commodore's dog, Grouse, will eat him before morning--mine will not quarrel with him, but Grouse will to a certainty."

"Then for a sartainty I'll shoot Grouse, and wallop Grouse's master, and that 'ill be two right things done one mornin'; the first would be a most darned right one, any how, and kind too! for then A--- would be forced to git himself a good, nice setter dog, and not go shootin' over a great old fat bustin' pinter, as isn't worth so much as I be to hunt birds!"

"Ha! ha! ha!" shouted the Commodore, whom nothing can, by any earthly means, put out of temper, "ha! ha! ha! I should like to see you shoot Grouse, Tom, for all the store you set by me, you'd get the worst of that game. You had better take Archer's advice, I can tell you."

"Archer's advice, indeed! it's likely now that I'd have left my nice little dog to be spiled by your big brutes, now aint it? Come, come, here's supper."

"Get something to drink, Jem, along with Timothy, and come in when we've got through supper."

"Yes, sir," replied the knight of the cut-throat; "I've got some news to tell you, too, Tom, if you'll wait a bit."

"Cuss you, and your news too," responded Tom, "you're sich a thunderin' liar, there's no knowin' when you do speak truth. We'll not be losin' our supper for no lies, I guess! Leastways I won't! Come Archer."

And with a right good appetite they walked into the parlor; every thing was in order; every article placed just as it had been when Frank went up to spend his first week in the Woodlands; the gun-case stood on the same chairs below the window; the table by the door was laid out with the same display of powder-flasks, shot-pouches, and accoutrements of all sizes. The liquor-stand was placed by Harry's chair, open, containing the case-bottles, the rummers being duly ranged upon the board, which was well lighted by four tall wax candles, and being laid with Harry's silver, made quite a smart display. The rabbits smoked at the head, smothered in a rich sauce of cream, and nicely shredded onions; the pork chops, thin and crisply broiled, exhaled rich odors at the bottom; the English snipe, roasted to half a turn, and reposing on their neat squares of toast, were balanced by a dish of well-fried sausages, reclining on a bed of mashed potatoes; champagne was on the table, un-resined and unwired, awaiting only one touch of the knife to release the struggling spirit from its transparent prison. Few words were spoken for some time, unless it were a challenge to champagne, the corks of which popped frequently and furious; or a request for another snipe, or another spoonful of the sauce; while all devoted themselves to the work in hand with a sincere and business-like earnestness of de-meanor, that proved either the excellence of Tom Draw's cookery, or the efficacy of the Spartan sauce which the sportsmen had brought to assist them at their meal. The last rich drops of the fourth flask were trickling into Tom's wide-lipped rum-mer, when Harry said:

"Come, we have done, I think, for one night; let's have the eatables removed, and we will have a pipe, and hear what Jem has got to say; and you have told us nothing about birds, either, you old elephant; what do you mean by it? That's right, Tim, now bring in my cigars, and Mr. Forester's cheroots, and cold iced water, and boiling-hot water, and sugar, out of my box, and lemons. The shrub is here, and the Scotch whiskey; will you have another bottle of champagne, Tom? No! Well, then, look sharp, Timothy, and send Jem in."

And thereupon Jem entered, thumbing his hat assiduously, and sat down in the corner, by the window, where he was speedily accommodated with a supply of liquor, enough to temper any quantity of clay.

"Well, Jem," said Archer, "unbutton your bag now; what's the news?"

"Well, Mr. Aircher, it ben't no use to tell you on't, with Tom, there, puttin' a body out, and swearin' it's a lie, and dammin' a chap up and down. It ben't no use to tell you, and yet I'd kind o' like to, but then you won't believe a fellow, not one on you!"

"In course not," answered Forester; and at the same instant Tom struck in like-wise--

"It's a lie, afore you tell it; it's a lie, cuss you, and you knows it. I'd sooner take a nigger's word than yours, Jem, any how, for the darned niggers will tell the truth when they can't git no good by lyin', but you, you will lie all times! When the truth would do the best, and you would tell it if you could, you can't help lyin'!"

"Shut up, you old thief; shut up instantly, and let the man speak, will you; I can see by his face that he has got something to tell; and as for lying, you beat him at it any day."

Tom was about to answer, when Harry, who had been eagerly engaged in mixing a huge tumbler-full of strong cold shrub punch, thrust it under his nose, and he, unable to resist the soft seductive odor, seized it incontinently, and neither spoke nor breathed again until the bottom of the rummer was brought parallel to the ceiling; then, with a deep heart-felt sigh, he set it down; and, with a calm placid smile, exclaimed, "Tell on, Jem." Whereupon that worthy launched into his full tide of narrative, as follows:

"Well, you sees, Mr. Aircher, I tuk up this mornin' clean up the old crick side, nigh to Vernon, and then I turned in back of old Squire Vandergriff's, and druv the mountains clear down here till I reached Rocky Hill; I'd pretty good sport, too, I tell you; I shot a big gray fox on Round Top, and started a raal rouser of a red one down in the big swamp, in the bottom, and them sluts did keep the darndest ragin' you ever did hear tell on. Well, they tuk him clean out across the open, past Andy Joneses, and they skeart up in his stubbles three bevies, I guess, got into one like! there was a drove of them, I tell you, and then they brought him back to the hills agin, and run him twice clean round the Rocky Hill, and when they came round the last time, the English sluts warn't half a rod from his tail no how, and so he tried his last chance, and he holed; but my! now, Mr. Aircher, by darn, you niver did see nothin' like the partridges; they kept a brushin' up and brushin' up, and treein' every little while; I guess if I seen one I seen a hundred; why, I killed seven on 'em with coarse shot up in the pines, and I daredn't shoot exceptin' at their heads. If you'd go up there now, to-morrow, and take the dogs along, I know as you'll git fifty."

"Well, if that's all your news, Jem, I won't give you much for it; and, as for going into the mountains to look after partridges, you don't catch me at it, that's all!" said Harry. "Is that all?"

"Not by a great shot!" answered Jem, grinning, "but the truth is, I know you won't believe me; but I can tell you what, you can kill a big fat buck, if you'll git up a little afore daylight!"

"A buck, Jem! a buck near here?" inquired Forester and Archer in a breath.

"I told you, boys, the critter couldn't help it; he's stuck to truth just so long, and he was forced to lie, or else he would have busted!"

"It's true, by thunder," answered Jem; "I wish I mayn't eat nor drink nother, if there's one bit of lie in it; d--n the bit, Tom! I'm in airnest, now, right down; and you knows as I wouldn't go to lie about it!"

"Well! well! where was't, Jem?"

"Why, he lies, I guess, now, in that little thickest swamp of all, jist in the eend of the swale atween Round Top and Rocky Hill, right in the pines and laurels; least-ways I druv him down there with the dogs, and I swon that he never crossed into the open meadow; and I went round, and made a circle like clean round about him, and darn the dog trailed on him no how; and bein' as he's hard hot, I guess he'll stay there since he harbored."

"Hard hit, is he! why, did you get a shot at him?"

"A fair one," Jem replied; "not three rod off from me; he jumped up out of the channel of Stony Brook, where, in a sort o' bend, there was a lot of bushes, sumac and winter-green, and ferns; he skeart me, that's a fact, or I'd a killed him. He warn't ten yards off when he bounced up first, but I pulled without cocking, and when I'd got my gun fixed, he'd got off a little piece, and I'd got nauthen but fox-shot, but I hot him jist in the side of the flank; the blood flew out like winkin', and the hounds arter him like mad, up and down, and round and back, and he a kind of weak like, and they'd overhauled him once and again, and tackled him, but there was only four on them, and so he beat them off like every time, and onned again! They couldn't hold him no how, till I got up to them, and I couldn't fix it no how, so as I'd git another shot at him; but it was growin' dark fast, and I flogged off the sluts arter a deal o' work, and viewed him down the old blind run-way into th' swale eend, where I told you; and then I laid still quite a piece; and then I circled round, to see if he'd quit it, and not one dog tuk track on him, and so I feels right sartain as he's in that hole now, and will be in the mornin', if so be we goes there in time, afore the sun's up.

"That we can do easily enough," said Archer, "what do you say, Tom? Is it worth while?"

"Why," answered old Draw instantly, "if so be only we could be sartain that the darned critter warn't lyin', there couldn't be no doubt about it; for if the buck did lay up there this night, why he'll be there to-morrow; and if so be he's there, why we can get him sure!"

"Well, Jem, what have you got to say now," said the Commodore; "is it the truth or no?"

"Why, darn it all," retorted Jem, "harn't I just told you it was true; it's most blamed hard a fellow can't be believed now--why, Mr. Aircher, did I ever lie to you?"

"Oh! if you ask me that," said Harry, "you know I must say 'Yes!'--for you have, fifty times at the least computation. Do you remember the day you towed me up the Decker's run to look for woodcock?"

"And you found nothing," interrupted Tom, "but..."

"Oh shut up, do, Tom," broke in Forester, "and let us hear about this buck. If we agree to give you a five dollar bill, Jem, in case we do find him where you say, what will you be willing to forfeit if we do not?"

"You may shoot at me!" answered Jem, "all on you--ivery one on you--at forty yards, with rifle or buckshot!"

"It certainly is very likely that we should be willing to get hanged for the sake of shooting such a mangy hound as you Jem," answered Forester, "when one could shoot a good clean dog--Tom's Dash, for example--for nothing!"

"Could you though?" Tom replied, "I'd like to catch you at it, my dear boy--I'd wax the little hide off of you. But come, let us be settling. Is it a lie now, Jem; speak out--is it a lie, consarn you? for if it be, you'd best jest say 't out now, and save your bones to-morrow. Well, boys, the critter's sulky, so most like it is true--and I guess we'll be arter him. We'll be up bright and airly, and go a horseback, and if he be there, we can kill him in no time at all, and be right back to breakfast. I'll start Jem and the captain here, and Dave Seers, with the dogs, an hour afore us! and let them come right down the swale, and drive him to the open--Harry and Forester, you two can ride your own nags, and I'll take old Roan, and A--- here shall have the colt."

"Very well! Timothy, did they feed well to-night? if they did, give them their oats very early, and no water. I know it's too bad after their work to-day, but we shall not be out two hours!"

"Weel! it's no matter gin they were oot six," responded Timothy, "they wadna be a pin the waur o't!"

"Take out my rifle, then--and pick some buckshot cartridges to fit the bore of all the double guns. Frank's got his rifle; so you can take my heavy single gun--your gauge is 17, A---, quite too small for buckshot; mine is 11, and will do its work clean with Ely's cartridge and pretty heavy powder, at eighty-five to ninety yards. Tom's bore is twelve, and I've brought some to fit his old double, and some, too, for my own gun, though it is almost too small!"

"What gauge is yours, Harry?"

"Fourteen; which I consider the very best bore possible for general shooting. I think the gunsmiths are running headlong now into the opposite of their old error--when they found that fifteens and fourteens outshot vastly the old small calibres--fifty years since no guns were larger than eighteen, and few than twenty; they are now quite out-doing it. I have seen late-imported guns of seven pounds, and not above twenty-six inches long, with eleven and even ten gauge calibres! you might as well shoot with a blunderbus at once!"

"They would tell at cock in close summer covert," answered A---.

"For a man who can't cover his bird they might," replied Harry; "but you may rely on it they lose three times as much in force as they gain in the space they cover; at forty yards you could not kill even a woodcock with them once in fifty times, and a quail, or English snipe, at that distance never!"

"What do you think the right length and weight, then, for an eleven bore?"

"Certainly not less than nine pounds, and thirty inches; but I would prefer ten pounds and thirty-three inches; though, except for a fowl-gun to use in boat-shooting, such a piece would be quite too ponderous and clumsy. My single gun is eleven gauge, eight pounds and thirty-three inches; and even with loose shot executes superbly; but with Ely's green cartridge I have put forty BB shot into a square of two and a half feet at one hundred and twenty-five yards; sharply enough, too, to imbed the shot so firmly in the fence against which I had fixed my mark, that it required a good strong knife to get them out. This I propose that you should use to-morrow, with a 1 1/2 oz. SG cartridge, which contains eighteen buck-shot, and which, if you get a shot any where within a hundred yards, will kill him as dead, I warrant it, as an ounce bullet."

"Which you intend to try, I fancy," added Frank.

"Not quite! my rifle carries eighteen only to the pound; and yours, if I forget not, only thirty-two."

"But mine is double."

"Never mind that; thirty-two will not execute with certainty above a hundred and fifty yards!"

"And how far in the devil's name would you have it execute, as you calls it," asked old Tom.

"Three hundred!" replied Harry, coolly.

"Thunder!" replied Draw, "don't tell me no sich thunderin' nonsense; I'll stand all day and be shot at, like a Christmas turkey, at sixty rods, for six-pence a shot, any how."

"I'll bet you all the liquor we can drink while we are here, Tom," answered Harry, "that I hit a four foot target at three hundred yards to-morrow!"

"Off hand?" inquired Tom, with an attempt at a sneer.

"Yes, off hand! and no shot to do that either; I know men--lots of them --who would bet to hit a foot square at that distance!"[8]

"Well! you can't hit four, no how!"

"Will you bet?"

"Sartain!"

"Very well--Done--Twenty dollars I will stake against all the liquor we drink while we're here. Is it a bet?"

"Yes! Done!" cried Tom--"at the first shot, you know; I gives no second chances."

"Very well, as you please!--I'm sure of it, that's all--Lord, Frank, how we will drink and treat--I shall invite all the town up here to-morrow-- Come!--One more round for luck, and then to bed!"

---

8   When this was written strong exception was taken to it by a Southern writer in the Spirit of the Times. Had that gentleman known what is the practice of the heavy Tyrolese rifle he would not have written so confidently. But it is needless to go so far as to the Tyrol. There is a well known rifle-shot in New York, who can perform the feat, any day, which the Southern writer scoffed at as utterly impossible. Scrope on Deerstalking will show to any impartial reader's satisfaction, that stags in the Highlands are rarely killed within 200 and generally beyond 300 yards' distance.

"Content!" cried A---; "but I mean Mr. Draw to have an argument to-morrow night about this point of Setter vs. Pointer! How do you say, Harry?--which is best?"

"Oh! I'll be Judge and Jury,"--answered Archer--"and you shall plead before me; and I'll make up my mind in the meantime!"

"He's for me, any how,"--shouted Tom--"Darn it all, Harry, you knows you wouldn't own a pinter--no, not if it was gin you!"

"I believe you are about right there, old fellow, so far as this country goes at least!"--said Archer--"different dogs for different soils and seasons--and, in my judgment, setters are far the best this side the Atlantic--but it is late now, and I can't stand chattering here--good night--you shall have as much dog-talk as you like to-morrow."

THE OUTLYING STAG

It was still pitch dark, although the skies were quite clear and cloudless, when Harry, Frank, and the Commodore re-assembled on the following morning, in Tom's best parlor, preparatory to the stag hunt which, as determined on the previous night, was to be their first sporting move in the valley.

Early, however, as it was, Timothy had contrived to make a glorious fire upon the hearth, and to lay out a slight breakfast of biscuits, butter, and cold beef, flanked by a square case-bottle of Jamaica, and a huge jorum of boiled milk. Tom Draw had not yet made his appearance, but the sound of his ponderous tramp, mixed with strange oaths and loud vociferations, showed that he was on foot, and ready for the field.

"I'll tell you what, Master A---," said Archer as he stood with his back to the fire, mixing some rum with sugar and cold water, previous to pouring the hot milk into it--"You'll be so cold in that light jacket on the stand this morning, that you'll never be able to hold your gun true, if you get a shot. It froze quite hard last night, and there's some wind, too, this morning."

"That's very true," replied the Commodore, "but devil a thing have I got else to wear, unless I put on my great coat, and that's too much the other way--too big and clumsy altogether. I shall do well enough, I dare say; and after all, my drilling jacket is not much thinner than your fustian."

"No," said Harry, "but you don't fancy that I'm going out in this, do you? No! no! I'm too old a hand for that sort of thing--I know that to shoot well, a man must be comfortable, and I mean to be so. Why, man, I shall put on my Canadian hunting shirt over this,"--and with the word he slipped a loose frock, shaped much like a wagoner's smock, or a Flemish blouse, over his head, with large full sleeves, reaching almost to his knees, and belted round his waist, by a broad worsted sash. This excellent garment was composed of a thick coarse homespun woollen, bottle-green in color, with a fringe and bindings of dingy red, to match the sash about his waist. From the sash was suspended an otter skin pouch, containing bullets and patches, nipple wrench and turn-screw, a bit of dry tow, an oiled rag, and all the indispensables for rifle cleaning; while into it were thrust two knives--one a broad two-edged implement, with a stout buck-horn haft, and a blade of at least twelve inches--the other a much smaller weapon, not being, hilt and all, half the length of the other's blade, but very strong, sharp as a razor, and of surpassing temper. While he was fitting all these in their proper places, and slinging under his left arm a small buffalo horn of powder, he continued talking:

"Now," he said, "if you take my advice, you'll go into my room, and there, hanging against the wall, you'll find my winter shooting jacket, I had it made last year when I went up to Maine, of pilot cloth, lined throughout with flannel. It will fit you just as well as your own, for we're pretty much of a size. Frank, there, will wear his old monkey jacket, the skirts of which he razeed last winter for the very purpose. Ah, here is Brower--just run up, Brower, and bring down my shooting jacket off the wall from behind the door--look sharp, will you! Now, then, I shall load, and I advise you both to do likewise; for it's bad work doing that same with cold fingers."

Thus saying, he walked to the corner, and brought out his rifle, a short heavy double barrel, with two grooves only, carrying a bitted ball of twelve to the pound, quite plain but exquisitely finished. Before proceeding, however, to load, he tried the passage of the nipple with a fine needle--three or four of which, thrust into a cork, and headed with sealing wax, formed a portion of the contents of his pouch--brushed the cone, and the inside of the hammer, carefully, and wiped them, to conclude, with a small piece of clean white kid--then measuring his powder out exactly, into a little charger, screwed to the end of his ramrod, he inverted the piece, and introduced the rod upward till the cup reached the chamber; when, righting the gun, he withdrew it, leaving the powder all lodged safely at the breech, without the loss of a single grain in the groovings. Next, he chose out a piece of leather, the finest grained kid, without a seam or wrinkle, slightly greased with the best watch-maker's oil--selected a ball perfectly round and true--laid the patch upon the muzzle, and placing the bullet exactly in the centre over the bore, buried it with a single rap of a small lignum vita mallet, which hung from his button-hole; and then, with but a trifling effort, drove it home by one steady thrust of the stout copper-headed charging rod. This done, he again inspected the cone, and seeing that the powder was forced quite up into sight, picked out, with the same anxious scrutiny that had marked all of his proceedings, a copper cap, which he pronounced sure to go, applied it to the nipple, crushed it down firmly, with the hammer, which he then drew back to half-cock, and bolted. Then he set the piece down by the fireside, drained his hot jorum, and...

"That fellow will do his work, and no mistake," said he. "Now A--- here is my single gun"--handing to him, as he spoke, one of the handsomest Westley Richards a sportsman ever handled--"thirty-three inches, nine pounds and eleven gauge. Put in one-third above that charger, which is its usual load, and one of those green cartridges, and I'll be bound that it will execute at eighty paces; and that is more than Master Frank there can say for his Manton Rifle, at least if he loads it with bullets patched in that slovenly and most unsportsmanlike fashion."

"I should like to know what the deuce you mean by slovenly and unsportsman-like," said Frank, pulling out of his breast pocket a couple of bullets, carefully sewed up in leather--"it is the best plan possible, and saves lots of time--you see I can just shove my balls in at once, without any bother of fitting patches."

"Yes," replied Harry, "and five to one the seam, which, however neatly it is drawn, must leave a slight ridge, will cross the direction of the grooving, and give the ball a counter movement; either destroying altogether the rotatory motion communicated by the rifling, or causing it to take a direction quite out of the true line; accordingly as the counteraction is conveyed near the breech, or near the muzzle of the piece."

"Will so trifling a cause produce so powerful an effect?" inquired the Commodore.

"The least variation, whether of concavity or convexity in the bullet, will do so unquestionably--and I cannot see why the same thing in a covering superinduced to the ball should not have the same effect. Even a hole in a pellet of shot, will cause it to leave the charge, and fly off at a tangent. I was once shooting in the fens of the Isle of Ely, and fired at a mallard sixty or sixty-five yards off, with double B shot, when to my great amazement a workman--digging peat at about the same distance from me with the bird, but at least ninety yards to the right of the mallard--roared out lustily that I had killed him. I saw that the drake was knocked over as dead as a stone, and consequently laughed at the fellow, and set it down as a cool trick to extort money, not uncommon among the fen men, as applied to members of the University. I had just finished loading, and my retriever had just brought in the dead bird, which was quite riddled, cut up evidently by the whole body of the charge--both the wings broken, one in three places, one leg almost dissevered, and several shots in the neck and body--when up came my friend, and sure enough he was hit--one pellet had struck him on the cheek bone, and was imbedded in the skin. Half a crown, and a lotion of whiskey--not applied to the part, but taken inwardly--soon proved a sovereign medicine, and picking out the shot with the point of a needle, I found a hole in it big enough to admit a pin's head, and about the twentieth part of an inch in depth. This I should think is proof enough for you--but, besides this, I have seen bullets in pistol-shooting play strange vagaries, glancing off from the target at all sorts of queer angles."

"Well! well!" replied Frank, "my rifle shoots true enough for me--true enough to kill generally--and who the deuce can be at the bother of your pragmatical preparations! I am sure it might be said of you, as it was of James the First, of most pacific and pedantic memory, that you are 'Captain of arts and Clerk of arms'--at least you are a very pedant in gunnery."

"No! no!" said A---; "you're wrong there altogether, Master Forester; there is nothing on earth that makes so great a difference in sportsmanship as the observation of small things. I don't call him a sportsman who can walk stoutly, and kill well, unless he can give causes for effects--unless he knows the haunts and habits both of his game and his dogs--unless he can give a why for every wherefore!"

"Then devil a bit will you ever call me one,"--answered Frank--"For I can't be at the trouble of thinking about it."

"Stuff--humbug--folly"--interrupted Archer--"you know a great deal better than that--and so do we, too!--you're only cranky! a little cranky, Frank, and given to defending any folly you commit without either rhyme or reason--as when you tried to persuade me that it is the safest thing in nature to pour gunpowder out of a canister into a pound flask, with a lighted cigar between your teeth; to demonstrate which you had scarcely screwed the top of the horn on, before the lighted ashes fell all over it--had they done so a moment sooner, we should all have been blown out of the room."

By this time, the Commodore had donned Harry's winter jacket, and Frank, grumbling and paradoxizing all the while, had loaded his rifle, and buttoned up his pea-jacket, when in stalked Tom, swathed up to his chin in a stout dreadnought coat.

"What are ye lazin' here about!" he shouted, "you're niver ready no how. Jem's been agone these two hours, and we'll jest be too late, and miss gittin' a shot--if so be there be a buck--which I'll be sworn there arn't!"

"Ha! ha!" the Commodore burst out; "ha! ha! ha! I should like to know which side the laziness has been on this morning, Mister Draw."

"On little wax skin's there," answered the old man, as quick as lightning; "the little snoopin' critter carn't find his gloves now; though the nags is at the door, and we all ready. We'll drink, boys, while he's lookin' arter 'em--and then when he's found them, and's jest a gittin' on his horse, he'll find he's left his powder-horn or knife, or somethin' else, behind him; and then we'll drink agin, while he snoops back to fetch it."

"You be hanged, you old rascal," replied Forester, a little bothered by the huge shouts of laughter which followed this most strictly accurate account of his accustomed method of proceeding; an account which, by the way, was fully justified not twenty minutes afterward, by his galloping back, neck or nothing, to get his pocket handkerchief, which he had left "in course," as Tom said, in his dressing-gown beside the fire.

"Come, bustle--bustle!" Harry added, as he put on his hunting cap and pulled a huge pair of fen boots on, reaching to the midthigh, which Timothy had garnished with a pair of bright English spurs. In another minute they were all on horseback, trotting away at a brisk pace toward the little glen, wherein, according to Jem's last report, the stag was harbored. It was in vain that during their quick ride the old man was entreated to inform them where they were to take post, or what they were to do, as he would give them no reply, nor any information whatever.

At last, however, when Forester rejoined them, after his return to the village, he turned short off from the high road to the left, and as he passed a set of bars into a wild hill pasture, struck into a hard gallop.

Before them lay the high and ridgy head of Round Top, his flanks sloping toward them, in two broad pine-clad knobs, with a wild streamlet brawling down between them, and a thick tangled swamp of small extent, but full of tall dense thornbushes, matted with vines and cat-briers, and carpeted with a rich undergrowth of fern and wintergreen, and whortleberries. To the right and left of the two knobs or spurs just mentioned, were two other deep gorges, or dry channels, bare of brushwood, and stony--rockwalled, with steep precipitous ledges toward the mountain, but sloping easily up to the lower ridges. As they reached the first of these, Tom motioned Forester to stop.

"Stand here," he whispered, "close in here, jest behind this here crag-- and look out hereaways toward the village. If he comes down this runway, kill him, but mind you doosn't show a hair out of this corner; for Archer, he'll stand next, and if so be he crosses from the swamp hole hereaways, you'll chance to get a bullet. Be still, now, as a mouse, and tie your horse here in the cove!--Now, lads"

And off he set again, rounded the knob, and making one slight motion toward the nook, wherein he wished that Harry should keep guard, wheeled back in utter silence, and very slowly--for they were close to the spot wherein, as they supposed, the object of their chase was laid up; and as yet but two of his paths were guarded toward the plain; Jem and his comrades having long since got with the hounds into his rear, and waiting only for the rising of the sun to lay them on, and push along the channel of the brook.

This would compel him to break covert, either directly from the swamp, or by one of the dry gorges mentioned. Now, therefore, was the crisis of the whole matter; for if--before the other passes were made good--the stag should take alarm, he might steal off without affording a chance of a shot, and get into the mountains to the right, where they might hunt him for a week in vain.

No marble statue could stand more silently or still than Harry and his favorite gray, who, with erected ears and watchful eye, trembling a little with excitement, seemed to know what he was about, and to enjoy it no less keenly than his rider. Tom and the Commodore, quickening their pace as they got out of ear-shot, retraced their steps quite back to the turnpike road, along which Harry saw them gallop furiously, in a few minutes, and turn up, half a mile off, toward the further gulley--he saw no more, however; though he felt certain that the Commodore was, scarce ten minutes after he lost sight of them, standing within twelve paces of him, at the further angle of the swamp--Tom having warily determined that the two single guns should take post together, while the two doubles should be placed where the wild quarry could get off encountering but a single sportsman.

It was a period of intense excitement before the sun rose though it was of short duration--but scarcely had his first rays touched the open meadow, casting a huge gray shadow from the rounded hill which covered half the valley, while all the farther slope was laughing in broad light, the mist wreaths curling up, thinner and thinner every moment, from the broad streamlet in the bottom, which here and there flashed out exultingly from its wood-covered margins--scarcely had his first rays topped the hill, before a distant shout came swelling on the air, down the ravine, announcing Jem's approach. No hound gave tongue, however, nor did a rustle in the brake, or any sound of life, give token of the presence of the game--louder and nearer drew the shouts--and now Harry himself began to doubt if there were any truth in Jem's relation, when suddenly the sharp, quick crack of Forester's rifle gave token that the game was afoot--a loud yell from that worthy followed.

"Look out! Mark--back--mark back!"

And keenly Archer did look out, and warily did he listen--once he detected, or fancied he detected, a rustling of the under-wood, and the crack of a dry stick, and dropping his reins on the horse's neck, he cocked his rifle--but the sound was not repeated, nor did any thing come into sight--so he let down the hammer once again, and resumed his silent watch, saying to himself...

"Frank fired too quick, and he has headed up the brook to Jem. If he is forward enough now, we shall have him back instantly, with the hounds at his heels; but if he has loitered and hung back, `over the hills and far away' is the word for this time."

But Jem was in his place, and in another moment a long whoop came ringing down the glen, and the shrill yelping rally of the hounds as they all opened on a view together! Fiercer and wilder grew the hubbub! And now the eager watcher might hear the brushwood torn in all directions by the impetuous passage of the wild deer and his inveterate pursuers.

"Now, then, it is old Tom's chance, or ours," he thought, "for he will not try Forester again, I warrant him, and we are all down wind of him-- so he can't judge of our whereabouts."

In another second the bushes crashed to his left hand, and behind him, while the dogs were raving scarcely a pistol-shot off, in the tangled swamp. Yet he well knew that if the stag should break there it would be A---'s shot, and, though anxious, he kept his eye fixed steadily on his own point, holding his good piece cocked and ready.

"Mark! Harry, mark him!"--a loud yell from the Commodore.

The stag had broken midway between them, in full sight of A---, and seeing him, had wheeled off to the right. He was now sweeping onward across the open field with high graceful bounds, tossing his antlered head aloft, as if already safe, and little hurt, if anything, by Jem Lyn's boasted shot of the last evening. The gray stood motionless, trembling, however, palpably, in every limb, with eagerness--his ears laid flat upon his neck, and cowering a little, as if he feared the shot, which it would seem his instinct told him to expect. Harry had dropped his reins once more, and leveled his unerring rifle--yet for a moment's space he paused, waiting for A--- to fire; there was no hurry for himself, nay a few seconds more would give him a yet fairer shot, for the buck now was running partially toward him, so that a moment more would place him broadside on, and within twenty paces.

"Bang!" came the full and round report of A---'s large shotgun, fired before the beast was fifteen yards away from him. He had aimed at the head, as he was forced to do, lest he should spoil the haunches, for he was running now directly from him--and had the buck been fifty paces off he would have killed him dead, lodging his whole charge, or the best part of it, in the junction of the neck and skull--but as it was, the cartridge--the green cartridge--had not yet spread at all; nor had one buckshot left the case! Whistling like a single ball, as it passed Harry's front eight or nine yards off, it drove, as his quick eye discovered, clean through the stag's right ear, almost dissevering it, and making the animal bound six feet off the green sward.

Just as he touched the earth again, alighting from his mighty spring, with an aim sure and steady, and a cool practiced finger, the marksman drew his trigger, and, quick, as light, the piece--well loaded, as its dry crack announced--discharged its ponderous missile! But, bad luck on it, even at that very instant, just in the point of time wherein the charge was ignited, eighteen or twenty quail, flushed by the hubbub of the hounds, rose with a loud and startling whirr, on every side of the gray horse, under his belly and about his ears, so close as almost to brush him with their wings--he bolted and reared up--yet even at that disadvantage the practiced rifleman missed not his aim entirely, though he erred somewhat, and the wound in consequence was not quite deadly.

The ball, which he had meant for the heart, his sight being taken under the fore-shoulder, was raised and thrown forward by the motion of the horse, and passed clean through the neck close to the blade bone. Another leap, wilder and loftier than the last! yet still the stag dashed onward, with the blood gushing out in streams from the wide wound, though as yet neither speed nor strength appeared to be impaired, so fleetly did he scour the meadow.

"He will cross, Frank yet!" cried Archer. "Mark! mark him, Forester!"

But, as he spoke, he set his rifle down against the fence, and halloaed to the hounds, which instantly, obedient to his well known and cheery whoop, broke co-vert in a body, and settled, heads up and sterns down, to the blazing scent.

At the same moment A--- came trotting out from his post, gun in hand; while at a thundering gallop, blaspheming awfully as he came on, and rating them for "know-nothins, and blunderin' etarnal spoil-sports," Tom rounded the farther hill, and spurred across the level. By this time they were all in sight of Forester, who stood on foot, close to his horse, in the mouth of the last gorge, the buck running across him sixty yards off, and quartering a little from him toward the road; the hounds were, however, all midway between him and the quarry, and as the ground sloped steeply from the marksman, he was afraid of firing low--but took a long, and, as it seemed, sure aim at the head.

The rifle flashed--a tine flew, splintered by the bullet, from the brow antler, not an inch above the eye.

"Give him the other!" shouted Archer. "Give him the other barrel!"

But Frank shook his head spitefully, and dropped the muzzle of his piece.

"By thunder! then, he's forgot his bullets--and hadn't nothen to load up agen, when he missed the first time!"

"Ha! ha! ha!" roared once again the Commodore--"ha! ha! hah!--ha! ha!" till rock and mountain rang again.

"By the Etarnal" exclaimed Draw, perfectly frantic with passion and excite-ment--"By thunder! A---, I guess you'd laugh if your best friends was all a dyin' at your feet. You would for sartain! But look, look! what the plague's Harry goin' at?"

For when he saw that Forester had now, for some reason or other, no farther means of stopping the stag's career, Archer had set spurs to his horse, and dashed away at a hard furious gallop after the wounded buck. The hounds, which had lost sight of it as it leaped a high stone wall with much brush round the base of it, were running fast and furious on the scent--but still, though flagging somewhat in his speed, the stag was leaving them. He had turned, as the last shot struck his horns, down hill, as if to cross the valley; but immediately, as if perceiving that he had passed the last of his enemies, turned up again toward the mountain, describing an arc, almost, in fact, a semi-circle, from the point where he had broken covert to that--another gully, at perhaps a short mile's distance--from which he was now aiming.

Across the chord, then, of this arc, Harry was driving furiously, with the intent, as it would seem, to cut him off from the gully--the stone wall crossed his line, but not a second did he pause for it, but gave his horse both spurs, and lifting him a little, landed him safely at the other side. Frank mounted rapidly, dashed after him, and soon passed A---, who was less aptly mounted for a chase--he likewise topped the wall, and disappeared beyond it, though the stones flew, where the bay struck the coping with his heels.

All pluck to the back-bone, the Commodore craned not nor hesitated, but dashed the colt, for the first time in his life, at the high barrier--he tried to stop, but could not, so powerfully did his rider cram him-- leaped short, and tumbled head over heels, carrying half the wall away with him, and leaving a gap as if a wagon had passed through it--to Tom's astonishment and agony--for he supposed the colt destroyed forever.

Scarcely, however, had A--- gained his feet, before a sight met his eyes, which made him leave the colt, and run as fast as his legs could carry him toward the scene of action.

The stag, seeing his human enemy so near, had strained every nerve to escape, and Harry, desperately rash and daring, seeing he could not turn or head him, actually spurred upon him counter to broadside, in hope to ride him down; foiled once again, in this--his last hope, as it seemed-- he drew his longest knife, and as--a quarter of a second too late only-- he crossed behind the buck, he swung himself half out of his saddle, and striking a full blow, succeeded in hamstringing him; while the gray, missing the support of the master-hand, stumbled and fell upon his head.

Horse, stag, and man, all rolled upon the ground within the compass of ten yards--the terrified and wounded deer striking out furiously in all directions--so that it seemed impossible that Archer could escape some deadly injury--while, to increase the fury and the peril of the scene, the hounds came up, and added their fresh fierceness to the fierce confusion. Before, however, A--- came up, Harry had gained his feet, drawn his small knife--the larger having luckily flown many yards as he fell--and running in behind the struggling quarry, had seized the brow antler, and at one strong and skilful blow, severed the weasand and the jugular. One gush of dark red gore--one plunging effort, and the superb and stately beast lay motionless forever--while the loud death halloo rang over the broad valley--all fears, all perils, utterly forgotton in the strong rapture of that thrilling moment.

SNIPE ON THE UPLAND

Now then, boys, we've no time to loose," said Archer, as he replaced his knives, which he had been employed in wiping with great care, in their respective scabbards, "it's getting toward eight o'clock, and I feel tolerably peckish, the milk punch and biscuits notwithstanding; we shall not be in the field before ten o'clock, do our best for it. Now, Jem," he continued, as that worthy, followed by David Seers and the Captain made their appearance, hot and breathless, but in high spirits at the glorious termination of the morning's sport-- "Now, Jem, you and the Captain must look out a good strong pole, and tie that fellow's legs, and carry him between you as far as Blain's house--you can come up with the wagon this afternoon and bring him down to the village. What the deuce are you pottering at that colt about, Tom? He's not hurt a pin's value, on the contrary--"

"Better for 't, I suppose, you'll be a tellin' me torights; better for that all-fired etarnal tumble, aint he?" responded the fat chap, with a lamentable attempt at an ironical smile, put on to hide his real chagrin.

"In course he is," replied Frank, who had recovered his wonted equanimity, and who, having been most unmercifully rallied by the whole party for leaving his bullets at home, was glad of an opportunity to carry the war into the enemy's country, "in course he is a great deal better--if a thing can be said to be better which, under all circumstances, is so infernally bad, as that brute. I should think he was better for it. Why, by the time he's had half a dozen more such purls, he'll leap a six foot fence without shaking a loose rail. In fact, I'll bet a dollar I carry him back over that same wall without touching a stone." And, as he spoke, he set his foot into the stirrup, as if he were about to put his threat into immediate execution.

"Quit, Forester--quit, I say--quit, now--consarn the hide on you"-- shouted the fat man, now in great tribulation, and apprehending a second edition of the tumble-

-"quit foolin', or by h--l I'll put a grist of shot, or one of they green cartridges into you stret away--I will, by the Etarnal!" and as he spoke he dropped the muzzle of his gun, and put his thumb upon the cock.

"I say quit foolin', too," cried Harry, "both of you quit it; you old fool, Tom, do you really suppose he is mad enough to ride that brute of yours again at the wall?"

"Mad enough!--Yes, I swon he be," responded Tom; "both of you be as mad as the hull Asylum down to York. If Frank arn't mad, then there aint such a word as mad!" But as he spoke he replaced his gun under his arm, and walked off to his horse, which he mounted, without farther words, his example being followed by the whole party, who set off on the spur, and reached the village in less than half an hour.

Breakfast was on the table when they got there--black tea, produced from Harry's magazine of stores, rich cream, hot bread, and Goshen butter-- eggs in abundance, boiled, roasted, fried with ham--an omelet au fines herbes, no inconsiderable token of Tim's culinary skill--a cold round of spiced beef, and last, not least, a dish of wood-duck hot from the gridiron.

"By George," said Harry, "here's a feast for an epicure, and I can find the appetite."

"Find it"--said Forester, grinning, who, pretending to eat nothing, or next to nothing, and not to care what was set before him, was really the greatest gourmet and heaviest feeder of the party--"Find it, Harry? it's quite new to me that you ever lost it. When was it, hey?"

"Arter he'd eat a hull roast pig, I reckon--leastwise that might make Harry lose his'n; but I'll be darned if two would be a sarcumstance to set before you, Frank, no how. Here's A---, too, he don't never eat."

"These wood-duck are delicious," answered the Commodore, who was very busily employed in stowing away his provant, "What a capital bird it is, Harry."

"Indeed, is it," said he, "and this is, me judice, the very best way to eat it, red hot from the gridiron, cooked very quick, and brown on the outside, and full of gravy when you cut; with a squeeze of a lemon and a dash of cayenne it is sublime. What say you, Forester?"

"Oh, you wont ketch him sayin' nauthen, leastwise not this half hour-- but the way he'll keep a feedin' wont be slow, I tell you--that's the way to judge how

Forester likes his grub--jest see how he takes hold on 't."

"Are there many wood-duck about this season, Tom?" asked Forester, affecting to be perfectly careless and indifferent to all that had passed. "Did you kill these yourself?"

"There was a sight on them a piece back, but they're gittin' scase-- pretty scase now, I tell you. Yes, I shot these down by Aunt Sally's big spring-hole a Friday. I'd been a lookin' round, you see, to find where the quail kept afore you came up here--for I'd a been expectin' you a week and better--and I'd got in quite late, toward sundown, with an outsidin' bevy, down by the cedar swamp, and druv them off into the big bog meadows, below Sugarloaf, and I'd killed quite a bunch on them-- sixteen, I reckon, Archer; and there wasn't but eighteen when I lit on 'em--and it was gittin' pretty well dark when I came to the big spring, and little Dash was worn dead out, and I was tired, and hot, and thunderin' thirsty, so I sets down aside the outlet where the spring water comes in good and cool, and I was mixin' up a nice long drink in the big glass we hid last summer down in the mudhole, with some great cider sperrits--when what should I hear all at once but whistle, whistlin' over head, the wings of a whole drove on 'em, so up I buckled the old gun; but they'd plumped down into the crick fifteen rod off or better, down by the big pin oak, and there they sot, seven ducks and two big purple-headed drakes--beauties, I tell you. Well, boys, I upped gun and tuck sight stret away, but just as I was drawin', I kind o' thought I'd got two little charges of number eight, and that to shoot at ducks at fif-teen rod wasn't nauthen. Well, then, I fell a thinkin', and then I sairched my pock-ets, and arter a piece found two green cartridges of number three, as Archer gave me in the Spring, so I drawed out the small shot, and inned with these, and put fresh caps on to be sarten. But jest when I'd got ready, the ducks had floated down with the stream, and dropped behind the pint--so I downed on my knees, and crawled, and Dash along side on me, for all the world as if the darned dog knowed; well, I crawled quite a piece, till I'd got under a bit of alder bush, and then I seen them--all in a lump like, except two--six ducks and a big drake-- feedin', and stickin' down their heads into the weeds, and flutterin' up their hinder eends, and chatterin' and jokin'--I could have covered them all with a handkercher, exceptin' two, as I said afore, one duck and the little drake, and they was off a rod or better from the rest, at the two different sides of the stream--the big bunch warn't over ten rods off me, nor so far; so I tuck sight right at the big drake's neck. The water was quite clear and still, and seemed to have caught all the little light as was left by the sun, for the skies had got pretty dark, I tell you; and I could see his head quite clear agin the water--well, I draw'd trigger, and the hull charge ripped into 'em--and there was a scrabblin' and a squatterin' in the water now, I tell you--but not one on 'em riz-- not the darned one of the hull bunch; but up jumped both the others, and I drawed on the drake--more by the whistlin' of his wings, than that I seen him--but I drawed stret, Archer, any ways; and arter I'd pulled half a moment I hard him plump down into the creek with a splash, and the water sparkled up like a fountain where he fell. So then I didn't wait to load, but ran along the bank as hard as I could strick it, and when I'd got down to the spot, I tell you, little Dash had got two on 'em out afore I came, and was in with a third. Well, sich a cuttin' and a splashin' as there was you niver did see, none on you--I guess, for sartin--leastwise I niver did. I'd killed, you see, the drake and two ducks, dead at the first fire, but three was only wounded, wing-tipped, and leg-broken, and I can't tell you what all. It was all of nine o'clock at night, and dark as all out doors, afore I gathered them three ducks, but I did gather 'em; Lord, boys, why I'd stay till mornin, but I'd a got them, sarten. Well, the drake I killed flyin' I couldn't find him that night, no how, for the stream swept him down, and I hadn't got no guide to go by, so I let him go then, but I was up next mornin' bright and airly, and started up the stream clean from the bridge here, up through Garry's backside, and my boghole, and so on along the meadows to Aunt Sally's run--and looked in every willow bush that dammed the waters back, like, and every bunch of weeds, and brier-brake, all the way, and sure enough I found him, he'd been killed dead, and floated down the crick, and then the stream had washed him up into a heap of broken sticks and briers, and when the waters fell, for there had been a little freshet, they left him there breast uppermost--and I was glad to find him--for I think, Archer, as that shot was the nicest, prettiest, etarnal, darndest, long good shot, I iver did make, anyhow; and it was so dark I couldn't see him."

"A sweet shot, Tom," responded Forester, "a sweet pretty shot, if there had only been one word of truth in it, which there is not--don't answer me, you old thief--shut up instantly, and get your traps; for we've done feeding, and you've done lying for the present, at least I hope so--and now we'll out, and see whether you've poached up all the game in the country."

"Well, it be gettin' late for sartain," answered Tom, "and that'll save your little wax skin for the time; but see, jest see, boy, if I doesn't sarve you out, now, afore sundown!"

"Which way shall we beat, Tom," asked Harry, as he changed his riding boots for heavy shooting shoes and leggins; "which course to-day?"

"Why, Timothy's gittin' out the wagon, and we'll drive up the old road round the ridge, and so strike in by Minthorne's, and take them ridges down, and so across the hill--there's some big stubbles there, and nice thick brush holes along the fence sides, and the boys does tell us there be one or two big bevies--but, cuss them, they will lie!--and over back of Gin'ral Bertolf's barns, and so acrost the road, and round the upper eend of the big pond, and down the long swamp into Hell hole, and Tim can meet us with the wagon at five o'clock, under Bill Wisner's white oak--does that suit you?"

"Excellently well, Tom," replied Harry, "I could not have cut a better day's work out myself, if I had tried. Well, all the traps are in, and the dogs, Timothy, is it not so?"

"Ey! ey! Sur," shouted that worthy from without, "all in, this half-hour, and all roight!"

"Light your cigars then, quick, and let us start--hurrah!"

Within two minutes, they were all seated, Fat Tom in the post of honor by Harry's side upon the driving box, the Commodore and Frank, with Timothy, on the back seat, and off they rattled--ten miles an hour without the whip, up hill and down dale all alike, for they had but three miles to go, and that was gone in double quick time.

"What mun Ay do wi' t' horses, Sur?" asked Tim, touching his castor as he spoke.

"Take them home, to be sure," replied Harry, "and meet us with them under the oak tree, close to Mr. Wisner's house, at five o'clock this evening."

"Nay! nay! Sur!" answered Tim, with a broad grin, eager to see the sport, and hating to be sent so unceremoniously home, "that winna do, I'm thinking--who'll hug t' gam bag, and carry t' bottles, and make t' loonchun ready; that winna do, Sur niver. If you ple-ease, Sur, Ay'll pit oop t' horses i' Measter Minthorne's barn here, and shak' doon a bite o' hay tull 'em, and so gang on wi' you, and carry t' bag whaile four o' t' clock, and then awa back and hitch oop, and draive doon to t' aik tree!"

"I understand, Tim," said his master, laughing; "I understand right well! you want to see the sport."

"Ayse oophaud it!" grinned Timothy, seeing at once that he should gain his point.

"Well! well! I don't care about it; will Minthorne let us put up the beasts in his barn, Tom?"

"Let us! let us!" exclaimed the fat man; "by gad I'd like to see Joe Minthorne, or any other of his breed, a tellin' me I should'nt put my cattle where I pleased; jest let me ketch him at it!"

"Very well; have it your own way, Tim, take care of the beasts, and overtake us as quick as you can!" and as he spoke, he let down the bars which parted a fine wheat stubble from the road, and entered the field with the dogs at heel. "We must part company to beat these little woods, must we not, Tom?"

"I guess so--I'll go on with A---; his Grouse and my Dash will work well enough, and you and Frank keep down the valley hereaways; we'll beat that little swamp-hole, and then the open woods to the brook side, and so along the meadows to the big bottom; you keep the hill-side coverts, and look the little pond-holes well on Minthorne's Ridge, you'll find a cock or two there anyhow; and beat the bushes by the wall; I guess you'll have a bevy jumpin' up; and try, boys, do, to git 'em down the hill into the boggy bottom, for we can use them, I tell you!" and so they parted.

Archer and Forester, with Shot and Chase at heel, entered the little thicket indicated, and beat it carefully, but blank; although the dogs worked hard, and seemed as if about to make game more than once. They crossed the road, and came into another little wood, thicker and wetter than the first, with several springy pools, although it was almost upon the summit of the hill. Here Harry took the left or lower hand, bidding Frank keep near the outside at top, and full ten yards ahead of him.

"And mind, if you hear Tom shoot, or cry 'mark,' jump over into the open field, and be all eyes, for that's their line of country into the swamp, where we would have them. Hold up, good dogs, hold up!"

And off they went, crashing and rattling through the dry matted briers, crossing each other evenly, and quartering the ground with rare accuracy. Scarcely, however, had they beat ten paces, before Shot flushed a cock as he was in the very act of turning at the end of his beat, having run in on him down wind, without crossing the line of scent. Flip--flip--flap rose the bird, but as the dog had turned, and was now running from him, he perceived no cause for alarm, fluttered a yard or two onward, and alighted. The dog, who had neither scented nor seen the bird, caught the sound of his wing, and stood stiff on the instant, though his stern was waved doubtfully, and though he turned his sagacious knowing phiz over his shoulder, as if to look out for the pinion, the flap of which had arrested his quick ear. The bird had settled ere he turned, but Shot's eye fell upon his master, as with his finger on the trigger-guard, and thumb on the hammer, he was stepping softly up in a direct line, with eye intently fixed, toward the place where the woodcock had dropped; he knew as well as though he had been blessed with human intellect, that game was in the wind, and remained still and steady. Flip--flap again up jumped the bird.

"Mark cock," cried Forester, from the other side of the wood, not having seen any thing, but hearing the sound of the timber doodle's wing somewhere or other; and at the self-same moment bang! boomed the full report of Harry's right hand barrel, the feathers drifting off down wind toward Frank, told him the work was done, and he asked no question; but ere the cock had struck the ground, which he did within half a second, completely doubled up--whirr, whirr-r-r! the loud and startling hubbub of ruffed grouse taking wing at the report of Harry's gun, succeeded-- and instantly, before that worthy had got his eye about from marking the killed woodcock, bang! bang! from Forester. Archer dropped butt, and loaded as fast as it was possible, and bagged his dead bird quietly, but scarcely had he done so before Frank hailed him.

"Bring up the dogs, old fellow; I knocked down two, and I've bagged one, but I'm afraid the other's run!"

"Stand still, then--stand still, till I join you. He-here, he-here good dogs," cried Harry, striding away through the brush like a good one.

In a moment he stood by Frank, who was just pocketing his first, a fine hen grouse.

"The other was the cock," said Frank, "and a very large one, too; he was a long shot, but he's very hard hit; he flew against this tree before he fell, and bounded off it here; look at the feathers!"

"Ay! we'll have him in a moment; seek dead, Shot; seek, good dogs; ha! now they wind him; there! Chase has him--no! he draws again--now Shot is standing; hold up, hold up, lads, he's running like the mischief, and won't stop till he reaches some thick covert."

Bang! bang! "Mark--ma-ark!" bang! bang! "mark, Harry Archer, mark," came down the wind in quick succession from the other party, who were beating some thick briers by the brook side, at three or four fields' distance.

"Quick, Forester, quick!" shouted Archer; "over the wall, lad, and mark them! those are quail; I'm man enough to get this fellow by myself. Steady, lads! steady-y-y!" as they were roading on at the top of their pace. "Toho! toho-o-o, Chase; fie, for shame--don't you see, sir, Shot's got him dead there under his very nose in those cat-briers. Ha! dead! good lads--good lads; dead! dead! fetch him, good dog; by George but he is a fine bird. I've got him, Forester; have you marked down the quail?"

"Ay! ay! in the bog bottom!"

"How many?"

"Twenty-three!"

"Then we'll have sport, by Jove!" and, as he spoke, they entered a wide rushy pasture, across which, at some two or three hundred yards, A--- and fat Tom were seen advancing toward them. They had not made three steps before both dogs stood stiff as stones in the short grass, where there was not a particle of covert.

"Why, what the deuce is this, Harry?"

"Devil a know know I," responded he; "but step up to the red dog, Frank --I'll go to the other--they've got game, and no mistake!"

"Skeap--ske-eap!" up sprang a couple of English snipe before Shot's nose, and Harry cut them down, a splendid double shot, before they had flown twenty yards, just as Frank dropped the one which rose to him at the same moment. At the sound of the guns a dozen more rose hard by, and fluttering on in rapid zig-zags, dropped once again within a hundred yards--the meadow was alive with them.

"Did you ever see snipe here before, Tom? asked Harry, as he loaded.

"Never in all my life--but it's full now--load up! load up! for heaven's sake!"

"No hurry, Tom! Tom--steady! the birds are tame and lie like stones. We can get thirty or forty here, I know, if you'll be steady only--but if we go in with these four dogs, we shall lose all. Here comes Tim with the couples, and we'll take up all but two!"

"That's right," said A---; "take up Grouse and Tom's dog, for they won't hunt with yours--and yours are the steadiest, and fetch--that's it, Tim, couple them, and carry them away. What have you killed, Archer?" he added, while his injunctions were complied with.

"One woodcock and a brace of ruffed grouse! and Frank has marked down three-and-twenty quail into that rushy bottom yonder, where we can get every bird of them. We are going to have great sport to-day!"

"I think so. Tom and I each killed a double shot out of that bevy!"

"That was well! Now, then, walk slowly and far apart--we must beat this three or four times, at least--the dogs will get them up!"

It was not a moment before the first bird rose, but it was quite two hours, and all the dinner horns had long blown for noon, before the last was bagged--the four guns having scored, in that one meadow, forty-nine English snipe--fifteen for Harry Archer--thirteen for Tom Draw--twelve for the Commodore, and only nine for Forester, who never killed snipe quite so well as he did cock or quail.

"And now, boys," exclaimed Tom, as he flung his huge carcase on the ground, with a thud that shook it many a rod around--"there's a cold roast fowl, and some nice salt pork and crackers, in that 'ar game bag-- and I'm a whale now, I tell you, for a drink!"

"Which will you take to drink, Tom?" inquired Forester, very gravely-- "fowl, pork, or crackers? Here they are, all of them! I prefer whiskey and water, myself!" qualifying, as he spoke, a moderate cup with some of the ice-cold water which welled out in a crystal stream from a small basin under the wreathed roots of the sycamore which overshadowed them.

"None of your nonsense, Forester--hand us the liquor, lad--I'm dry, I tell you!"

"I wish you'd tell me something I don't know, then, if you feel communicative; for I know that you're dry--now and always! Well! don't be mad, old fellow, here's the bottle--don't empty it--that's all!"

"Well! now I've drinked," said Tom, after a vast potation, "now I've drinked good--we'll have a bite and rest awhile, and smoke a pipe; and then we'll use them quail, and we'll have time to pick up twenty cock in Hell-hole arterwards, and that won't be a slow day's work, I reckon."

THE QUAIL

Certainly this is a very lovely country," exclaimed the Commodore suddenly, as he gazed with a quiet eye, puffing his cigar the while, over the beautiful vale, with the clear expanse of Wickham's Pond in the middle foreground, and the wild hoary mountains framing the rich landscape in the distance.

"Truly, you may say that," replied Harry; "I have traveled over a large part of the world, and for its own peculiar style of loveliness, I must say that I never have seen any thing to match with the vale of Warwick. I would give much, very much, to own a few acres, and a snug cottage here, in which I might pass the rest of my days, far aloof from the Fumum et opes strepitumque Romae."

"Then, why the h--l don't you own a few acres?" put in ancient Tom; "I'd be right glad to know, and gladder yit to have you up here, Archer."

"I would indeed, Tom," answered Harry; "I'm not joking at all; but there are never any small places to be bought hereabout; and, as for large ones, your land is so confounded good, that a fellow must be a nabob to think of buying."

"Well, how would Jem Burt's place suit you, Archer?" asked the fat man. "You knows it--just a mile and a half 'tother side Warwick, by the crick side? I guess it will have to be sold anyhow next April; leastways the old man's dead, and the heirs want the estate settled up like."

"Suit me!" cried Harry, "by George! it's just the thing, if I recollect it rightly. But how much land is there?"

"Twenty acres, I guess--not over twenty-five, no how."

"And the house?" "Well, that wants fixin' some; and the bridge over the crick's putty bad, too, it will want putty nigh a new one. Why, the house is a story and a half like; and it's jist an entry stret through the middle, and a parlor on one side on't, and a kitchen on the t'other; and a chamber behind both on 'em."

"What can it be bought for, Tom?"

"I guess three thousand dollars; twenty-five hundred, maybe. It will go cheap, I reckon; I don't hear tell o' no one lookin' at it.

"What will it cost me more to fix it, think you?"

"Well, you see, Archer, the land's ben most darned badly done by, this last three years, since old 'squire's ben so low; and the bridge, that'll take a smart sum; and the fences is putty much gone to rack; I guess it'll take hard on to a thousand more to fix it up right, like you'd like to have it, without doin' nothin' at the house."

"And fifteen hundred more for that and the stables. I wish to heaven I had known this yesterday; or rather before I came up hither," said Harry.

"Why so?" asked the Commodore.

"Why, as the deuce would have it, I told my broker to invest six thousand, that I have got loose, in a good mortgage, if he could find one, for five years; and I have got no stocks that I can sell out; all that I have but this, is on good bond and mortgage, in Boston, and little enough of it, too."

"Well, if that's all," said Forester, "we can run down tomorrow, and you will be in time to stop him."

"That's true, too," answered Harry, pondering. "Are you sure it can be bought, Tom?"

"I guess so," was the response.

"That means, I suppose, that you're perfectly certain of it. Why the devil can't you speak English?"

"English!" exclaimed Frank; "Good Lord! why don't you ask him why he can't speak Greek? English! Lord! Lord! Lord! Tom Draw and English!"

"I'll jist tell Archer what he warnts to know, and then see you, my dear little critter, if I doosn't English you some!" replied the old man, waxing wroth. "Well, Archer, to tell heaven's truth, now, I doos know it; but it's an etarnal all-fired shame of me to be tellin' it, bein' as how I knows it in the way of business like. It's got to be selled by vandoo in April[9].

"Then, by Jove! I will buy it," said Harry; "and down I'll go to-morrow. But that <u>need not take you away, boys; you can stay and finish out the week</u> here, and go

9 Vendue. Why the French word for a public auction has been adopted throughout the Northern and Eastern States, as applied to a Sheriff's sale, deponent saith not.

home in the Ianthe; Tom will send you down to Nyack."

"Sartain," responded Tom; "but now I'm most darned glad I told you that, Archer. I meant to a told you on't afore, but it clean slipped out of my head; but all's right, now. Hark! hark! don't you hear, boys? The quails hasn't all got together yit--better luck! Hush, A--- and you'll hear them callin'--whew-wheet! whew-wheet! whe-whe-whe;" and the old Turk began to call most scientifically; and in ten minutes the birds were answering him from all quarters, through the circular space of Bog-meadow, and through the thorny brake beyond it, and some from a large ragwort field further yet.

"How is this, Frank--did they scatter so much when they dropped?" asked Harry.

"Yes; part of them 'lighted in the little bank on this edge, by the spring, you know; and some, a dozen or so, right in the middle of the bog, by the single hickory; and five or six went into the swamp, and a few over it."

"That's it! that's it! and they've been running to try to get together," said the Commodore.

"But was too skeart to call, till we'd quit shootin'!" said Tom. "But come, boys, let's be stirrin', else they'll git together like; they keeps drawin', drawin', into one place now, I can hear."

No sooner said than done; we were all on foot in an instant, and ten minutes brought us to the edge of the first thicket; and here was the truth of Harry's precepts tested by practice in a moment; for they had not yet entered the thin bushes, on which now the red leaves hung few and sere, before old Shot threw his nose high into the air, straightened his neck and his stern, and struck out at a high trot; the other setter evidently knowing what he meant, though as yet he had not caught the wind of them. In a moment they both stood steady; and, almost at the same instant, Tom Draw's Dash, and A---'s Grouse come to the point, all on different birds, in a bit of very open ground, covered with wintergreen about knee deep, and interspersed with only a few scattered bushes.

Whir-r-r-r--up they got all at once! what a jostle--what a hubbub! Bang! bang! crack! bang! crack! bang! Four barrels exploded in an instant, almost simultaneously; and two sharp unmeaning cracks announced that, by some means or other, Frank Forester's gun had missed fire with both barrels.

"What the deuce is the matter, boys" cried Harry, laughing, as he threw up his gun, after the hubbub had subsided, and dropped two birds--the only two that fell, for all that waste of shot and powder.

"What the deuce ails you?" he repeated, no one replying, and all hands looking bashful and crest-fallen. "Are you all drunk? or what is the matter? I asked merely for information."

"Upon my life! I believe I am!" said Frank Forester. "For I have not loaded my gun at all, since I killed those two last snipe. And, when we got up from luncheon, I put on the caps just as if all was right--but all is right now," he added, for he had repaired his fault, and loaded, before A--- or fat Tom had done staring, each in the other's face, in blank astonishment.

"Step up to Grouse, then," said Archer, who had never taken his eye off the old brown pointer, while he was loading as fast as he could. "He has got a bird, close under his nose; and it will get up, and steal away directly. That's a trick they will play very often."

"He haint got no bird," said Tom, sulkily. And Frank paused doubtful.

"Step up, I tell you, Frank," said Harry, "the old Turk's savage; that's all."

And Frank did step up, close to the dog's nose; and sent his foot through the grass close under it. Still the dog stood perfectly stiff; but no bird rose.

"I told you there warn't no quails there;" growled Tom.

"And I tell you there are!" answered Archer, more sharply than he often spoke to his old ally; for, in truth, he was annoyed at his obstinate pertinacity.

"What do you say, Commodore? Is Grouse lying? Kick that tussock--kick it hard, Frank."

"Not he," replied A---; "I'll bet fifty to one, there's a bird there."

"It's devilish odd, then, that he won't get up!" said Frank.

Whack! whack! and he gave the hard tussock two kicks with his heavy boot, that fairly made it shake. Nothing stirred. Grouse still kept his point, but seemed half inclined to dash in. Whack! a third kick that absolutely loosened the tough hassock from the ground, and then, whirr-r, from within six inches of the spot where all three blows had been delivered, up got the bird, in a desperate hurry; and in quite as desperate a hurry Forester covered it--covered it before it was six yards off! His finger was on the trigger, when Harry quietly said, "Steady, Frank!" and the word acted like magic.

He took the gun quite down from his shoulder, nodded to his friend, brought it up again, and turned the bird over very handsomely, at twenty yards, or a little further.

"Beautifully done, indeed, Frank," said Harry. "So much for coolness!"

"What do you say to that, Tom?" said the Commodore, laughing.

But there was no laugh in Tom; he only muttered a savage growl, and an awful imprecation; and Harry's quick glance warned A--- not to plague the old Trojan further.

All this passed in a moment; and then was seen one of those singular things that will at times happen; but with regard to quail only, so far as I have ever seen or heard tell. For as Forester was putting down the card upon the powder in the barrel which he had just fired, a second bird rose, almost from the identical spot whence the first had been so difficultly flushed, and went off in the same direction. But not in the least was Frank flurried now. He dropped his ramrod quietly upon the grass, brought up his piece deliberately to his eye, and killed his bird again.

"Excellent--excellent! Frank," said Harry again. "I never saw two prettier shots in all my life. Nor did I ever see birds lie harder."

During all this time, amidst all the kicking of tussocks, threshing of bog-grass, and banging of guns, and, worst of all, bouncing up of fresh birds, from the instant when they dropped at the first shot, neither one of Harry's dogs, nor Tom's little Dash, had budged from their down charge. Now, however, they got up quickly, and soon retrieved all the dead birds. "Now, then, we will divide into two parties," said Harry. "Frank, you go with Tom; and you come with me, Commodore. It will never do to have you two jealous fellows together, you wont kill a bird all day," he added, in a lower voice. "That is the worst of old Tom, when he gets jealous he's the very devil. Frank is the only fellow that can get along with him at all. He puts me out of temper, and if we both got angry, it would be very disagreeable. For, though he is the very best fellow in the world, when he is in a rage he is untamable. I cannot think what has put him out, now; for he has shot very well to-day. It is only when he gets behindhand, that he is usually jealous in his shooting; but he has got the deuce into him now."

By this time the two parties were perhaps forty yards apart, when Dash came to a point again. Up got a single bird, the old cock, and flew directly away from Tom, across Frank's face; but not for that did the old chap pause. Up went his cannon to his shoulder, there was a flash and a roar, and the quail, which was literally not twelve feet from him, disappeared as if it had been resolved into thin air. The whole of Tom's concentrated charge had struck the bird endwise, as it flew from him; and except the extreme tips of his wings and one foot, no part of him could be found.

"The devil!" cried Harry, "that is too bad!"

"Never mind," said the Commodore, "Frank will manage him."

As he spoke a second bird got up, and crossed Forester in the same manner, Draw doing precisely as he had done before; but, this time, missing the quail clear, which Forester turned over.

"Load quick! and step up to that fellow. He will run, I think!" said Archer.

"Ay! ay!" responded Frank, and, having rammed down his charge like lightning, moved forward, before he had put the cap on the barrel he had fired.

Just as he took the cap out of his pocket between his finger and thumb, a second quail rose. As cool and self-possessed as it is possible to conceive, Frank cocked the left hand barrel with his little finger, still holding the cap between his forefinger and thumb, and actually contrived to bring up the gun, some how or other, and to kill the bird, pulling the trigger with his middle finger.

At the report a third quail sprang, close under his feet; and, still unshaken, he capped the right hand barrel, fired, and the bird towered!

"Mark! mark! Tom--ma-ark Timothy!" shouted Harry and A--- in a breath.

"That bird is as dead as Hannibal now!" added Archer, as, having spun up three hundred feet into the air, and flown twice as many hundred yards, it turned over, and fell plumb, like a stone, through the clear atmosphere.

"Ayse gotten that chap marked doon roight, ayse warrant un!" shouted Timothy from the hill side, where with some trouble, he was holding in the obstreperous spaniels. "He's doon in a roight laine atwixt 't gray stean and yon hoigh ashen tree."

"Did you ever see such admirable shooting, though?" asked A---, in a low voice. "I did not know Forester shot like that."

"Some times he does. When he's cool. He is not certain; that is his only fault. One day he is the coolest man I ever saw in a field, and the next the most impetuous; but when he is cool, he shoots splendidly. As you say, A---, I never saw anything better done in my life. It was the perfection of coolness and quickness combined."

"I cannot conceive how it was done at all. How he brought up and fired that first barrel with a cap between his thumb and forefinger! Why, I could not fire a gun so, in cold blood!"

"Nor could he, probably. Deliberate promptitude is the thing! Well, Tom, what do you think of that? Wasn't that pretty shooting?"

"It was so, pretty shootin'," responded the fat man, quite delighted out of his crusty mood. "I guess the darned little critter's got three barrels to his gun some-how; leastwise it seems to me, I swon, 'at he fired her off three times without loadin' I guess I'll quit tryin' to shoot agin Frank, to-day."

"I told you so!" said Harry to the Commodore, with a low laugh, and then added aloud--"I think you may as well, Tom--for I don't believe the fellow will miss another bird to-day."

And in truth, strange to say, it fell out, in reality, nearly as Archer had spoken in jest. The whole party shot exceedingly well. The four birds, which Tom and the Commodore had missed at the first start, were found again in an old ragwort field, and brought to bag; and of the twenty-three quail which Forester had marked down into the bog meadow, not one bird escaped, and of that bevy not one bird did Frank miss, killing twelve, all of them double shots, to his own share, and beating Archer in a canter.

But that sterling sportsman cared not a stiver; too many times by far had he had the field, too sure was he of doing the same many a time again, to dislike being beaten once. Besides this, he was always the least jealous shot in the world, for a very quick one; and, in this instance, he was perhaps better pleased to see his friend "go in and win," than he would have been to do the like himself.

Exactly at two o'clock, by A---'s repeater, the last bird was bagged; making twenty-seven quail, forty-nine snipe, two ruffed grouse, and one woodcock, bagged in about five hours.

"So far, this is the very best day's sport I ever saw," said Archer; "and two things I have seen which I never saw before; a whole bevy of quail killed without the es-cape of one bird, and a whole bevy killed entirely by double shots, except the odd bird. You, A---, have killed three double shots--I have killed three--Tom Draw one double shot, and the odd bird; and Master Frank there, confound him, six double shots running--the cleverest thing I ever heard of, and, in Forester's case, the best shooting possible. I have missed one bird, you two, and Tom three."

"But Tom beant a goin' to miss no more birds, I can tell you, boy. Tom's drinked agin, and feels kind o' righter than he did--kind o' first best! You'd best all drink, boys--the spring's handy, close by here; and after we gits down acrost the road into the big swamp, and Hell-Hole, there arn't a drop o' water fit to drink, till we gits way down to Aunt Sally's big spring-hole, jest to home."

"I second the motion," said Harry; "and then let us be quick, for the day is wearing away, and we have got a long beat yet before us. I wish it were a sure one. But it is not. Once in three or four years we get a grand day's sport in the big swamp; but for one good day we have ten bad ones. However, we are sure to find a dozen birds or so in Hell-Hole; and a bevy of quail in the Captain's swamp, shan't we, Tom?"

"Yes, if we gits so far; but somehow or other I rather guess we'll find quite a smart chance o' cock. Captain Reed was down there a' Satterday, and he saw heaps on 'em."

"That's no sure sign. They move very quickly now. Here today and there to-morrow," said Archer. "In the large woods especially. In the small places there are plenty of sure finds."

"There harn't been nothing of frosts yet keen enough to stir them," said Tom. "I guess we'll find them. And there harn't been a gun shot off this three weeks there. Hoel's wife's ben down sick all the fall, and Halbert's gun busted in the critter's hand."

"Ah! did it hurt him?"

"Hurt him some--skeart him considerable, though. I guess he's quit shootin' pretty much. But come--here we be, boys. I'll keep along the outside, where the walkin's good. You git next me, and Archer next with the dogs, and A--- inside of all. Keep right close to the cedars, A---; all the birds 'at you flushes will come stret out this aways. They never flies into the cedar swamp. Archer, how does the ground look?"

"I never saw it look so well, Tom. There is not near so much water as usual, and yet the bottom is all quite moist and soft."

"Then we'll get cock for sartain."

"By George!" cried A--- "the ground is like a honey-comb, with their borings;

and as white in places with their droppings, as if there had been a snow fall!"

"Are they fresh droppings, A---?"

"Mark! Ah! Grouse! Grouse! for shame. There he is down. Do you see him, Harry?"

"Ay! ay! Did Grouse flush him?"

"Deliberately, at fifty yards off. I must lick him."

"Pray do; and that mercifully."

"And that soundly," suggested Frank, as an improvement.

"Soundly is mercifully," said Harry, "because one good flogging settles the business; whereas twenty slight ones only harass a dog, and do nothing in the way of correction or prevention."

"True, oh king" said Frank, laughing. "Now let us go on; for, as the bellowing of that brute is over, I suppose 'chastisement has hidden her head.'"

And on they did go; and sweet shooting they had of it; all the way down to the thick deep spot, known by the pleasing sobriquet of Hell-Hole.

The birds were scattered everywhere throughout the swamp, so excellent was the condition of the ground; scattered so much, that, in no instance did two rise at once; but one kept flapping up after another, large and lazy, at every few paces; and the sportsmen scored them fast, although scarcely aware how fast they were killing them. At length, when they reached the old creek-side, and the deep black mud-holes, and the tangled vines and leafy alders, dogs were thrown into it, Frank was sent forward to the extreme point, and the Commodore out into the open field, on the opposite side from that occupied by fat Tom.

On the signal of a whistle, from each of the party, Harry drove into the brake with the spaniels, the setters being now consigned to the care of Timothy; and in a moment, his loud "Hie cock! Hie cock! Pur-r-r--Hie cock! good dogs!" was succeeded by the shrill yelping of the cockers, the flap of the fast rising birds, and the continuous rattling of shots.

In twenty minutes the work was done; and it was well that it was done; for, within a quarter of an hour afterwards, it was too dark to shoot at all.

In that last twenty minutes twenty-two cock were actually brought to bag, by the eight barrels; twenty-eight had been picked up, one by one, as they came down the long swamp, and one Harry had killed in the morning. When Timothy met them, with the horses, at the big oak tree, half an hour afterward--for he had gone off across the fields, as hard as he could foot it to the farm, as soon as he had received the setters --it was quite dark; and the friends had counted their game out regularly, and hung it up secundum artem in the loops of the new game bag.

It was a huge day's sport--a day's sport to talk about for years afterward--Tom Draw does talk about it now!

Fifty-one woodcock, forty-nine English snipe, twenty-seven quail, and a brace of ruffed grouse. A hundred and twenty-nine head in all, on unpreserved ground, and in very wild walking. It is to be feared it will never be done any more in the vale of Warwick. For this, alas! was ten years ago.

When they reached Tom's it was decided that they should all return home on the morrow; that Harry should attend to the procuring his purchase money; and Tom to the cheapening of the purchase.

In addition to this, the old boy swore, by all his patron saints, that he would come down in spring, and have a touch at the snipe he had heerd Archer tell on at Pine Brook.

A capital supper followed; and of course lots of good liquor, and the toast, to which the last cup was quaffed, was LONG LIFE TO HARRY ARCHER, AND LUCK TO HIS SHOOTING BOX, to which Frank Forester added: "I wish he may get it."

And so that party ended; all of its members hoping to enjoy many more like it, and that very speedily.

www.bookjungle.com *email: sales@bookjungle.com fax: 630-214-0564 mail: Book Jungle PO Box 2226 Champaign, IL 61825*

The Codes Of Hammurabi And Moses
W. W. Davies

QTY

The discovery of the Hammurabi Code is one of the greatest achievements of archaeology, and is of paramount interest, not only to the student of the Bible, but also to all those interested in ancient history...

Religion   ISBN: *1-59462-338-4*   Pages:132

MSRP $12.95

The Theory of Moral Sentiments
Adam Smith

QTY

This work from 1749. contains original theories of conscience amd moral judgment and it is the foundation for systemof morals.

Philosophy   ISBN: *1-59462-777-0*   Pages:536

MSRP $19.95

Jessica's First Prayer
Hesba Stretton

QTY

In a screened and secluded corner of one of the many railway-bridges which span the streets of London there could be seen a few years ago, from five o'clock every morning until half past eight, a tidily set-out coffee-stall, consisting of a trestle and board, upon which stood two large tin cans, with a small fire of charcoal burning under each so as to keep the coffee boiling during the early hours of the morning when the work-people were thronging into the city on their way to their daily toil...

Childrens   ISBN: *1-59462-373-2*   Pages:84

MSRP $9.95

My Life and Work
Henry Ford

QTY

Henry Ford revolutionized the world with his implementation of mass production for the Model T automobile. Gain valuable business insight into his life and work with his own auto-biography... "We have only started on our development of our country we have not as yet, with all our talk of wonderful progress, done more than scratch the surface. The progress has been wonderful enough but..."

Biographies/   ISBN: *1-59462-198-5*   Pages:300

MSRP $21.95

www.bookjungle.com *email: sales@bookjungle.com fax: 630-214-0564 mail: Book Jungle PO Box 2226 Champaign, IL 61825*

The Art of Cross-Examination
Francis Wellman

QTY

I presume it is the experience of every author, after his first book is published upon an important subject, to be almost overwhelmed with a wealth of ideas and illustrations which could readily have been included in his book, and which to his own mind, at least, seem to make a second edition inevitable. Such certainly was the case with me; and when the first edition had reached its sixth impression in five months, I rejoiced to learn that it seemed to my publishers that the book had met with a sufficiently favorable reception to justify a second and considerably enlarged edition. ..

Reference   ISBN: *1-59462-647-2*

Pages:412

MSRP $19.95

On the Duty of Civil Disobedience
Henry David Thoreau

QTY

Thoreau wrote his famous essay, On the Duty of Civil Disobedience, as a protest against an unjust but popular war and the immoral but popular institution of slave-owning. He did more than write—he declined to pay his taxes,   and was hauled off to gaol in consequence. Who can say how much this refusal of his hastened the end of the war and of slavery ?

Law   ISBN: *1-59462-747-9*

Pages:48

MSRP $7.45

Dream Psychology Psychoanalysis for Beginners
Sigmund Freud

QTY

Sigmund Freud, born Sigismund Schlomo Freud (May 6, 1856 - September 23, 1939), was a Jewish-Austrian neurologist and psychiatrist who co-founded the psychoanalytic school of psychology. Freud is best known for his theories of the unconscious mind, especially involving the mechanism of repression; his redefinition of sexual desire as mobile and directed towards a wide variety of objects; and his therapeutic techniques, especially his understanding of transference in the therapeutic relationship and the presumed value of dreams as sources of insight into unconscious desires.

Psychology   ISBN: *1-59462-905-6*

Pages:196

MSRP $15.45

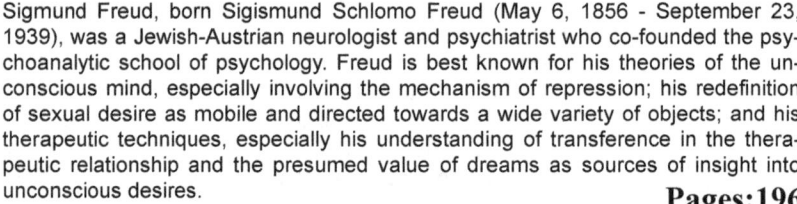

The Miracle of Right Thought
Orison Swett Marden

QTY

Believe with all of your heart that you will do what you were made to do. When the mind has once formed the habit of holding cheerful, happy, prosperous pictures, it will not be easy to form the opposite habit. It does not matter how improbable or how far away this realization may see, or how dark the prospects may be, if we visualize them as best we can, as vividly as possible, hold tenaciously to them and vigorously struggle to attain them, they will gradually become actualized, realized in the life. But a desire, a longing without endeavor, a yearning abandoned or held indifferently will vanish without realization.

Pages:360

Self Help   ISBN: *1-59462-644-8*

MSRP $25.45

The Rosicrucian Cosmo-Conception Mystic Christianity *by Max Heindel*   ISBN: *1-59462-188-8* **$38.95**
The Rosicrucian Cosmo-conception is not dogmatic, neither does it appeal to any other authority than the reason of the student. It is: not controversial, but is: sent forth in the, hope that it may help to clear...   *New Age/Religion Pages 646*

Abandonment To Divine Providence *by Jean-Pierre de Caussade*   ISBN: *1-59462-228-0* **$25.95**
"The Rev. Jean Pierre de Caussade was one of the most remarkable spiritual writers of the Society of Jesus in France in the 18th Century. His death took place at Toulouse in 1751. His works have gone through many editions and have been republished...   *Inspirational/Religion Pages 400*

Mental Chemistry *by Charles Haanel*   ISBN: *1-59462-192-6* **$23.95**
Mental Chemistry allows the change of material conditions by combining and appropriately utilizing the power of the mind. Much like applied chemistry creates something new and unique out of careful combinations of chemicals the mastery of mental chemistry...   *New Age Pages 354*

The Letters of Robert Browning and Elizabeth Barret Barrett 1845-1846 vol II   ISBN: *1-59462-193-4* **$35.95**
by Robert Browning and Elizabeth Barrett   *Biographies Pages 596*

Gleanings In Genesis (volume I) *by Arthur W. Pink*   ISBN: *1-59462-130-6* **$27.45**
Appropriately has Genesis been termed "the seed plot of the Bible" for in it we have, in germ form, almost all of the great doctrines which are afterwards fully developed in the books of Scripture which follow...   *Religion/Inspirational Pages 420*

The Master Key *by L. W. de Laurence*   ISBN: *1-59462-001-6* **$30.95**
In no branch of human knowledge has there been a more lively increase of the spirit of research during the past few years than in the study of Psychology, Concentration and Mental Discipline. The requests for authentic lessons in Thought Control, Mental Discipline and...   *New Age/Business Pages 422*

The Lesser Key Of Solomon Goetia *by L. W. de Laurence*   ISBN: *1-59462-092-X* **$9.95**
This translation of the first book of the "Lernegton" which is now for the first time made accessible to students of Talismanic Magic was done, after careful collation and edition, from numerous Ancient Manuscripts in Hebrew, Latin, and French...   *New Age/Occult Pages 92*

Rubaiyat Of Omar Khayyam *by Edward Fitzgerald*   ISBN:*1-59462-332-5* **$13.95**
Edward Fitzgerald, whom the world has already learned, in spite of his own efforts to remain within the shadow of anonymity, to look upon as one of the rarest poets of the century, was born at Bredfield, in Suffolk, on the 31st of March, 1809. He was the third son of John Purcell...   *Music Pages 172*

Ancient Law *by Henry Maine*   ISBN: *1-59462-128-4* **$29.95**
The chief object of the following pages is to indicate some of the earliest ideas of mankind, as they are reflected in Ancient Law, and to point out the relation of those ideas to modern thought.   *Religion/History Pages 452*

Far-Away Stories *by William J. Locke*   ISBN: *1-59462-129-2* **$19.45**
"Good wine needs no bush, but a collection of mixed vintages does. And this book is just such a collection. Some of the stories I do not want to remain buried for ever in the museum files of dead magazine-numbers an author's not unpardonable vanity..."   *Fiction Pages 272*

Life of David Crockett *by David Crockett*   ISBN: *1-59462-250-7* **$27.45**
"Colonel David Crockett was one of the most remarkable men of the times in which he lived. Born in humble life, but gifted with a strong will, an indomitable courage, and unremitting perseverance...   *Biographies/New Age Pages 424*

Lip-Reading *by Edward Nitchie*   ISBN: *1-59462-206-X* **$25.95**
Edward B. Nitchie, founder of the New York School for the Hard of Hearing, now the Nitchie School of Lip-Reading, Inc, wrote "LIP-READING Principles and Practice". The development and perfecting of this meritorious work on lip-reading was an undertaking...   *How-to Pages 400*

A Handbook of Suggestive Therapeutics, Applied Hypnotism, Psychic Science   ISBN: *1-59462-214-0* **$24.95**
by Henry Munro   *Health/New Age/Health/Self-help Pages 376*

A Doll's House: and Two Other Plays *by Henrik Ibsen*   ISBN: *1-59462-112-8* **$19.95**
Henrik Ibsen created this classic when in revolutionary 1848 Rome. Introducing some striking concepts in playwriting for the realist genre, this play has been studied the world over.   *Fiction/Classics/Plays 308*

The Light of Asia *by sir Edwin Arnold*   ISBN: *1-59462-204-3* **$13.95**
In this poetic masterpiece, Edwin Arnold describes the life and teachings of Buddha. The man who was to become known as Buddha to the world was born as Prince Gautama of India but he rejected the worldly riches and abandoned the reigns of power when...   *Religion/History/Biographies Pages 170*

The Complete Works of Guy de Maupassant *by Guy de Maupassant*   ISBN: *1-59462-157-8* **$16.95**
"For days and days, nights and nights, I had dreamed of that first kiss which was to consecrate our engagement, and I knew not on what spot I should put my lips..."   *Fiction/Classics Pages 240*

The Art of Cross-Examination *by Francis L. Wellman*   ISBN: *1-59462-309-0* **$26.95**
Written by a renowned trial lawyer, Wellman imparts his experience and uses case studies to explain how to use psychology to extract desired information through questioning.   *How-to/Science/Reference Pages 408*

Answered or Unanswered? *by Louisa Vaughan*   ISBN: *1-59462-248-5* **$10.95**
Miracles of Faith in China   *Religion Pages 112*

The Edinburgh Lectures on Mental Science (1909) *by Thomas*   ISBN: *1-59462-008-3* **$11.95**
This book contains the substance of a course of lectures recently given by the writer in the Queen Street Hall, Edinburgh. Its purpose is to indicate the Natural Principles governing the relation between Mental Action and Material Conditions...   *New Age/Psychology Pages 148*

Ayesha *by H. Rider Haggard*   ISBN: *1-59462-301-5* **$24.95**
Verily and indeed it is the unexpected that happens! Probably if there was one person upon the earth from whom the Editor of this, and of a certain previous history, did not expect to hear again...   *Classics Pages 380*

Ayala's Angel *by Anthony Trollope*   ISBN: *1-59462-352-X* **$29.95**
The two girls were both pretty, but Lucy who was twenty-one who supposed to be simple and comparatively unattractive, whereas Ayala was credited, as her Bombwhat romantic name might show, with poetic charm and a taste for romance. Ayala when her father died was nineteen...   *Fiction Pages 484*

The American Commonwealth *by James Bryce*   ISBN: *1-59462-286-8* **$34.45**
An interpretation of American democratic political theory. It examines political mechanics and society from the perspective of Scotsman James Bryce   *Politics Pages 572*

Stories of the Pilgrims *by Margaret P. Pumphrey*   ISBN: *1-59462-116-0* **$17.95**
This book explores pilgrims religious oppression in England as well as their escape to Holland and eventual crossing to America on the Mayflower, and their early days in New England...   *History Pages 268*

www.bookjungle.com *email: sales@bookjungle.com fax: 630-214-0564 mail: Book Jungle PO Box 2226 Champaign, IL 61825*

QTY

The Fasting Cure by *Sinclair Upton*　　　　　　　　　　　　ISBN: *1-59462-222-1*　**$13.95**
In the Cosmopolitan Magazine for May, 1910, and in the Contemporary Review (London) for April, 1910, I published an article dealing with my experiences in fasting. I have written a great many magazine articles, but never one which attracted so much attention... New Age/Self Help/Health Pages 164

Hebrew Astrology by *Sepharial*　　　　　　　　　　　　　ISBN: *1-59462-308-2*　**$13.45**
In these days of advanced thinking it is a matter of common observation that we have left many of the old landmarks behind and that we are now pressing forward to greater heights and to a wider horizon than that which represented the mind-content of our progenitors... Astrology Pages 144

Thought Vibration or The Law of Attraction in the Thought World　　ISBN: *1-59462-127-6*　**$12.95**
by *William Walker Atkinson*　　　　　　　　　　　　　　　　　*Psychology/Religion Pages 144*

Optimism by *Helen Keller*　　　　　　　　　　　　　　　ISBN: *1-59462-108-X*　**$15.95**
Helen Keller was blind, deaf, and mute since 19 months old, yet famously learned how to overcome these handicaps, communicate with the world, and spread her lectures promoting optimism. An inspiring read for everyone... Biographies/Inspirational Pages 84

Sara Crewe by *Frances Burnett*　　　　　　　　　　　　　ISBN: *1-59462-360-0*　**$9.45**
In the first place, Miss Minchin lived in London. Her home was a large, dull, tall one, in a large, dull square, where all the houses were alike, and all the sparrows were alike, and where all the door-knockers made the same heavy sound... Childrens/Classic Pages 88

The Autobiography of Benjamin Franklin by *Benjamin Franklin*　　ISBN: *1-59462-135-7*　**$24.95**
The Autobiography of Benjamin Franklin has probably been more extensively read than any other American historical work, and no other book of its kind has had such ups and downs of fortune. Franklin lived for many years in England, where he was agent... Biographies/History Pages 332

Name	
Email	
Telephone	
Address	
City, State ZIP	

☐ **Credit Card**　　　　　☐ **Check / Money Order**

Credit Card Number	
Expiration Date	
Signature	

Please Mail to:　Book Jungle
　　　　　　　　　PO Box 2226
　　　　　　　　　Champaign, IL 61825
or Fax to:　　　630-214-0564

ORDERING INFORMATION

web*: www.bookjungle.com*
email*: sales@bookjungle.com*
fax*: 630-214-0564*
mail*: Book Jungle PO Box 2226 Champaign, IL 61825*
or PayPal *to sales@bookjungle.com*

Please contact us for bulk discounts

DIRECT-ORDER TERMS

**20% Discount if You Order
Two or More Books**
Free Domestic Shipping!
Accepted: Master Card, Visa,
Discover, American Express

www.ingramcontent.com/pod-product-compliance
Lightning Source LLC
Chambersburg PA
CBHW080730020726
47503CB00010B/2863